SING,
WILD
BIRD,
SING

ALSO BY JACQUELINE O'MAHONY

A River in the Trees (Quercus, 2019)

SING, WILD BIRD, SING

A Novel

JACQUELINE O'MAHONY

LAKE UNION
PUBLISHING

Published by Lake Union Publishing, Seattle

www.apub.com

Amazon, the Amazon logo, and Lake Union Publishing are trademarks of Amazon.com, Inc., or its affiliates.

ISBN-13: 9781662512186 (paperback)
ISBN-13: 9781662512179 (digital)

Cover design by Lesley Worrell
Cover image: ©Nella / Shutterstock; ©Sybille Sterk / ArcAngel
Interior image: ©Cat_arch_angel / Shutterstock

Printed in the United States of America

To Mike

No feeling is final . . .
Nearby is the country they call life.

—Rilke

PROLOGUE

AMERICA

OREGON TERRITORY, 1854

She rested her hand against her stomach and leaned toward the window so that she stood with her shoulder against the frame, looking down at the street below her. The light, at this hour, was yellow and heavy. At home, before the close of day, the air would turn to a deeper blue, and then the blue would darken to the color of ink, but it was rare the night that the sky was a solid, simple thing. The night at home always had something in it of the evening it had just left behind, and of the morning to come. It had a light of its own; it was never entirely dark. The night here was a different place entirely from the day, and its silent sky was domed and black as a bird's eye and dotted only sometimes with cold stars.

The town was quiet now. In the distance, she could see the line of the prairie against the line of that early-evening sky.

"Are we done?" he said.

She turned to face him. He was half sitting up, his back against the iron bedstead. He was naked from the waist up, but he'd kept on his white long johns, and he sat with one leg bent up and the other stretched out in front of him. He'd pushed his hair back from his face, and it stood up at odd angles all over his head. He was young, and strong, and though he was not handsome, there was a good, clean smell from him. He had an easy manner and a pleasant, singsong way of speaking. It was hard to imagine him angry; he had shown her kindness where others would have used her apparent vulnerability to their advantage. He had seen some things, she imagined, but from them he had learned compassion instead of cruelty. A person's true nature was quickly revealed when they had no reason to hide it. Not much was hidden from her in this room.

"We are," she said. "You are."

She turned back to the window. She could feel him watching her, waiting for her to do something.

"You sure do like looking out that window," he said. "Every time I come here, seems like you can't wait to get back to that window."

She didn't say anything.

"They told me you're from Ireland."

The word sounded like a mistake when he said it. His way of pronouncing it was all wrong: he leaned too heavily on the first part of the word, breaking it in two, like the word itself was something too big for his mouth that he was trying to swallow. But still she said nothing. If you didn't speak when people expected you to, they'd speak to fill the space themselves. The less you said, the more others spoke, and the more they spoke, the more you understood about them and the less they understood about you, and that was only for the good, as far as she was concerned.

Recently, she had found that she was falling back into old habits, and the less she spoke, the less she wanted to speak. It was as if she were losing the knack of speaking altogether. More and more often now, a whole day could go by when she didn't say a word to anyone in this house full of people. The less you said, the less you had to say, the less people expected you to say, and on it went.

"You've come a long way," he said. "I've come from out of Tennessee, and I thought that was a long way, but you come even farther." He waited. "You come all that way on your own?"

4

He was the only person she'd ever known who asked her questions about herself like he wanted to know the answer. That was no small thing, she supposed.

She moved back to the bed and sat on the edge of it. She smoothed the cover with the flat of her hand. The bedcover was a good white linen, hemmed in lace. She washed the cover herself every week and bleached it and ironed it, though it was no easy thing to iron such a linen. The other girls laughed at her for taking such care, but she took pleasure from the job. She would not easily have surrendered the task of treating the linen until it was white and clean and as good as if it had never been used.

When he understood that she was not going to answer him, he gave her the crooked smile she had come to know.

"Well, all right," he said. "I know you don't like questions. I keep going with them, though. I guess I figure you'll answer when I ask a question you like."

He swung his legs off the side of the bed and came toward her so that he was standing in front of her. Her hair hung over her shoulder loosely, and he picked it up and twisted it very gently in his hand so that it glinted in the light.

"If I want to go again, how does it work?" he said. "You answer me that question?"

"You pay again," she said. "That's how it works. You leave the money over there, same as before."

"You want to go again, Nell?" he said very quietly. His voice caught on her name. He kept twisting her hair around his hand, slowly, carefully.

She didn't look at him. She didn't want to see the need on his face and to have to pity him for it. It was hard enough to hear it in his voice.

"Leave the money over there," she said, nodding at the hatstand by the door.

"I have to leave it now, before?" he said.

"I have to see that you have the money," she said. "That's the rule. You might not have the money. You might just be saying you do. You have to leave the money first."

He let go of her hair.

"Well, I guess that's the most I've ever heard you say."

He stood there, looking at her. When she didn't look up at him, he turned away and went to pick up his pants from the chair by the window.

"Nell," he said.

He was going through his pockets, and he was beginning, she saw, to become agitated in the search. Then he swung about, and before she had understood what he meant to do, he had kicked the chair against the wall, so hard that one of its spindles cracked. She stood up from the bed. The door was behind her, and locked; she always locked it from the inside and then put the key in the drawer of the stand. She began to move toward the stand. She wanted that key in her hand.

"I been coming here nine months straight now, I'd say. I come every Friday, at dusk. Soon as I get paid, I come straight here. The foreman gives me my money. I wash up. I get on my horse. I ride directly here. When I come here, I see only you, and sometimes I have to sit out in that corridor and wait for the man who is in here to finish, and I have to nod at him when he walks out of this room like we are acquaintances, when what I want to do is—" He threw the pants to the ground and went to the window, and he put a hand on either side of it and leaned forward so that his head was hanging down between his outstretched arms.

She watched his bare back rise and fall with his breath. He had a long, ugly scar down his backbone: his horse, frightened by a rattle-snake, had thrown him, he'd told her, and, losing its balance, had fallen back on him as it had reared. He'd landed on a rock, the horse on top of him, and his back had split open from top to bottom like a cut fish, he said. It had taken many months before that opening had closed up

6

and he could walk again properly. She kept that image in her mind as she opened the drawer in the stand and took out the key: the rearing horse, the falling horse. In her mind she made the horse rear and fall, over and over, in a loop. He'd had to shoot that horse after it fell, he'd told her. It had broken its leg clean through to the bone. He was sorry about his back, he'd said, but he'd been sorrier about the horse. It had been a good, loyal friend and didn't deserve its end.

"I'm sorry about the chair," he said. "I'll fix it."

He turned so that he was facing her. She understood that he was readying himself to speak.

"First time I saw you was on the main street, end of last summer. That's one year ago now. You were carrying a load of laundry, and straight off I thought to myself that's a heavy load for such a small-boned girl. I went to help you, but one of the boys told me where you were coming from with the laundry, and I held back then, in my surprise. You were wearing a blue cotton dress, and you had your hair in a braid all the way down your back, and it was braided nice and careful."

She was still standing next to the stand. She held the cold key so tightly in her hand that its edges were cutting into her palm. She squeezed the key tighter, then tighter still.

"I asked around, but no one knew anything about you except when you came here, and that you came from Ireland. No one knows more now, I guess. Not me, certainly."

He took a step toward her.

"I came here to find you, Nell. I never been to a place like this before I saw you, and I reckon you don't fit in here, either. I know that the circumstances of our meetings are not something to be proud of. Neither of us, I guess, got much to be proud of being here. But here we are. Question is now, Where do we go from here?"

She waited.

"Do you know anyone in this country, Nell?" he said.

She shook her head, no. She knew no one outside the walls of this house.

"You got no one waiting for you to come home?"

"No," she said. "There's no one left where I come from."

"Well," he said. "Seeing as how you are free, as such, to make your own decisions, would you consider, Nell, setting up with me?"

She didn't answer.

"I have some money put by," he said. "We can head out West. We can set up. We can marry, Nell."

She put the key down on the stand. It had cut into her palm; there was blood on her hand.

I don't know anyone in this country, she thought, outside this house, but I know myself.

I know myself.

"My name is not Nell," she said.

PART I

IRELAND

1849

I

A robin in the house is a *piseog*. It's bad luck, a curse. When Honora O'Neill's mother was birthing her, a robin flew in the open door and around the room and back out the door. It was in the house only minutes, but that was long enough to put a darkness on the room and the people in it. Her mother died very soon after she was born, and she was fed on milk from the goat because none of the local women would put her to the breast, on account of the piseog. She reared herself, the neighbors told each other, because she had no mother to look after her, and her father preferred it when she wasn't within his sight. But she grew strong on the goat's milk, stronger than the other children her age; she could outrun even the older boys, and she was quicker to learn than all of them. She kept herself apart from the people, lived to a different time from them, even: from when she was very small, she spent the nights out in the woods, and she slept during the day—in the long grass in low fields in the summer, or on the floor in her father's cottage in the winter, for she had no bed—and she came to know the secret ways of the fields and the woods and all the things that lived in them better than most. She had her own rhythms, her own ways. The neighbors grew used to her comings and goings; they thought of her as a half-wild thing who lived between their world and the world of the woods, which was another world, hardly visited. She was dark haired, and her eyes were very light colored, and some of the other children called her a *sioga* and laughed at her without fear of retribution. She didn't mind their laughter. Worse things had happened to her than being laughed at. Worse things are happening to her now, every day, because of the hunger.

～

Ta an ocras orm. The hunger is on me. The hunger was on everyone, but it is worse for her than it is for the others; she is sure of that. Everyone is hungry, but she has been hungry forever, for all of her twenty years, because she has always been a greedy girl. You're a savage, her father had said to her once when she was very small. Your eyes are bigger than your belly. The image had frightened her enough to appear in her dreams, and for a long time after he had said that to her, she would wake crying because she had seen herself with huge round eyes and a strange small round belly, and in the dreams, every time, her eyes were so big that they were too heavy for her head, and the weight of them would make her fall over, face-first, onto the wet ground, and on falling, she would wake, crying out in the darkness to no one.

Always, she had wanted, and always, she wants, still.

Now it is William who despairs of her and her wants, as her father had before. Though they have been married only a year, he is already tired from her, and of her, it seems.

He was mad for her in the beginning, and especially before they married. Once he had come to her father's house with an armful of pale wildflowers for her—primroses, honeysuckle—and she'd put the flowers around the dark cottage, and even her father had marveled at their scent. And he'd written her three letters, which were accounts of what he did between their meetings (*today the father and myself dug a rill by the lower wall*) rounded off with strangely formal declarations of devotion (*I look forward with great longing to the day when we will be joined as one*). It had cost him to write those letters, she knew: William could barely hold a pen; it would have been very difficult for him to find paper. So, though they were very poorly done, and it made her burn with embarrassment for William, for herself, to read them, she'd kept the letters. She had them still, hidden behind a stone in a hole in the cottage wall.

It was hard to imagine William writing her letters now. More and more often, she caught him looking at her like she was a problem he couldn't fix. She is half-wild, people had warned him. The father won't give her a pot for a dowry. She won't know how to keep a house for you. But he'd told her how he'd lain awake in his bed at night as if taken by a fever, seeing only her light-colored eyes and thinking of her moving like a ghost through the trees, her feet barely touching the ground. He loved the smell of her—he said that after they'd been together, the smell of her on him made him want to punch a hole in a wall—and though everyone was against even the idea of them, they'd married in his father's house only weeks after meeting. She had walked out of her father's house to her wedding with her hands hanging to her, alone, without a backward glance.

She'd looked only ahead.

But it had not been easy to stand alone before William's family, a hungry girl in a poor girl's dress. She read the first glimmerings of doubt on William's face as he looked at her barefoot in his father's house on their wedding day; she saw him begin to understand then the full extent of her loneliness. It was no small thing, she knew, to take a wife who was so alone in the world. It's lucky you are, Honora, she told herself, to be living in these strange times, when strange things can happen because of the hunger, when someone like you can marry a son of the O'Donoghues, and get away with it too. The rules are easily broken now, and that's only to your favor.

People shook their heads and clicked their tongues disapprovingly, but it was the hunger, they told each other, that made an O'Donoghue wedding such a poor show of a thing. No one blamed Honora.

But the hunger didn't always change things, Honora knew; it only revealed them as they really were. There was no wedding breakfast, but there would have been no wedding breakfast anyway if it had been up to her father, even in the best of times. And she had no wedding dress, because her mother's had been sold a long time since for the rent.

These things stood, hunger or no hunger.

She remembered how she felt on the day of the wedding, but the small details of it—those were mostly lost to her now. It was becoming harder, every day, to hold on to such details: time and memory had become slippery things. She could recall the color of the bowl that she ate from as a child, the feel of the rough edge against her mouth, the smell of its clay, but she couldn't remember exactly what had happened to her last week. Days, weeks, slid by, made indistinct by the hunger.

Every day, William worked his father's land, digging for something that wasn't there, and it seemed to her that it was dark all the time, and they were never properly in the light.

They had married in the spring, and after their wedding, there had been a long stretch of unusually good weather, and those days, it seemed—and it seemed still—had been filled with light. It was easier to bear the hunger in the summer, and they had the hope, though faint, of a good crop ahead of them, and the hope gave them strength. During the day, they had worked side by side under the high lavender sky, and the blue evenings they'd spent walking the fields, coming back to the cottage just as darkness fell. Every night in that cottage had been like a present. They had a house, a bed, each other, and all they had wanted, in those days, was to be together. Before they had married, they had lain together in the long grass in the woods, always fearful of being discovered, disgraced, and it was a wondrous thing to have the peace of a place of their own; that room, that cottage, had been a whole world to them. The things they had done, in that cottage—she blushed still at the memory of them. They used to fall asleep holding hands, and when they woke in the morning, still holding hands, they would turn to each other and smile. She marveled at that now, the holding of hands; when she tried to see herself as she had been then, it was like trying to make out a distant figure across a river. The world they inhabited, for that summer, had been colored differently, and them as different people in it.

But the summer had passed, and in the autumn the crop had failed, and they couldn't pay the rent, so the landlord had evicted them before Christmas and had the cottage leveled. All of their happiness went away then. They were luckier than most, William kept telling her: they had no children to care for, and they had a roof over their heads in his father's house, and all they had to do was to keep working and hoping for the best, but it was very hard to watch their cottage being knocked down and their wedding bed being taken away, and it was hard to live in Donal Og's house—William was not good at being a son and a husband at the same time, and his loyalty, his attention, she soon found, he gave to his father.

After only days of moving to Donal Og's cottage, she began to sleep out in the woods again, to keep her hours of old. She grew more silent, spoke less. No one remarked on her absence or her silence. She began to feel that she could slip into the world of the woods and stay there altogether and that no one would even notice that she had gone away.

When she did return to the cottage, when the nights grew too cold for the woods, she had to lie with William in his narrow childhood bed. They had a corner of the room, behind a blanket that they tacked up onto the ceiling and against the wall. It had been months— three, maybe four—since they had been together as husband and wife, because William feared they'd make a noise that his father might overhear. And William was very tired from the work, and they were both too weak from the hunger to turn to each other at night, too tired to hold hands, even.

She often didn't sleep, despite her tiredness, and so through the long nights she lay perfectly still, not making a sound, pretending at being asleep, and trying to think, trying to understand how she could survive, and all the while she had to listen to William's father's snoring, and to William pulling at himself under the blanket, making enough noise to raise a dead man.

It was hard, though, to think. It was as if there were a big hole inside her that no food could ever fill now, and what was inside her was outside, too, and all there was, was absence, and that absence was melting the world like ice melted before the sun. Her hunger began to grow nearly unbearable, unmanageable as the days passed, and it was her greed, she knew, that made it so.

Her greed, her hunger, made her impatient where before she was quick in thought, and unkind, she feared, ready to act out of anger, and alert to intent. She had become too hasty in thought and action, and sharp and unpredictable, given to the unexpected. She was far, now, from who she once was, and getting farther and farther away all the time. She lay awake at night, next to William but not touching him, and she began to worry at what she could and might do. She began to think that she did not know herself.

~

They started walking to the town too late in the day. That was clear to her from the outset. The people were to walk together to the town, more than twelve miles away, to be seen by the landlord's inspectors, and if they were judged there to be sufficiently wanting, they would be granted relief. The relief would be three pounds of grain to the person, enough food for weeks, if managed properly. Those who failed to appear for inspection would be struck from the relief list, and that meant no food at all.

The hunger and the worry of the hunger had made the people simple, it seemed to her. They were made childlike by their weakness. Walk, the landlord said, and so they walked. There were no questions asked anymore of the why of everything. Why must we walk? Why can no one come to us? Why only three pounds of grain? Why are we hungry? Why is this happening to us? The people were concerned now only with the how. How will we manage the walk? How will we be judged? How can we make the grain last until we next get food? It was entirely the wrong way to think about it all, she thought, and how that was not clear to the others was astonishing to her. But the people could not question their lot, she knew, for one why would only lead to a bigger why, and on and on to whys so big you would drown in them. The people could only manage the how of things now, and even the how was too much for them, for to make such a simple mistake as to wait until the best part of the day had gone was fatal, surely.

~

It was a wickedly cold day and getting colder, and it had been raining since the morning. The men—William, and his father, Donal Og, among them—had decided to wait until the rain stopped before leaving. There's worse coming than rain, she had said to them. She knew from the look of the sky that bad weather was rising from beyond the mountains. But the men hadn't listened to her, and so she had cried out in frustration. Oh, would that I could go on my own and not have to wait for all of you sitting around here like a load of sleeping cows, and they had laughed at her then, and William had given her a terrible look and, because the others were watching him, had raised his fist up to her. Stop, the raised fist had meant. Be quiet. He was angry and ashamed that she had spoken so loudly in front of the gathering, but she feared neither his nor the men's anger: her own anger at their wrongheadedness left no room for fear. They would not listen to her, though they were wrong and she was right and that was that. It was as simple a wrong as all the other wrongs in her life.

She left the room of men after they had silenced her and went to stand outside the cottage with her back to the wall. The wall was cold and damp—she could feel it through her dress—and the trees were black and wet and beautiful against the lavender sky, and she lifted her face to the wind and closed her eyes. She felt something in her open out and rise up. She loved this spot, where the corner of the cottage gave onto the field, and she loved especially to be out there when the wind was high. She had never been on a boat out on the sea, though she saw the shine of the sea in the distance every day, but she thought that to be out in the wild wind must be very like being out on the great sea in a small boat. Even today, with all the trouble about her, there was a wonder to standing against the wind like this. Even as the moment was passing her, she saw the glory in it. I have the wind and its wildness, she thought, and glad I am that I hear its voice and am not deaf to its secrets. I have that, at least.

She stood there for a long time, until the wind changed direction so that it started to come in from the mountains, and then it had a bad sound to it that was like a lament. She was very tired, the kind of tiredness that made her want to lie down on the ground and go to sleep for a long time, and always, and above everything else, she was hungry. Her tongue felt swollen, like it was too big for her mouth, and she had a strange taste like metal in her mouth. She felt then that she would retch. This had started to happen to her, and to some of the other people, too—being sick from the hunger. She felt the warning wave of heat begin to rise in her stomach, and she was forced then to stand with her head against the wall and wait until the heat and the sickness passed.

When she felt steady enough, she turned her face from the wind and began to walk away across the field and toward the woods. She wanted to get into the trees and away from the cottage, from the men, from herself.

Below her were the valley and, in the distance, the black lake, with the white road running beside it and away from it and over the mountains. Beyond the mountains was the town. The rain was steady now, and getting colder, and the sky had a heavy dark look to it that told you all you needed to know. There wasn't a break anywhere in the sky, nor a bird flying in it, nor an animal on the land. She was by the woods now, and they were singing to her, and she threw her arms out wide and her head back to the wind.

"Honora."

William was coming up the field toward her, shouting to make himself heard above the wind. His face was contorted from the effort of shouting and running and trying to do both at the same time. He was not a natural runner—he was too big, too heavy—and for a moment, she considered running away from him and having him chase her through the woods in a kind of mad game. He would not be able to catch her, and he would grow very angry, and there might be some amusement to be had from that. But it would not be worth it, she knew, and she was too tired and too hungry for such games, in any case.

He came up to her, drawing himself up like a horse in the traces, and he stood with his hands on his hips, breathing very heavily and looking down at the valley as if he were taking his time to admire the view and not trying at all to steady his breathing. He did not look at her, except out of the side of his eye.

"I knew you'd be up here," he said. "You can't get enough of these old woods."

He wiped the back of his hand across his mouth.

She said nothing; she waited.

"We'll wait a few hours," he said eventually. "It will lift by evening."

"It won't," she said, but quietly, because he could see the mushroom-colored sky above them as well as she could, and they both knew what it meant.

"We can't walk any distance in this rain," he cried, as if they had been arguing for a very long time and this were the end of the argument and he could take no more. She knew that if she looked down, he would be holding his hands in tight balls, and he'd be rubbing his thumb against the top of his fingers like he was trying to rub something dirty off them.

"There's a bad light over the mountains," she said. "Something is coming."

"You sound like an old witch when you say things like that," he said.

Whatever feeling there had been between them was all finished, all put away now. Now when she looked at William, she saw someone slow and weak. He moved slowly; he spoke slowly; he thought slowly. Sometimes he took so long finishing a sentence that she thought he'd forgotten what he wanted to say, and often she would shout, "What?" just as he was starting to speak again, startling both of them. She was embarrassed by him, and ashamed of her embarrassment, but every time she looked at him, she felt only panic and worry. He had married her out of a wrongheaded love, the kind that ran out of road quickly.

"Do as you want, William," she said into the wind. "Do as you will, as you always do."

"Ah, Honora," he said.

She turned to look at him straight on.

"You're afraid to speak honestly to the men. You're a coward."

She was amazed that she had said this out loud. That's it now, Honora, she said to herself. That is too far, even for William.

William made as if to walk away, and then, pausing, he turned and said under his breath, but loudly enough so that she heard, "Stupid motherless bitch."

She knew that he was repeating what they had both heard others say—the local boys she spurned, the local girls she outwitted, outran. But to hear William say it nearly broke something in her. She thought of his letters to her, saw him bent over the paper, trying to write to her by the poor candlelight and him not even knowing how to hold the pen properly, and she felt, suddenly, terribly, that she might cry. As a child she had never cried; she had been known for it. But in these recent months, she had often felt that she could cry at any moment, that to not cry was a thing nearly beyond her managing. The tears were something she had to work at keeping back, all the time. But now, oh surely, the tears would come and disgrace her.

To stop the tears, she put her head back and looked up at the great dark-domed sky above her, and then she lifted one hand up into the air and moved her fingers together so that her hand looked like a bird, and she moved the bird against the sky, black against the gray light. Fly away, bird, she thought. If I could, I would free myself from this body and rise up and away into the high sky, higher and higher until all the world below is a memory.

"Honora," William said. He was standing in front of her now, watching her, and he sounded very tired, as tired as she felt. He put his hand out and took hold of her hand moving through the air. "It will clear soon. This weather. And anyway, this light is terribly poor; it is not as if we are wasting good light. We do better to wait."

Oh! she thought. William! You don't want to go into the town, and that is why you look for reasons to wait. It is not because of the weather; it is because you are afraid to go. As long as you do not go, there is hope to hold on to; there is the hope of going another day. What William thought was strength—to persist, to wait, always to wait—was weakness, because it was so wrong. They were fighting shadows now.

"It will be a long walk with these bare feet, when we do go," she said, to say something easy, to help him.

She had no shoes; none of them had now. They were as barefoot as small children in the summer. The walk would be through bog and bracken, and the white road was only a goat track, really; it would be very hard on their feet. And their clothes were no good. Once they'd had a loom in the townland and they'd had clothes from it, but the loom was long gone, and everything they wore now was thin with age and hard with dirt. They would need to find shelter on the road, from the cold, and the night.

They stood before each other in the rain and the wind. She remembered the first time she had seen William, and the energy that had come from him like heat, the force he had been. He wasn't that person anymore.

He was still holding her hand tightly, and he shook it gently now, as if he wanted to shake an answer from her.

"When this is all over, Honora, we'll go into Galway, and we'll buy ourselves the finest shoes. Won't we?"

"William," she said. She would try one more time. "Please. It is a mistake to wait. I know this. Will you trust me, William? If we are to go, we should go now. It is twelve miles to the town. That is five hours' fast walk on a good day. If we leave now, we will be there while it is still light, at least."

He dropped her hand, and looked away from her.

"It's been decided," he said. "We wait for the rain to lift. And you should not come. I don't know if you're able for it, Honora. You don't look right. It's days now since you ate anything decent."

"I am able," she said. "I'm as able as anyone. I won't be left behind. I must be counted."

~

She did what she could to prepare for the walk. Under the ditch in the back field there was a hole big enough to sleep in, and she went there to rest. There was nowhere to lie in the cottage, with the men there, and if she were to walk any distance, she would need to rest first. The earth was fine and dry in the hole, like sand, and she was warm enough—she was warm, nearly always, these days, which was a strange thing she didn't understand. The hunger had rendered her body a foreign thing to her: it did unexpected things, behaved in unexpected ways that she didn't question. She gave no consideration to questions that couldn't be answered. There was no point to them. She lay down on her side and put her hands under her face and said out loud to herself, as she had since she was a child, "Go to sleep now, Honora," and soon enough, she did.

When she woke, she ate what she had hidden in her apron. She had a bit of biscuit, a handful of meal; she ate it as slowly as she could bear. The others would take whatever food they had on the walk, and they would share it with her when they saw that she had nothing; this food was hers alone. She drank water, fast, after she'd eaten, to make her feel full; she drank until the skin on her stomach felt stretched and taut, and then she tapped her fingers against the skin to make it thrum like a drum. Then she saw to her feet. She tore two long strips from the hem of her dress—they came away easily in her hand, like the petals of old flowers—and tied knots in the strips so that they would hold longer. This way, she thought, she might get through the worst of the white road if the luck was with her. She wound the strips round and round her feet until they were bound up like bundles. She put her hair on top of her head and twisted it until it was in a tight bun. She didn't want wet hair in her face or down the back of her neck while she was walking; that was a feeling she hated. Her hair was hard with the dirt, and there was a terrible smell from her body when she moved. She was ashamed of that, as she was of everything else she had, and was, and stood for. Shame, shame, Honora, her father would cry when she had done something wrong when she was a little girl, and she thought, Yes, Dada, oh, the shame, the shame.

II

She was afraid to look at the faces of the children who had come from across the mountains. It was not so bad yet in William's townland that the children starved, but the people living out in the hills—they were near death from the hunger, and their children looked old, like tiny, wizened, ancient people. Their faces had collapsed inward. They were gray from the hunger, and their eyes were huge and their mouths small and pinched. Some of them, the younger ones, were naked. The older children wore rags. They were all barefoot. She saw a girl from her own townland, who'd had glorious dark red hair down to her waist that she'd worn loose summer and winter. Someone had sheared her hair off, and what was left was a dull brown. She had gone up to the girl and said, Ann, is it you? But the girl had looked at her without recognition as if it were she, Honora, who was so terribly changed. There was no expression at all in the girl's eyes. She said nothing, though she looked at Honora for a long time, so long that Honora started to wonder if the girl was able to reason at all, and then the girl began to cry, silently. She put her hand on her hair, and Honora put her hand on her arm, and neither of them said anything, not a word. There was nothing to say. That was the thing she thought she would remember: the silence. None of the children made any noise. Even the babies did not cry. They were too weak, and anyway, they'd learned that it made no difference to cry. Nothing would change if they did.

~

The rain had stopped late in the afternoon, quite suddenly, and then the pale winter sun had come out and shone weakly through the rain, and Honora had thought, on seeing the sun and rain together, All in this world is wrong. The wind rose and cleared the sky to an empty brilliant blue, and though it was so cold that it was hard to breathe, the people had cheered at the sun, and William had said, You'd be better off keeping your weather predictions to yourself next time there, Honora.

People had begun to gather at the bottom of the hill below the cottage after the rain stopped, and now there was a great crowd. She had never seen so many people in one place: there were a hundred people now, surely, maybe more, and the number was growing all the time. She watched the crowd, and after a while, she realized that she was watching because she was looking for her father. It was not impossible that he was here: Ann was, and she recognized others from her townland too. She had not seen her father since the morning of her wedding, when she had walked out of his cottage and away, without looking back. He had closed the door behind her as soon as she walked through it: she remembered that the bang it made was loud enough to make her jump.

She had received no word of him since, though that was not a strange thing; her village was many an hour's walk back over the mountains. There were no marts being held now where people might meet to exchange information, and in the last months, the regular patterns of life had fallen away; there were no harvests to celebrate, no weddings or funerals held, no gatherings of any kind. There were people here whom she knew from her village—girls she had played with when they were only children, women whose tables she had eaten at—and there were people she had never seen before, though they all had a look to them of her own people. But she could not see her father; he was not here. She knew that instinctively, even as she searched for him. If he did not come, it was because he could not. She put her hand to her heart and said, "Oh," out loud, to let some of the tightness in her chest out. He had been glad to have her married and gone from the house: he'd told her that. He'd been glad to be rid of the piseog, of course. But she would have welcomed the chance to see him again.

The light of the day was fading fast, and as it faded, the noise from the people grew stronger. They were growing impatient now; they were eager to leave. Many of them, those who had come from across the fields and down from the mountains, had already walked in the rain and the wind for hours to reach this spot. She was afraid to be with so many people; there were too many faces to look at, and each face told a terrible story. She began to push her way out of the crowd.

"Honora!"

It was the schoolmaster who had taught her to read and write and had given her his own buttermilk at dinnertime when she had nothing else and once, even, had given her an old dress of his wife's that she'd worn without altering because she didn't know how; its skirts had trailed after her in the schoolyard and the other children had laughed at her, but she had gloried in the delicately sprigged pale colored cotton. She had been afraid to wash the dress, she remembered; she had worried she would wash the flowers away, so she'd worn it winter and summer until it fell apart in her hands, like a fading flower. She thought of that as she watched the schoolmaster advance toward her. The dress, the schoolroom, the buttermilk—these were things now from a different life, and it was entirely confusing to see the schoolmaster here, in this life; it was not right. He had his hand up in the air and was waving at her and trying to make his way to her through the people. She understood from the urgent way he was advancing that he had something he wanted to say to her. She backed away from him and then fell suddenly down, tripping over her own feet.

The schoolmaster came to stand above her. He held out his hand to her. She took it and stood up and then shook his hand, pretending to both of them that she hadn't fallen over like a child. She did not want the schoolmaster to think her so weak, so clumsy.

"Honora," he said. "How are you."

He did not put this as a question, but as an acknowledgment of the circumstances in which they found themselves, in this field, under this sky.

"I'm all right, sir," she said. "Thank you."

"I'm sorry to see you here," he said. "I knew, of course, that you had married and that you lived here with Donal O'Donoghue's people, but I am sorry to see you . . ."

He stopped. He put his hand up to his eyes, and his hand was shaking and his whole body too. Honora saw that he was crying. She took a step back from him.

"You were a great girl. You were the best student I ever had; I always said it to Frances. I never knew a child to learn as quick as you. You'd only have to tell you something the one time and you had it. Some of them you could be talking to for years, and it has no effect on them at all, but you . . ."

He was crying and laughing, and she put her head down so she wasn't looking at him. To see the schoolmaster cry like this was as unnatural as seeing him stand naked before her.

"Sir," she said.

"Did they tell you about your father, Honora?" he said.

There was something wild looking in his eyes. He was moving and looking at her and at the sky and at the crowd but seeing nothing, she realized. There was blood on his left hand, and his face was dark with dirt.

"No, sir," she said. "I have had no word from my father, or of him, since my wedding."

"No, of course. No one would have told you. They're a backward people, Honora; I always said it. A backward, inward-looking people."

He put his hand on her arm.

"He was weak from the hunger, and then the fever came and took him fast, very fast. I'm sorry to have to tell you."

"Thank you, sir," she said.

She waited to feel something, but nothing came. She felt as if someone had opened a door inside her and everything had rushed out and she was completely empty, open to the wind, light as a feather, and insubstantial as light. I am standing now, she thought, in an empty room, and I am getting smaller and smaller, and the room is getting bigger, and soon I will disappear, and only the empty room will be left.

"Where is he buried?" she said, because the schoolmaster was waiting for her to say something.

"Oh," he said. He was rocking from side to side now and slapping his hands against his thighs. "Oh, there is no money for burials, Honora. When Frances went, I wrapped her in her shawl, and the men came and took her on the cart toward Galway with the rest of them, and they did the same for your father. I'm sorry to say it, Honora; I'm sorry."

He leaned toward her and took hold of her hand.

"You must leave this place, Honora," he said. "There is nothing for you here. Do you hear what I say to you? We are finished as a people. Go away from here and don't come back."

He dropped her hand as if he had suddenly realized that it was too heavy for him to hold.

"Go away, Honora," he said. "And don't look back."

~

She went back up the hill to the cottage. When she got to the door, she felt as if her legs would give way from under her; she had to sit down heavily and suddenly on the ground. She drew her knees up to her chest, and then without knowing what she was doing, she began to tear at the earth between her legs like she was digging for something

28

hidden in the ground until she said to herself, Stop, Honora. Her hands were black with earth, and she pressed them to her face; the earth was cool, and it had a good, clean smell. "Dada," she said, out loud, and she thought, That is the last time I say that word aloud, or even in my head. That word is going in the earth now. She pushed the earth back into the hole she had made, and then she stood up.

The mass of people at the bottom of the hill was swelling and shifting like a cloud of birds in the evening sky at that moment when the day tips into the violet night. The time to leave was near; the crowd could sense it. She took a step forward and into the path of a robin flying slowly past her. She put her hand up to her cheek; the bird's wing had touched her face. The robin landed on the ground before her, in front of the open door of the cottage, and began to rearrange itself with care, and as it did so, it put its head on one side and, calm, unblinking, regarded her.

She got down onto her haunches, and she looked at the bird, and the bird watched her back, as if waiting for something to happen.

"Hello, bird," she said. "Hello, my friend."

She felt something settle silently beside her then, like a cold shadow.

"Do you know why the breast of the robin is so red these days?"

Honora kept her eyes on the eyes of the bird.

"It's because he feeds on the dead he finds lying in the fields and on the roads. Don't you, birdy? That's what makes the robin so fat and so red. Bird is fat from the flesh and red from the blood of the dead. Isn't that right, birdy birdy?"

Old Alice had crouched down so that she was level with Honora. She put a finger out and traced a line down Honora's bare arm with her long nail.

"Hello, girly," she said, softly.

Honora stood up. Her sudden movement made the robin take flight. It flew slowly to the top of the open door and landed there with a shake. It kept its eye, though, on Honora.

Old Alice laughed.

"Birdy likes you," she said, standing. She was as small as a child and so old that her eyes were milky pale and her skin was the color of the earth. "Knows you hear the things others don't hear; knows you see the sights unseen."

"I hear, and more than you know, and what's more, I understand what I hear, what I see," said Honora, with her eyes fixed on the bird and her back to Alice.

The people were afraid of Alice and said she would give you the evil eye if you looked at her wrong. They were right, thought Honora, to fear her. They didn't fear her enough. But that fear had to be hidden from Alice, because fear was a weakness, and Alice fed off all that was weak, exposed, vulnerable.

"Oh, she's a brazen one, this one," Alice shouted in delight. "As if she has all the world behind her and her all alone, as alone as a bird in the wind."

Better alone than with the wrong kind, like your kind, thought Honora, but she said nothing. It was better to say nothing now.

"There's a test coming for you down the road, girly," said Alice quietly. It was worse when she spoke quietly. It was more frightening. The words landed on Honora like stones dropped into a deep well.

"Birdy knows," said Alice. "Birdy is waiting."

It would not do to run away, though the urge to break into a run was very strong. I wish more than anything that I could run from Alice and this place and the people here, she thought, and I wish, too, that I could run from the dirt and the tiredness and the hunger. As a child she had run everywhere, barefoot, across fields, through the woods, chased by no one and with nowhere to run to. She had run for the feeling of it alone. It had been a long time since she had had the strength to run, or a reason for running. But she could not run from Alice, and she couldn't run down the hill like a mad person to William and the gathered people. It would tell them all something about her that she didn't want them to know.

She lifted her skirts so that they were above her knees in a kind of nod to the memory of running, and she began to walk away as slowly as she could make herself from Alice.

"Stop," said Alice. "Foolish girl. You have no reason to fear me. Not you. Look now and see what I have for you."

Honora stopped. She should not keep her back to Alice for so long. She turned and saw that Alice was bending and reaching behind her, and when she straightened up, she was holding a black stick that stood higher than her.

"Blackthorn," Alice said, looking up at the stick. She held it out to Honora then and shook it at her. "Tree of the dark half of the year. Fairy tree."

"You cut the blackthorn," said Honora.

It was a sin to cut the blackthorn, and bad luck beyond knowing to those who profited from its cutting.

"Ah," cried Alice. "I've no fear of that world and its rules. It's a good, powerful tree and a protector to all those who carry it." She laughed. "Not to those who cut it, but to those who carry it."

She shook the stick again at Honora.

"Take it," she said impatiently. "You need this where you are going. Trouble is coming down the road for you. Help yourself, girl."

She had no mother. Her father had preferred not to have her in the house. The people from her townland, from William's, had long talked about her in low voices when she walked by. All this she had borne. But to be marked out by Alice as one of her own was something that Honora had never been able to countenance. *Leave me be,* she wanted to shout. *You will not put your mark on me. Am I not marked enough, already?*

"I need nothing from you," said Honora. "You cut that tree to make sticks for cursing and I'll have no part in your doings."

31

Alice stepped toward her. Don't move away, Honora, she told herself. Stand your ground. Alice was looking at her now, as if deciding something. If she touches me, I will not be able to stop myself pushing her away and running, she thought. Let her not try to touch me. Alice put both hands on the stick and held it up to her again.

"Take the stick, girl," she said. "It would be bad cess to you to turn it down; you know that well. And I give it to you without asking anything back. Take the stick and help yourself."

It was a good strong stick. She was weak. The way to the town was long. She put a hand down to it: the blackthorn was as cool to the touch as dark water. Without looking at Alice, she took hold of the stick and held it against her. It reached to the top of her shoulder and was nearly as light to carry as a flower.

Alice nodded.

"I won't see you again," she said. "Go well."

"Where are you going?" said Honora, before she could stop herself. Where could Alice go? There was nowhere for her beyond this place.

Alice laughed. She was laughing at her; Honora knew.

"Go on, now, girl," she said. "Go away from me."

Honora turned and faced the hill. She could feel Alice watching her. Don't turn around, she said to herself. Don't look back at her. Her father would have warned her to keep her head down, to not look back. Keep your eyes to the ground, Honora, he used to say to her. Don't give any trouble, and don't look for trouble. But nothing he had ever said had helped her, and she had followed her own counsel, and she would follow it still, and a stronger voice in her head said to her then, Turn, Honora, and before she could give herself more time to think, she turned around so that she was facing Alice.

"What is to come?" The wind was blowing, shoving at her, but she stood as straight as she could manage with her back to the wind and her feet apart and the stick in her hand by her side. "What is this test? You know, and you should tell me. It's my story to know."

Alice looked at her without expression, without giving her any sign or gesture.

"Will you tell me what is to come?" said Honora desperately, because there was no point in trying to hide her need now that she had asked twice.

The robin, still on top of the open cottage door, put its head on the side and watched her.

She bent and picked up a stone, breathed in, then aimed and threw it at the bird. The stone bounced off the door, and the robin took flight, flew to the top of the roof, and settled there, watching her still.

I wish I'd hit it, she thought. I wish I'd hit it on the head and closed its eyes finally. I've had enough of being watched and judged in this world, she thought, and then she told herself, You're a long way from yourself now, Honora, wishing ill on a small bird of the woods who never did you harm.

"What's a curse to one is a blessing to another," said Alice.

"What does that mean?" said Honora, and her hand opened and closed against the stick.

The wind was crying out now like a child, and the sky was darkening, and it felt like the very earth beneath her had a pulse of its own.

"Beware the one who won't set you free," said Alice. Her eyes were closed, and her face, without the pale light of her eyes, was a dark emptiness. "Look for the one who sees the blessing."

"I don't know what that means," said Honora, and the words sounded strangled, strange in her mouth. Don't start crying, she warned herself. Don't you start crying now, Honora.

"That's all there is, girl," said Alice, and she sounded almost regretful. "I see no more."

Honora put her head down, against the stick. When she lifted it, Alice was standing directly in front of her, and she was holding her hand out toward her in a fist. She opened her hand. There was a feather on her palm, gray on one side of the shaft, white on the other, the tips of the plumes black as if they had been dipped in paint.

Alice took Honora's hand in hers, laid the feather against her palm, and closed Honora's hand around it.

"Trouble coming," she said in a whisper, sadly. She was still holding Honora's hand. She closed her eyes again and put her lips together and made a soft smacking sound, *put-put.*

Honora pulled her hand away from Alice.

"Trouble is here already," she said. She put her clenched hand to her chest. When Alice had held it, she had felt something like a light run through her, and she felt that too-bright light in her still, and it frightened her.

Alice opened her eyes and laughed hard.

"You always had fire in your belly," she said. "Since you were a small child that no one wanted. It will serve you, that fire. Go on now, girl."

Alice put her hand out toward her, palm up; it was as brown as the bark of the blackthorn tree. Honora knew that Alice didn't mean for her to take her hand; the open hand was only an invitation to go away from her. Such a thing, she thought—to live in expectation of never being touched, and then she thought, You know well how it is to be not wanted, not touched, Honora. You know how it is to live so alone.

Something turned itself over in Honora's mind, opened itself up. See what you are, Honora, she said to herself. Be brave, now, and raise yourself up. She closed her eyes, and then she put her hand on top of Alice's hand. She felt Alice go very still, and then she heard her make a sound like aahhh, and she breathed out and pushed her hand very gently up against Honora's hand.

"You were a friend to me when I was a small child," said Honora. "I don't forget it."

From watching Alice, she had learned how to live in the woods. Alice had fed her, more than once. She had never done her harm. The people spurned Alice because they feared her, but they turned from

Honora, too, and in time, they would put a word on why, and it was as likely as not that the word would be *fear*. She had been a coward, all these years, to have refused Alice's attention. And she hadn't said good-bye to her father, or to the people in the townland of her birth—she hadn't known when she'd last seen them that she would not see them again. Alice is right, she thought. We will not see each other again. Lucky we are when we know we're doing something or seeing someone for the last time.

"Goodbye, Alice," Honora said. *"Go raibh maith agat."*

Thank you. In the Irish, to say thank you was to say *may good be with you*, and she wished that, she realized; she wished Alice well.

"I'll do a powerful binding to keep you safe," said Alice, and the words came out of her in a rush. "You'll see, girl."

Her face was contorted with an emotion Honora couldn't, didn't want to name, and it frightened her, how the look on Alice's face made her feel, like someone was reaching down into her chest and touching her heart and turning it over.

She took her hand from Alice and turned away to the hill, and started down it, and this time she didn't look back. Alice, she said again, but to herself now, and she then heard Alice's voice in her head saying back, *Goodbye, girl. Go well.*

She made her way through the crowd to stand next to William.

He turned to look at her.

"Your face looks strange," he said. "What was the old witch saying to you?"

"Nothing," she said.

She wouldn't tell him what the schoolmaster had told her about her father. He would tell Donal Og, and then everyone would know and it would be too much to bear, the weight of everyone's attention on her. She would tell him after the walk, when they were back in the village. For now, if she didn't have to talk about it, she didn't have to think about it. And there was no point, at all, in telling him what Old Alice had said.

"Nothing," she said again, and she made herself sound more certain this time, and William, satisfied, turned his attention away from her, and while he looked away, she put the feather under her dress, against her heart, without even knowing why.

~

The people were standing in knots of three and four. William and the men—his father, and his cousin, Tim, and Sean O'Tuama, and all the rest of them—were at the head of the crowd. The people were growing quiet now in expectation of some instruction.

"What are we to do, Donal?" shouted out a man in the crowd.

"The weather is with us," called Donal Og. "We will go now and hope that we have an easy way of it."

"It's many a mile, and the day is nearly dead," said another man. "We will have a bad way of it in the dark."

"If we have to, we sleep on the road," Donal Og shouted. "We've no choice here, now. The strong will help the weak, and with the help of God, this time tomorrow we'll be home, and we'll have food enough to see us through the winter."

Without another signal, and quite abruptly, he turned and started on the white road that led from the village to the mountain, and the people, once they had organized themselves into families or groups of three or four, followed on, without a word.

III

The landlord's agents had repaired to the lord's lodge for the evening. It took her a moment to understand what the clerk was telling them, because the word *repair* meant "fix" to her. But she realized quickly, from the man's demeanor and from everything else he was saying, that what he meant was, the agents had gone.

They were too late. They had started walking too late in the day.

"What is he saying?" the people were asking each other. "What does he mean?"

The older ones had no English at all; many of the young people, even, spoke a mixture of Irish and English without even knowing which words were which. *An bhfuil cead agam dul go dti* the outhouse, the children in her class used to say to the schoolmaster. Please may I go to the outhouse. They lived between the two languages, fitfully, uncomfortably.

"He says that the agents are gone," Honora called out. She stood at the front of the crowd, next to William and his father. The man, a clerk for the agents, stood on a wooden box above them, looking down at them. What does he see when he looks at us? she wondered, and she answered herself: He sees a dirty mass, in rags, not able to speak his language, stinking of poverty, demanding help. I think that we are not even people to him. I think we are less to him than his horse. She looked up at the man and kept looking at him. *Look at me,* she wanted to shout. *Do you see me? Do you see us?* The man was pale with some emotion—fear, she thought. She hoped it was fear. "We are too late," she said to the crowd.

The man's eyes flicked down to her as she spoke, and then away again immediately.

"How can it be?" said Donal Og. "We were told to come today."

"The agents have gone to their dinner," said the clerk loudly, clearly. The agents hev gone to their din-ah.

English people spoke very slowly, it seemed to her. Irish people spoke quickly, whether they were speaking Irish or English, with the words falling over each other and the *t* swallowing the *h* after it and the sentences running into each other, oh sorry sorry sorry bye bye bye, like they were more than half-ashamed of what they were saying and were trying to get it over with as quickly as possible. English people gave every word plenty of time and space. Each word was given weight and significance, and they were never in a hurry to get those words out. They were confident in their audience's willingness to wait and listen while they practiced their perfect enunciation. Either that, she thought, or English people considered the Irish hard of hearing or slow in understanding, or both. Both, she told herself. Both.

"Does he say where they have gone, Honora?" said Donal Og.

"To the lord's hunting lodge," said the clerk, speaking to a spot in the air, above the people's heads. "They left word that if you came, you were to journey there to be inspected." He cleared his throat and tried to raise his voice. "You will be seen tonight, as promised."

"That lodge is many miles from here," shouted a man in the crowd.

"It is," cried a woman. "We have children with us."

"It's twelve miles, at least," said Donal Og, almost to himself.

"That's twelve miles too many," said Honora to him. "We cannot do it."

Donal Og turned to the people. "He says we have to walk, now, to the lord's lodge," he shouted, in Irish. "It's a hard twelve miles there, and we'll have that twelve miles back again and then the walk home across the mountain."

"What else can we do?" said William. "We have come this far. The worst is behind us, surely."

"And we'll have food on the way back where we have none now," said another young man.

"No," said Honora. She moved so that she was standing in front of William and speaking directly to Donal Og. "We must not. It's too far, Donal. It's night now, and the cold is too much."

Donal Og looked at her. He turned back to face the clerk. He took his cap off and smoothed his hair back with the flat of his hand and then bent his head forward in supplication. For a terrible moment, she thought he would kneel.

Don't beg! she wanted to shout. *Don't shame us more than we have already been shamed! We have nothing left now but our refusal to beg. Your people were the kings of this place once and asked for nothing. How has it happened that we are all so reduced that now you beg for us?*

"Would we sleep here, in the town, sir, and walk tomorrow morning?" said Donal. "There are many children and babies even among us and older people, too, who will find the going very hard. We could leave at first light and be with the landlord early in the day tomorrow."

"No," said the clerk, and at least he looked nearly sorry saying it, she thought. "The instruction is that you walk there tonight. I can say no more."

"So we go," said William to his father.

Donal Og straightened up slowly and put his cap back on his head like he was screwing a cork into a bottle.

"So we go," he said, and that was that.

~

Afterward, she thought of the walk as something that happened in stages. That helped her to put the memory of it into boxes. There was the walk to the town; that was the first part. She had some hope during that walk. The people talked. Some people had food. At the start of the walk, the children even ran alongside their parents, silently, but playing and hiding and excited to be in such a crowd. They stopped every hour for a rest, sitting down in small groups on the white road and waiting for the word from Donal Og before they rose again. They were a quiet, organized, purposeful group. She began to allow herself to think that perhaps everything would be all right; there seemed to be no reason, after all, why they would not make it to the town. They were brave, she supposed, to even attempt the walk, and surely such bravery would have its reward. Many a people would not have had such spirit, she told herself, and she saw in the faces of the others that they, too, were encouraged by the undertaking. It was encouraging to be taking action. It was encouraging to know that there would be an end to this trial, that the trial itself had a motive and that its end had its reward. It made the walk manageable—bearable, even. It was cold and dark, but when they tired, toward the end, they urged each other along with the thought of the food they would be given as soon as they got to the town. They kept up a good enough pace until the last minute.

The second part of the walk was from the town to the landlord's lodge. That walk started in darkness and ended in darkness. The ten miles felt longer than the first twelve they had done over the mountain; the first mile felt longer than the first twelve. The road was even rougher than the mountain road, and Honora's feet began to bleed nearly as soon as they left the town: she had worn through her bandages hours since, and every step was difficult. She was very tired now, from the walking and from the cold. She was surprised and frightened by how tired she was. Something is wrong with me, she thought. I am stronger than this. I should not be so tired already. Something is wrong.

The cold and the terrible pain in her feet slowed her, and the more slowly she walked, the more difficult it became to continue walking at all. She was grateful then for Alice's stick; it fitted well under her arm, and she leaned on it like a friend, and it took some of the weight of her. All around her, the people were moving on, leaning forward, down and into the wind as if they were pushing a great weight in front of them. Honora became conscious that now there was pain low down in her back, too, and that the pain was spreading around to her front and moving up her body. This is a new pain, she observed, as if considering the body of a stranger, and then, as the pain shot up and through her, she said, in fright and out loud, "Oh my God."

When she was a child, she had the habit of reciting her actions out loud, telling herself the story of her days as they went by. Honora is getting up for the day, she would say, And oh, ready as anything she is. Or, Look, Honora; there are fresh berries by the river already! It had been a comfort to her to hear her own voice when she was alone in the cottage all day or in the woods at night; the silence was often heavy to bear and needed shattering. It had been a long time since she'd allowed herself to indulge in the habit, which had begun to seem a sign of some unnamable weakness as she grew older.

But the childhood habit was rising to the surface suddenly, unbidden, seemingly uncontrollable, and she was afraid now, as afraid, perhaps, as she had ever been of anything; the fear moved through her body like cold water. It was as if some renegade part of her had detached itself brazenly from the hold of her body and had risen up and began addressing her own form as a separate thing, as if she were splitting into two things, the speaker and the listener, and the speaker said, aloof, almost disinterested, nearly mocking, Honora is hungry and cold, and now she begins to be in great pain, too: What will become of Honora? The pains in her back were growing worse, and together with the terrible rolling pains in her stomach, they robbed both speech and thought from her, and all that was left to her was the walking.

All around her the people walked in silence.

There was nothing to say.

~

She would never forget, she knew, coming over the top of the hill and seeing the lodge below her laid out in its own valley. It seemed to glow gold in the night, every room in it burning with candlelight. "We are saved," whispered a young woman next to her. She was carrying her baby tied to her chest, and she put her face down into her baby's hair and wept.

The young men began to run down the hill, whooping and jumping.

There was a great wall running around the lodge. Set into the wall were tall, iron gates; next to them hung a bell on a rope.

The men took hold of the rope and rang the bell, and the sound spilled out in the night, up to the people on the hill, and the hill picked up the ringing and threw it to the hills behind them so that all the world was ringing with the silver sound.

No one answered the bell.

The people came down the hill and stood with the young men, in front of the gates.

"Ring it again, William," said Donal Og.

William took hold of the rope and yanked it to himself. She knew from the violent, careless way he did it that he was near breaking now. They waited until the unspooling peals were swallowed into the silence of the black night, and even after silence had settled again, no one spoke for a long time.

"What will we do?" said Honora. "They do not come."

She looked up at the iron gates. They were beautifully decorated with elaborately detailed flowers and leaves and vines. She put her hand out to the sharp black flowers. Imagine living in a world where it was possible to make such things, where one might say, Let us make flowers for the gates, to make the gates look more beautiful, and then to put time and effort and money into making those flowers, while beyond the gates there were people who had nothing, made nothing, died from having nothing. She touched the tip of her finger to one of the flowers. They were sharp enough to make you bleed.

"We ring until they come, and if they do not come, we climb the gates," said William.

They would be easy enough to climb, thought Honora. She could step up on the flowers and the leaves and be over these gates in moments.

"Let us climb them now," shouted one of the young men, and the people, shouting agreement, began to push forward, toward the gates.

"Get back out of that," said a voice. Someone was coming across the gravel from the lodge to the gates.

They stopped and fell back as quickly and silently as errant children who'd expected, all along, to be found out.

Behind the gates stood a man in a servant's uniform. He was holding a candle high in front of him.

"We are here to see Lord Palmer and his inspectors," said Donal Og. "We were told to come."

"Donal Og," said the man, "he will not see you. It's after dinner; the men have drink taken. They will not come out in the cold. You will not be seen until morning, if then."

"Who are you?" called William. "How do you know us?"

"I'm Michael Carroll, from back by Doolough," said the man.

"You are one of us!" called William in amazement. "Will you not open the gates to us? Open these gates, man!"

He was holding on to the bars of the gates now and shaking them. The man came toward him, holding the candle to his face.

"I cannot," he said. "*A dhuine usaile.* I cannot. I have a wife and children."

"There are many children here!" cried William. "Open the gates!"

Donal Og stepped forward.

"Will they see us tomorrow?" he said to the man. "If we wait here?"

"I do not know," said the man. "They leave early to hunt. They will not want to lose time. It is better if you go home. Go back."

"They have guns and horses," said Donal Og to William. "We must go."

"Walk here; walk there; eat dirt; die in the dirt," cried William. "Are we no better than animals that must do their bidding?" He turned to the gates. "This will be remembered, Michael Carroll," said William. "Our children's children will speak of this. From this day, your family will be marked down as traitors to their own people, and there is no worse than that. You and yours are finished in this country now."

The woman standing next to Honora began to cry, quietly.

"Let us climb the gates," shouted William to the crowd.

"William," said Donal Og, "come away."

"I will not," said William. "I'm going over those gates. I'm not crawling away like a dog in the night. They'll have to look me in the face; they'll have to shoot me in the face if they want rid of me. I am no coward."

She saw his eyes flicker toward her. He would not forget what she had called him earlier, in the woods. He would show her that he was not afraid.

"They will shoot you," said Michael Carroll, backing away from the gates. "They'll shoot every one of you, man, woman, and child."

"Come away, William," said Donal Og.

"It would be better to be shot than to have to wait here like beggars outside these gates," shouted one of the young men, and many called out in agreement that it would, it would.

"We will change our way back so we have an easier way of it. We will go around the black lake," said Donal to the people, and Honora could hear the desperation in his voice now. "There is shelter there. Let us go and have no trouble."

"No," said William. He moved so that he was standing before Donal Og, and though he kept his voice low, the people grew silent to hear what he said. "We will not turn back with nothing, and we will not heed, anymore, what you say, because what you have said and done has led us to this."

Before anyone could speak, William turned to Honora. She could see that he was near tears; his face was stretched tight with emotion.

"You were never one to shy away from the fight," he said. "Will we go over the gates? Are you with me, Honora?"

The pain took hold of her then, circling around her chest like an iron band and pushing the air out of her so she could not speak, but she put her stick down slowly onto the ground, stepped forward, and took hold of the gates. She put her head down on her hands and tried to steady her breathing. The pain was very bad now. I am dying, perhaps, she thought. This is what it must feel like to be dying.

"I cannot," she said in a whisper.

"What?" said William. "You can! You've made it this far. And I've seen you climb higher than this a hundred times! You go over first, and I will follow. Go on, Honora!"

"William!" shouted Donal Og. "No!"

He came toward William and put his hand on his arm, but William threw his hand off so viciously that Donal Og fell back from him, and the people gasped and one man cried out, "Shame." William took hold of Honora by her shoulders and pulled her to him, and he put his face down so that it was level with hers. His breath smelled so sour that she had to turn her face away from him. It was sour because it was rising up from his empty stomach; hers smelled the same, she knew.

"They will not shoot a woman," he said to her. "Even the English will not shoot a woman in cold blood before all these people. Go on, Honora."

"I'll do it."

It was Maura O'Leary, William's childhood sweetheart. When Honora had first married William, many people had been keen to tell her that Maura was the girl he was meant to marry, that it was a matter of great surprise to everyone and not least to Donal Og that he had turned away from Maura and her obvious charms and toward Honora. Honora straightened herself up now and looked at Maura; Maura held her eye brazenly. She lived with her parents in a cottage that always had a fire burning; she had three strong older brothers, and in the good times, the family had had a donkey and a cart. Tonight, Maura wore a shawl that her mother had knitted her, crossed in an X on her breast like a shield. She had large, slightly protruding teeth that pushed her lips out into an O and dark, darting eyes.

Even now, here, she had to fight. It was a constant wonder to her how other people always wanted to diminish her, defeat her to make themselves more seen. Here we are, Maura, she felt like saying, fighting for our lives, and this is the battle you chose to spend your energies on? Honora put her head on one side and considered her, and she took her time doing it. Maura blinked, but she did not back away. She has been waiting for this, thought Honora. This is a big moment for her.

It has always been like this; there is something about her, she knows, that unsettles. People do not like her; women, especially, do not like her.

"It's all right, William," she said, still looking at Maura. She kept her face as empty as possible and her voice steady. This would enrage Maura, she knew, who had a reputation for liking a fight. "I will do it."

"Miss," said Michael Carroll, taking a step toward her. He put his hand out to her, as if he would grab her through the bars of the gates. "Do not."

"Go on, Honora," said William.

She looked at the gates.

The metal curves of the flowers would be too sharp for her to hold on to, so she moved to the smooth bars in the middle of the gates and took a good strong grip, and then in one motion, she pulled and pushed herself up so that she was standing on the latch, out of Michael Carroll's reach. She was well balanced on the latch with a bare foot on either side of it, and she had hold of a bar in each hand, and it felt for all the world like she was standing on a swing ready to swoop forward. She had been right: it would be easy to climb these gates. Whoever had made them had not expected that they would have to function as something to keep people out. They had been more concerned, she suspected, with the making of perfect flowers and leaves. She was already halfway up the gates, and she had barely begun. The night was black around her, and the wind blew strong and clear and cold, and she closed her eyes and lifted her chin. For a moment, she was back in the trees in the wood on the hill, out in the wind, free. She opened her eyes and looked down at the faces of the people watching her. Michael Carroll was holding the candle above his head, and it was casting a small pale pool of light on his upturned face. No one made a sound.

She looked up to the top of the gates. She was not strong enough to pull herself up to the top of it from where she stood, but if she swung her leg high and if luck was with her, she might be able to hook her foot into a narrow spot above, between a bar and a flower, and use the lever-age from there to pull herself to the top; once she was on the top, she could swing down the other side without difficulty. She took a breath, leaned down, pushed back, and lifted her leg, swinging it into the air. You are on a swing, she told herself. Swing high, Honora.

The pain hit her like a fist in the stomach, and she shouted out loud from the shock of it. Afterward, when she retold herself the story of that night, she would think that pain was like a knife twisting, but it wasn't; it wasn't. She used those words because they sounded right, and using them let her move on quickly to what happened afterward. But the pain had nothing clean or sharp about it that the idea of the twisting of a knife suggested. It was a dark, ugly, heavy, tearing pain that was a beginning and an end all at once and made her want to be sick and cry as freely as a child from what it might mean.

"Why have you stopped?" shouted William, and another man in the crowd called out, "You're nearly there," and other voices called to each other in agreement, "She is; she is."

"I cannot," she whispered to herself. Then she said, as loudly as she could manage, "I cannot. The gates are too high."

If she did not get down from these gates, she would fall down; she was too weak from the pain to hold on any longer. She ran her hands down the bars of the gates as far as she could and leaned out backward; then she pushed forward and jumped down and backward. She mistimed the jump, though: because she had hesitated for a moment, she didn't let go of the bars in time, and so she hindered her dismount and landed badly, falling heavily onto her side.

Donal Og took hold of her arm and pulled her to her feet, but he didn't look at her. He was looking only at William.

"Stop it, William," he said to him. "Think of the women and children. Come away."

William stood with his hands on his hips; he was looking down at the ground and breathing as quickly as if it were he who had tried to climb the gates. Behind him was the shadow of Maura O'Leary. She watched as Maura moved next to him, whispered something against his cheek. She will take her chance now, thought Honora, and show how she can go over the gates. But William turned away from her, and toward Honora. It is me he wants to climb the gates, she realized, because I am the one he thinks of, always. I am the one he cannot free himself of. I am the one he's trying to make sense of even as I make his heart heavy with unhappiness and worry, and it is the same for me. It is love, this thing between us, and a bad love it is, too, that burns darkly and serves neither of us well. She put her hand out to him. *Help me, William,* she wanted to say. *I cannot breathe. I am afraid of this pain, and I need help.* William hit her hand away from him.

"You could have climbed those gates," he said to her bitterly. "You've made a fool of us in front of everyone."

He walked away from her then, shoving against her with his shoulder as he went.

Honora went back to the gates and leaned against them, putting her head against the cold bars. Michael Carroll moved closer to the gates, holding the candle toward her.

"I would open the gates, miss, if it were in my power," he said. "I can't even give you this." She looked up at him, and he nodded at the candle. "They count the candles," he said.

She let her head fall down again between her outstretched arms. It was very hard to steady her breathing; her heart felt like it was running away from her. She put her hand to her heart, and then she felt a hand on her arm.

"Take this," Michael Carroll said to her.

She raised her head.

"It's a loaf of bread," he said. "From the table inside."

She stood up and let go of the gates, and took the bread from him. She opened up her shawl and put the bread against her chest and then wrapped the shawl around her body so that the bread was tight and secure, hidden, safe. She did not say thank you. It was right that he gave her the bread. If he had that, he had more, or he could get more.

"I would have opened the gates," said Michael Carroll, "but I have small children at home. Do you see, miss? Wouldn't you have done the same yourself?"

She made herself stand up very straight. She and Michael looked at each other through the gates. She was taller than he was. He was middle-aged, with a thin, gray face and small eyes, set too close together. The flame of the candle flickered weakly behind his cupped hand.

"No," she said. "I wouldn't. And that's why you're in there, and I'm out here."

IV

All that time afterward, when she was in a different place under a different name and she began telling parts of what had happened in Ireland so that she could put some kind of beginning and end to it to make of it a story as tidy as something that could be shut up in a box, he had interrupted her when she told him of the walk and had asked, What did the people say when it started to snow?

It was a night at the start of their first winter in the pine cabin, and they were sitting in front of the fire, waiting for the snows of the season to come. The people cried out, she had answered him, but as she had spoken, she'd turned away so that he couldn't see her face, because she couldn't remember, exactly, the sound the people had made. They must have cried out, she thought; that seemed the right answer to give, but in truth, she couldn't remember them making any sound at all. She had been alert only to the unnaturally loud sound of her own heart beating when the snow started to fall, and to the accompanying sound of the breathing as loud inside her head as if she were underwater.

Why do you want to know what the people said? she wanted to ask him, though she already knew the answer: he was interested in other people's responses to things he himself had experienced because those responses illuminated his own, and more than anything else, he was interested in himself and his own history. Most people, she had found, were interested in other people only in as much as they could relate directly to them or learn something about themselves from them. But it didn't matter to her what the people had said when the snow came, what sound they had made. What had mattered to her that night was the white of the snow, the black of the water of the lake, and the red of the blood on the snow. That was all that mattered then, and that was what stayed with her still from that night.

Those were the memories that wouldn't leave her alone.

~

In Honora's mind, the third part of the walk was the walk through the snow to the black lake. The people had waited outside the gates of the lodge all night, and the lord's inspectors had seen them after their breakfast, and the inspection had been quick, so quick, but still it had been noon by the time it was over. They had had no food since before they had left home the day before, no water, even—there are no provisions to be had here, one of the inspectors had told them—and they were very weak, from the cold and the hunger and the tiredness, even before they started home, and then the snow came.

The snow started to fall as they went back up the hill, away from the lodge. First the wind stopped quite suddenly as if someone had drawn it up into a bag. It grew very quiet and still, as if the land itself were holding its breath in anticipation of something, and then, almost as a release, as if a space had opened, the snow began. From the first moment, it fell fast and deep. Honora had not seen snow since she was a child. It was rare for snow to fall in this part of the country, for the weather they had came mostly from the sea; the weather from farther inland usually broke over the mountains before it reached them. And it was strange, too, for snow to fall in March, when the worst of the year was usually over and the spring seemed not too far away. The people must have cried out to each other in shock when the snow came; she thought after he'd asked her, that had certainly been the right answer to give because it had been such an unexpected thing, but she herself had stayed silent. She had known from early in the day that dangerous weather lay ahead, and Old Alice had warned her of trouble to come, and so she was glad, almost, when the snow started; at least she knew now what Alice had meant, she told herself. Better to know than to wait in fear.

So they walked through the falling snow. They could not risk stopping or even slowing. The road to the lake was easier than the mountain road they'd taken from the town to the lodge, nearly even underfoot, and they made good progress, spurred on by the thought of the shelter Donal Og had told them was waiting by the lake's sandy banks. The snow fell in beautifully fat flakes from the endless sky and brought with it a strange numinous light all of its own; the world, under its cover, was transformed. The snow had that light and its own sound that swallowed all other sound: the sound of the people's walking under the snow was muffled; the normal sounds of the country at night were erased. It was a marvel, thought Honora, the snow, and maybe it was a sign of some change to come and not a bad change in the end. Honora was for change; nothing had happened so far in her life to argue against it.

The snow on the easy road made the road even faster going, and Alice's stick helped her to steady herself through the unexpectedly deeper drifts by the side of the road. The snow was as soft as powder under her bare cut feet, and she was sure that it was less cold now than it had been before the snow had started, and after a while, Donal Og called out to them that they were not so far now from the lake.

A cheer went up then.

Honora put her face up to the falling flakes and opened her mouth and let the soft sweet crystals melt on her tongue. The pain in her stomach and back had eased, and the relief at being free from its grip was so great that she felt energized and nearly uplifted, suddenly thrumming and humming with life. A strange and wonderful warmth was radiating through her, and her body gave a strange jump, and then the warmth was running down her leg. She looked down at herself. What is this warmth? she wondered, and in the same moment she understood that it was liquid. Moving very quickly now, she grabbed at her skirts and lifted them and put her hands to her thighs, feeling herself: where was the liquid coming from? She had not wet herself; she was not a child. She looked at her hand: it was dark with something warm and wet. She put her hand to her nose to smell it. Her heart was beating very hard and fast. She got down onto the ground and put her hand on the snow, pressing it down. She lifted her hand up and looked at the mark she had left on the white snow.

It was blood. She was bleeding.

She stood up and took a step back from the bloody handprint, but the blood was running very quickly down her legs, and as she moved, the blood followed her in thick spatters across the snow. She stopped moving, and the blood began to pool around her feet.

The young woman—she was no more than a girl, really—with the baby at her breast who had cried out before when they had seen the lodge stopped next to her. She looked down at the blood at Honora's feet and put her hand on her baby's head as if she were protecting her from something. Then she looked up at Honora. She was younger than Honora, and she had a plain, honest face.

"Where's your husband?" she said.

Honora lifted her hand to point in William's direction, but she could not speak; the words wouldn't come.

"Where's this girl's husband?" shouted the girl, and Honora heard in her voice the panic and fear that she felt in her own chest. "Find the husband."

A woman stopped. Behind her were two very small, dirty children, holding on to her skirts.

"What's happening?" the woman said.

"She's bleeding from down below," answered the girl with the baby. "The blood is coming very fast."

The woman came to stand next to Honora. She put her arm around her waist and squeezed her.

"What is your name?" the woman said.

Then she put her cheek to Honora's and squeezed her waist again, gently. Her cheek felt like warm dough. Her behavior was so unexpected and so foreign in its open affection that for a moment Honora felt like resting her head on the woman's shoulder and weeping.

"Honora O'Donoghue," said Honora.

She was glad of such a question; it was easy to be able to get the words out for such a question.

"Are you with child, Honora?" the woman said.

"What?" said Honora. "No."

She felt her body sway and grow curiously light, and then she was falling down onto the snow and landing with a gentle bounce, all of her body as limp as if without bones. She hit the ground without even feeling it. The snow was very soft under her head, and it seemed as if she were sinking down into it, and she thought how nice it would be to fall asleep on the soft snow. If she could only sleep now, she thought, she would never ask for anything again. Then she remembered the bread in her sleeve. She put her hand across her arm, covering the lump of bread. If she fell asleep, someone would take the bread from her. She put her hands on the ground and began to try to get up on her knees.

The two women were standing above her and talking about her like she wasn't there.

"She must be the wife of William O'Donoghue," the older one was saying, and the girl was saying in a high, excited voice, "I was next to her, and I saw the blood on the snow, and oh, for a minute I thought it was coming from me until I saw her face." She saw then that Honora was trying to stand, and gave a shout of fright and called out, "Stay sitting down, for God's sake almighty," and the baby began to cry.

I must get up and eat the bread, thought Honora. It will give me a bit of strength. That was all that mattered to her in that moment: to stand, to eat the bread. She took hold of the stick that she'd dropped on the ground next to her as she'd fallen, and leaning on top of it, she tried to stand. She got no farther than halfway up—she couldn't straighten her legs or move up from her hips—before falling back down again as if she had been pushed. The baby was crying in wild jags now, like it couldn't catch its breath, and the women were shouting at her, and the pain was starting again, and this time it felt like she was being cut across the stomach with a knife. She rolled onto her side, drawing her knees up to her chest. There were more voices then, and someone was saying, "Here's the husband," and William was kneeling in the snow next to her saying, "Honora, what's wrong with you?" and shaking her by the arm and shouting at the women as if they had done something wrong, "What's wrong with her? Why is there all this blood?"

"She has a baby coming, I think," said a woman.

William took her by the shoulders and sat her up so that she was facing him.

"Is that right, Honora?" he said. "Is what she says true?"

She could tell that he was trying to keep his voice steady.

"It cannot be," said Honora to him.

She had not bled for months, but it was because she had had no food—that was the reason. She had heard other women whisper of it by the fire at night: none of them bled, because of the hunger. The hunger had stopped the blood. It was not because she was having a baby. She could not be having a baby. The bleeding now was from some injury she had done herself trying to climb the gates, or indeed from some old injury, or maybe the bleeding had started after all these months, and there was a lot of blood because it had gathered over time and was now being released.

She could not be having a baby.

"She doesn't look like she is carrying a baby," said William to the women. "Her stomach is as flat as mine."

"She could be carrying facing inward," said the girl. "I did myself."

55

William let go of her shoulders, and, very slowly, she lay back down on her side in the snow. He stood up.

"I have to talk to my father," said William.

"What you have to do is to get her to the lake," said the woman with the children at her skirt. "And fast. She has to have some shelter."

"She can't have the baby here in the snow," said the girl, and the other women agreed in a murmuring chorus, "She can't, she can't."

William stood leaning over Honora, considering her. Then he put his hand out to her.

"She can't walk," said a woman to him.

"She can't even stand," said another woman, indignantly, to the first woman, "not to mind walk."

"You have to carry her," said the woman with the children, and she spoke very impatiently, harshly even. In response, William kneeled down in front of Honora, and a woman fixed Honora's arms around his neck, and two other women lifted her onto his back as he pushed himself first onto his knees and from there to standing. He put one arm behind him, holding her up under her legs, and with the other hand he held her wrists under his chin so that she didn't fall backward from him. Then he started to walk, with the women walking behind him, following the trail of blood.

He was leaving Alice's stick behind in the snow, and she didn't have the strength to ask him to take it, and even if she had, she knew he would have said no.

No, Honora, no.

"What is it?" The woman with the children was next to her.

"I want my stick," she said.

The woman stopped and William kept walking, and then she remembered no more of the walk to the lake.

~

Set into the banks running alongside the lake were caves with sand floors. The caves were open to the lake, and from where she lay, she could see the snow falling on the black water and the small slow waves tapping the snowy shore.

"It is beautiful," she said. She was not ashamed now to say what she thought; she was beyond caring. She was usually careful to check and measure her words before she spoke, because she knew that the things she noticed and thought about were not things other people cared to give expression to. She was beyond thinking about things like that now.

"What is?" said William. He was sitting by her side, his chest heaving with the effort of having carried her for miles. He had blood on his hands, and on his shirt, and a streak of blood on his face. But she felt nothing, looking at him, and felt only mild surprise at feeling nothing. It was as if all of this were happening to someone else entirely.

"The snow on the black water," she said.

She had heard tell of this black lake since she was a child. The water was black all year round, black through to the bottom they said, like black glass.

"Jesus, Honora," said William.

"I've always wanted to see the black lake at night," she said.

She let her head fall back and closed her eyes. Everything below her waist felt numb and heavy, but she herself felt completely weightless. She had a sensation then like some essential part of her was beginning to rise up out of her body. It was as if she were suddenly able to concentrate herself into a small ball, and she was moving the ball, freeing it from her body. The ball, some essence of her, was suspended now above her body, and she could move it about the cave if she wanted, or out of the cave, over the black water. Her mind felt free and full of light. The pain in her stomach was moving lower and was a deeper kind of pain now, but in her mind, she felt like she was slipping away from the pain, like she was moving into another room, another place.

It was not an unpleasant or frightening feeling.

"Lift up her legs and hold them to either side," said a woman's voice.

There was a hand on both her thighs, lifting and pushing them apart. She felt herself descend back into her body, into the pain.

I have flowers in my bones, she thought, and they bleed, the flowers.

She cried out and tried to pull away by twisting her knees to the side.

"Honora," said a voice. "Look at me."

She made herself open her eyes. The woman with the children was kneeling next to her. Honora watched her wipe blood from her hand and arm onto her skirt. She'll dirty her skirt, she thought, and that stain will be hard to get out, for blood is hard to shift. She was thinking of that when the woman leaned forward, and she put her hand on Honora's forehead and smoothed her hair back and made a sound, tsk. Her hand was ice cold against Honora's burning skin, and Honora gave a start and pulled back from her. "Tsk, tsk," said the woman. Honora felt like she had failed at some important test she had been set. "Tsk, tsk."

"What's happening to me?" Honora said.

"You have a baby coming, all right," said the woman, and William said, "Honora!" as if she had played an unkind trick on him.

The woman looked across Honora at him.

"You'd be better off outside, I'd say," the woman said to him, "than here with your hands hanging to you. Go on off out to the men. And before you go, take off your jacket."

"What?" said William.

"She has to have something to lie on," she said. "Would you want to have a baby, lying on the sand with nothing under you?"

She turned to the girl with the baby. She was sitting by the entrance to the cave, with the baby at her breast.

"Take my children," she said to the girl, "and go and find Bridget Brady. Tell her what's happening here, and ask her to look after them."

"You'll need help," the girl said to her from over her shoulder as she left, but she sounded distracted, as if she were speaking from a dream. She had moved the baby from one breast to the other in an easy motion and she didn't lift her eyes from her for even a moment as she spoke; it was as if she couldn't raise her head to look away from the baby, as if she were locked into her.

"I've had two of my own," the woman said. "I'll do it alone. The fewer we are in here, the better."

William stood up, took off his jacket, and folded it over his arm, smoothing it out, and then put it carefully on the ground, next to Honora. He put his hands deep down in the pockets of his trousers and began to rock slowly forward onto his toes, then back onto his heels.

"I'll go, so," he said to Honora.

Oh, to be able to get up and go, she thought. When this is over, I will go, and I won't stop going, ever.

Because she hadn't answered him, he kept talking.

"You'll be all right," he said. "This woman here will look after you. Fear of you."

He did not even ask the woman her name, thought Honora, and that was deliberate; he did not want to acknowledge her as a person. He was trying to sound commanding, in control, and make their dependence on this—unknown—woman insignificant. In a minute, he would tell her that his father was Donal Og.

If I could stand, she thought, I would walk over to him and put my hand over his mouth and push his words back down his throat and push him and push him until he was gone from me, gone into the black water and away.

She felt a great wave of anger begin to rise up in her. All of this is beyond my comprehension, she thought. How can I have a baby and then feed the baby? What will become of us? What will become of me? It is ridiculous to think that I can have a baby, here, now, in this cave. It is not something that can happen.

She was a stranger to anger. Fear, worry, and shame she knew well, but she couldn't remember ever saying to herself, I am angry. Now her anger was as clear to her as a truth. I am all anger, she realized, and acknowledging that made everything feel purer, simpler, in its proper place. The anger made sense of all those other, weaker, emotions: it clarified and concentrated them. I am angry about William; I am angry about my mother and my father; I am angry that I am poor, and dirty, and weak; and I am angry that I am hungry, all the time. But most of all, I am angry that this is happening to me, in spite of me, like everything else in my life that happens to me and that I cannot control. My body is owned, possessed, beyond my managing, and so is my destiny, and I have had enough. I want possession; I want ownership.

She sat up so that she was leaning on her elbows.

The anger made her feel stronger. The anger made her ready for the fight.

She turned her face away from William to the woman. She would not speak to him. She would not make it easy for him to go. Let him leave without having had a word from her.

"What is your name?" she said to the woman.

Out of the tail of her eye, she saw William begin to move away from her.

"Nell," said the woman.

"How old are you?" said Honora.

"If I were you," said Nell, "I'd be doing less of the talking."

Then she looked at Honora, and her face changed: Honora saw that she understood what she was doing, that she was talking William out of the room.

"I'm twenty-five," she said. "I've two children, five and two. My husband went to Galway to look for work six months ago, and we haven't had word of him since."

William backed out of the cave, quietly and quickly.

"Now," said Nell as soon as he was gone, "we're better off without the men, aren't we?"

They were both facing the entrance to the cave. The whole world lay dark beyond them, out of reach. Honora looked across at this woman, this Nell who was to help her. She looked as young as a girl, and she had long golden hair tied up on her head: she had never seen hair of such a glorious color. Nell had been beautiful once, Honora thought. What must she have looked like with that hair loose down her back and color in her cheeks? For what felt like a long time, neither of them spoke.

"How long are you married?" said Nell then.

"Nearly a year," said Honora. "A year this spring."

"Where is your mother?" said Nell.

"I have no mother," said Honora, and then because of the way Nell had held her waist and put her face next to hers, because of her unexpected kindness, she added, "She died having me."

"We won't let that happen here to you, will we, Honora?" said Nell. "We'll look after you." She had turned to face Honora, and they looked at each other, considering each other.

"There's only you," said Honora.

"When I say *we*, I mean you and me," said Nell.

"I don't think that's enough," said Honora.

To Honora's surprise, Nell gave a laugh.

"You've spirit," she said. "You'll need that."

She took hold of Honora's hand.

"You're bleeding a lot, Honora. You're hot to the touch, so you have a fever, I think, maybe from an infection. The baby is very small, but it's coming." She put Honora's hand to her chest. "When the next wave of pain comes, you have to push down hard; push the baby down and forward like you're trying to put your foot into a boot that's too small for you. The baby has to come out. Once the baby is out, we hope the bleeding stops or that we can do something to stop it. Do you understand me?"

Without waiting for an answer, she put her face down so that her forehead lay against Honora's forehead.

"I'm sorry for you," she whispered, as if she were telling her a secret. She sounded sad, and Honora wished she didn't; she wished she sounded like she didn't care what happened to her. It was hard to bear her kindness. "I wish you strength."

Don't, she wanted to say. *Don't be sorry for me. I don't want your pity. Better me than you, with two children at your skirts and a husband in Galway.*

"I have bread," she said. She had to change the look on Nell's face, the tone of her voice. "I've it hidden in the sleeve of my dress."

Nell gave a laugh.

"Honora O'Donoghue," she said.

In reply, Honora put her hand up the sleeve of her dress and pulled the bread out.

"It's as hard as a rock," said Nell, taking it. "You'd be better off throwing it at someone than eating it."

"It will be all right after it's soaked in water," said Honora. "Take it."

"No," said Nell. She put the bread back in Honora's hand and closed her fingers around it. "I wouldn't take your bread from you even if it was fit for eating."

She was too thin, and Honora saw now that her skin had a strange, gray shine to it, and there was a bad, sour smell to her. She is nearer to death than me, Honora realized. She had seen that color on people before and smelled that smell, and she knew it meant that Nell had been hungry for too long and that if she did not eat soon, it would be too late for her. *You should not be here in this cave with me,* she wanted to say. *You should be saving yourself and your children and not spending what's left of your strength on me.*

It was important she told Nell this. She had to tell her to go away. She opened her mouth to speak, and then she gasped. The pain was back, tightening about her stomach. She began to push herself up into a sitting position to try to relieve the pressure on her stomach.

"That's good," said Nell. "Sit up."

"Nell," she said.

Nell had moved behind her and now sat with one leg on each side of her. She pulled Honora up into her lap.

"I know," she said. "I know. Poor girl."

Honora leaned back against her, trying to catch her breath, and Nell put her arms under Honora's and locked them across Honora's chest.

The pain had hold of her now like it was a dog and she was a rabbit between its teeth. The pain was stronger than her; she could do nothing in its grip.

"No, Nell," she said. She had to make her understand what she meant, that she wanted her to go, that she wanted to be left alone in the cave.

"Stop talking," said Nell, "and push now."

"I can't," she said.

"You can," said Nell. "Push down on the pain. Push the pain out."

The pain was moving up her body, strangling her. It was amazing to her that she could forget how bad the pain was when she was free of it, and yet when it descended upon her, it made her weak and sick to the stomach, and even if she pushed until she broke in two and the baby came, what then?

Don't think about that, and just push the pain out, Honora, she told herself.

Push.

The pain began to move away from her, like a wave pulling out from the shore. She was panting for breath like a fox she'd seen once silhouetted on a hill against the evening sky. It had been running from the dogs, and she'd felt sorry for it and for its poor slight body fighting to breathe.

"Honora," said Nell. "You're not trying."

"I am," cried Honora, but Nell was right; she wasn't. She didn't want to.

How would she feed a baby?

How would they live?

"If you don't push, Honora," said Nell, "you will die. Do you want to die here in this cave?"

I don't know, Nell, she wanted to shout. *I don't know. I am not strong, and I want this to stop because I can't do it; I can't do it; I can't fight this pain, and worse than this pain is the fear.*

"I'm afraid," she said.

"What?" said Nell. "What are you saying?"

"I said I'm afraid," she cried out. "I'm afraid of having the baby. I don't want to have it. I don't want it. You should leave me and let what happens happen and look out for yourself. Go away from me. Leave me be."

Nell unlocked her arms, first dropping and then shoving Honora away from her and onto the ground. She swung one leg high over Honora's head, and on her hands and knees, she crawled around her until she was next to her; then she took hold of Honora's face, digging her fingers into her chin and jaw and twisting her face toward her. She was holding her face too tightly; Honora could feel her sharp nails cutting into her skin, but when she tried to turn away, Nell pulled her face back toward her with such force that Honora cried out.

"You listen to me now," said Nell. She was crying, and her face was dark and too close to Honora's face, and Honora could smell Nell and feel her breath on her. "You're not dying here, today, because I won't have that on me as well as everything else. I can't feed my children. My husband is gone. Now I'm stuck here with you, and you're talking about what you want and what you don't want. I don't care what you want. What any of us wants is neither here nor there and never was and never will be in this country. We're all afraid. I'm afraid all the time, from morning to night. I'm afraid of everything around me, and most of all, I'm afraid of myself and what I might do any day now."

She let go of Honora's face and fell back onto her haunches. She put a hand over her mouth and the other hand behind her head and closed her eyes. When she spoke again, it was in a whisper.

"Honora, you are going to push this baby out, and by God if it's the last thing I do, I'm going to make you do it. Do you hear me?"

Honora said nothing.

"Please, Honora," said Nell quietly. "For God's sake."

Honora turned her face toward the lake. The snow was filling up the world outside the cave. The silence was a thing in itself, almost solid, colored whiter than the snow. She wished she could watch the snow falling until she felt her eyes grow tired and heavy and then close her eyes against the darkness and the strange empty light of the snow until only the silence was left. She wished she could slip away quietly into the silence. I would go if I could, she thought. I would choose the easy thing and leave this world as easily as you'd leave a room you don't want to be in anymore. But there is something in me, something I would deny with my last breath if I could, that won't let me go. There is something deep within me that makes me go on.

She turned back toward Nell.

"Sit me up," she said.

Nell looked back at her, saying nothing, and then she nodded.

"You're brave, Honora," she said.

"I'm not," she cried angrily, because Nell was wrong: to be brave was to choose the hard thing. There was no question of being able to make a choice here. There never has been for you, Honora, not yet.

Nell crawled behind her, and Honora pulled herself up so that she was half sitting, half lying against her. With one hand, she fixed William's jacket beneath her, and with the other, she pulled her skirt high up on her waist and bent her legs. She had the desire, for a moment, to laugh out loud at how ridiculous it all seemed. *This can't be what happens,* she wanted to say. *Surely everyone doesn't go through this.*

There was a terrible smell of blood and something else rotten that made her want to retch, but she closed her eyes and put her hand out, and Nell took it and squeezed it hard.

"Good girl," said Nell, and Honora realized that all her life she had wanted someone to say those words to her, and now they had, and it was too late, too late.

And then she began to push.

V

"There's something wrong," she said.

"It always feels like that toward the end," said Nell.

She could not have explained to Nell what was happening to her. She knew only that there had been a change, a shift inside her, and that it was at once nothing and something so significant that it seemed like she could touch the thing the change was, hold it in her hand if she could just reach it. It's as if I've moved from one room to another and in the new room there is a wholly different light or a different smell and it's a room I don't want to be in, she wanted to say.

"No," she said. "There's something wrong."

She was up on her elbows, more sitting than lying, her fingers digging into the sand and her legs bent and Nell between them. The pain was fading, she thought, and the wild energy that she had felt during the last hour of pushing was ebbing out of her body.

She had the feeling that something was passing, passing on.

Nell looked up at her. She thinks the same, thought Honora, or she would say otherwise, surely.

"We're nearly there," said Nell. "Stop talking and keep going."

Honora put her chin up and pushed down and forward.

"I can see the head," said Nell. "Push, Honora."

She pushed again, and then it felt like something unlocked inside her, click. She was very near the end now, one way or another.

"That's it," said Nell. "Go on."

She was pushing, and Nell had her hands inside her and was pulling, and then it was as if she had been opened up and emptied out.

"I have her," said Nell. "It's a little girl."

It was completely silent in the cave. She would remember that always, afterward, how the silence told the story. She could hear the waves from the lake slapping against the shore, and in the distance, a fox screamed out, the scream of a child in distress, but there was no sound from the baby, and nothing more from Nell. Get up, she told herself. Move, and she turned, and then a wave of nausea rose up in her, and she began to be violently sick, her body folding over to protect itself against the spasms. She fell back because it hurt too much to lie on her side, and then she was lying flat on the sand and had to turn her head to the side so that the terrible vomit ran out of her mouth and not down her throat. The waves of sickness continued, and still she could not hear the baby.

She was in great pain now. It seemed to her that her body could not take more, that it was broken in some fundamental way.

"Nell," she said, but her voice was very weak and too quiet to be heard.

"Nell," she said again.

"Stay lying down, and keep your head turned to the side," shouted Nell. "Don't sit up."

Honora put both hands on one side of her body and began to try to push herself up. Seeing the movement, Nell cried out.

"No," she shouted. "No, Honora."

She was sitting at Honora's feet with her back to her, bent over the baby in her lap. She half turned to look over her shoulder at her, and Honora saw that she was crying.

"Go away, Honora," she said.

"Give her to me," said Honora.

"She's just cold, I think," said Nell. "If we can warm her, or feed her, she will be all right."

On her hands and knees, Honora began to crawl toward Nell. She saw that Nell was rubbing the baby and breathing on her and then that she was unbuttoning her dress and putting the baby to her breast; she took her nipple between her thumb and her finger and squeezed it, and drops of milk came out and fell on the baby's face. She was trying now to put her nipple in the baby's mouth, and in the same motion she was wrapping her dress around her.

Honora was in front of Nell now. Nell looked up at her. Her face was empty, clean of emotion, as if what she was feeling were beyond expression. She opened her dress, took the baby from her breast, and passed her to Honora.

"Poor baby, poor baby," said Nell.

The baby was tiny, wonderful, a complete universe. Honora touched her perfect hand, her perfect fingers, her fingernails. She put her face down to the baby's perfect face and kissed her.

"Here," said Nell. She unwound the shawl that she wore in an X across her body and held it out to Honora.

Honora put the shawl over the baby, wrapped her in it. She fixed the folds of wool so that they framed her face. The baby, swaddled, looked like she was sleeping peacefully.

"It was too early for her," said Nell. "It wasn't her time." She was kneeling and had her hands on the ground, and she was looking down at the ground. "I'm very sorry, Honora," she said. "May God be with her. Poor baby."

Honora said nothing. She was looking at the baby. She hadn't expected her to be so beautiful, so formed. She touched her face, very gently.

"Will you give her a name?" said Nell. "She should have a name."

She sounded suddenly very angry, as if she had just realized something, as if she had just learned of a wrong that had to be righted.

"I should get your husband," she said then, when Honora didn't answer her.

69

"No," said Honora, without looking up from the baby. She didn't want the outside world coming into the cave. She wanted everything in the cave to stay as it was, never changing, untouched.

She was hot, too hot, and she rested her face against the baby's cheek, which was wonderfully cooling. She closed her eyes. She felt as if she were spinning around, slowly, gently, and it was becoming hard to see, so she lay down on her back with the baby on her chest, holding on to her very tightly. I am still bleeding, she thought distractedly, because I can feel the hot stickiness of it, and I know that smell now, and Nell was wrong to say that the bleeding would stop when the baby came, because it's getting worse; I'm sure it's pumping out of me now. She moved the baby so that she was lying with her face next to hers.

She heard Nell say, as if she were calling to her from far away, "Honora," and then, "Oh my God," and then, she slept.

~

When she woke, it was completely dark in the cave. Her hands were empty. She rolled onto her stomach and then got up onto all fours. Where was the baby? She began to crawl around the cave, feeling the sand with her hands. She was making a sound, uh, uh, that was panic and fear out loud, and she was crying in great silent jags. She could not find the baby. She crawled toward the weak light at the mouth of the cave. William was sitting outside, with his back to her, facing the lake.

"Where is the baby?" she whispered. It was hard to say those words, when what she wanted to do was scream and rend her clothes.

It was very early morning, and the snow had settled on the land, on the water, even. William had a small fire burning, and he was sitting leaning over it, poking at it with a small stick.

He dropped the stick.

"You're awake," he said.

"Where's the baby?" she said.

She tried to stand, but she could not. It was stunningly cold outside the cave.

"We buried her, Honora, by the side of the lake, farther down."

She half stood and began to move as best she could toward the lake. She could hardly walk: she was bent over, and her legs were like useless wooden sticks, and they would not move to her will, and her arms flailed about by her sides. She was like a broken doll, and she hit her legs with her fists, stupid legs, stupid broken body that had failed, and failed still. William moved after her and tried to grab at her.

"Stop," he said. "Stop it." He put his arms around her, and he pinned her arms to her side so that he was holding her tight in a lock. "You'll hurt yourself," he said. "Stop it."

"Where's Nell?" she said.

"You've been in that cave for three days," he said. "Everyone is gone. They left after the first night. Nell had word that the woman who was looking after her children had left in the night and taken the children with her, so she went after them. You've been very sick, Honora. You kept bleeding, and you were boiling hot and—"

He stopped. He let go of her. He was breathing very hard, and he turned from her and faced the water.

"She was a lovely baby," he said.

She was mine, she thought, mine alone, and you are not to even speak of her, and you took her from me and put her in the earth, and I will never see her face again, and I never even gave her a name.

Crows rose from the trees beyond the lake and began their slow circling around each other in the pink sky.

William turned toward her.

"I named her Aine, for my mother," he said, "and we said some words over her, and she was wrapped in Nell's shawl. Nell wouldn't take it back even though I told her to, and we laid her down, and she didn't suffer; she'll never know hunger, Honora, at least."

"Where is she?" said Honora.

"I don't know exactly," he said. "I wasn't thinking properly at the time. It was dark, and it was snowing when we buried her, and we put a stone marker on the spot, but it's all under snow now; it all looks the same to me. But, Honora—leave her rest. What does it matter now where she is? She's in a better place than us."

Very quietly she said, "I want her."

William looked at her. She saw him gather himself: she could see that he had registered something in her voice and that he was measuring his answer in response.

"You never had her, Honora," he said. "She was never of this world. She was too good for it."

He sounded like an old man with his worn-out words. All he was able to do was repeat things he had heard others say; everything he touched he diminished with his stupidity, his coarseness. She ran toward him with her fist raised. She would lower him to the ground as the baby had been lowered; she would wipe him from her sight.

He grabbed her hand before it landed on him and twisted her arm behind her. She shouted in pain, and then her legs went from under her, and she fell to her knees.

"Stop," he cried, letting her go. "You're sick, Honora. You'll kill yourself if you act like this."

She put her forehead down on the snow and her hands over her head and pulled herself into a ball. She would stay here, in this place by the lake, and let the snow come down and blanket her and wait for the earth to gather her back to it.

William was kneeling next to her now. He put his hand on her back, then on her head.

"We can't stay here," he said. "We have to find food; we have to go home. If we make good time, we might still meet the others on the way back."

"Go on without me," she said, turning her face to the side. "I'm not going with you."

"You are," he said, "because I'm not leaving you here."

He picked her up like a child, with one hand under her knees and the other behind her head and turned her toward him, so that he was holding her tight against his chest.

"If I have to carry you all the way back, I will," he said. "And that's the end of it."

"William," she said, "please. I've never said please to you before. I don't want to go on. I want to stay here."

He tossed her up, rearranging her in his arms, evening out the weight of her, and when he spoke again, it was as if he were telling a long-rehearsed story to an assembly: his voice had a strange, almost formal cadence to it.

"I married you when everyone said don't. I married you because I wanted you. I used to see you in the evening when the light was blue and fading away, and you were always moving, always going away, and it was the way you looked at me when you passed by like you knew me or you knew what I was thinking, and you were half laughing at me because of it, and I wanted you even though I knew that I'd be better off staying well away. I knew that, but I married you anyway. I wanted to be near you. I didn't want you going where I couldn't see you. And nothing's changed. I'm not leaving you now where I can't see you. I could have married Maura O'Leary and had an easy time of it, but I didn't, and I haven't gone through all of this to leave you behind me in the snow."

He started walking away from the cave.

"So that's that, Honora. That's that."

He looked down at her, checking her. He had always been unsure of her response. She would think more about this another time, when she was not so tired. She felt very tired now, beyond speech, or thought, even. Her father used to say, when she did something he didn't like,

Honora, I'm beyond caring. The set of those words had bothered her when she was a child, and they came back to her now like a line from a song that she wanted to forget.

She let her head fall back on William's arm, to try to silence the words in her head. She did not want to remember her father. The memory of him hurt her.

"Say goodbye to this place," he said. "You will never see it again."

He said that to make her feel better, she understood, and so she didn't say anything, but she knew that she would never not see the black water under the snow, the lightless cave that smelled of blood, the black crows circling in the pink sky and the baby's perfect face, her closed eyes and her tiny hands held in little fists like she was trying to hold on to something. She would never again be free from the sight of them.

William stopped.

"Wait," he said to himself.

He turned back toward the entrance of the cave, and, still holding her, leaned down and picked up her stick.

"Nell came back with this for you," he said. "She'd no sooner left than she was back with it—she said she saw a man walking off with it and knew it as yours. She'd a tussle to get it back, she said, and she made me promise to give it to you if you woke." He was smiling, pleased with himself. "There now," he said. "I remembered." He put the stick down on her chest so that it ran the length of her body, and she took hold of it with both hands. William looked at her, waiting for her to speak, but when she did not, he cocked his chin, looked out at the white road, and began to walk.

VI

After they had left the lake, she did not speak again, and for a long time, it seemed possible, not unlikely, that she would never speak again. I am struck dumb, she thought, in wonder and fear, for when she opened her mouth and tried to speak, words did not come. There were no words available to her, in Irish or in English, that could convey what she needed to say. She was gone beyond language: words slid, slipped away from her. In her mind, she thought in words: she was able to give things their name, to think in sentences. She could look at the snow and think, Snow, but she could not say it. When William slept, she tried to speak: she would open her mouth and try to say a word, and a noise, the sound of the word melting, a sound like *ahn*, would come. Sometimes she chose to simply make noises like a baby, *ba ba ba*, just to hear her voice, to test it out. But she could not make the words she wanted. Her mind had rejected language and its ordering, shaping force; she was silenced. The world before the baby had been full of the noise of talking and crying and singing and shouting, of the sound of water and the great wind and the birds calling to each other as they flew through it. But the baby had arrived silently, and the world after she came was made silent, too, emptied of people and their voices, without even the familiar sound of her own voice. The world was rent cleanly in two, divided between the absolutes of noise and silence. Not even the wind blew in this silent world, for the snow had swallowed it, and all was stilled.

Though she was frightened by the silence, she did not deplore it, for the silence outside mirrored the emptiness inside her, and there was a peace in that. And William seemed to accept, easily enough, her not speaking. She was not sure he understood that she tried to speak and could not; perhaps he thought that she simply chose not to speak. In any case, he did not question her silence, and his only response to it was to speak enough for both of them, and more than she had ever heard him speak before, answering his own questions to her, telling her stories. She suspected that he was talking to keep himself going, talking to convince himself that they were both there, alive, and not figures in a vision. She was not bothered by his talking; she would perhaps have done the same, she thought, in his place. His talk ran through the back of her mind like a track in the snow, and she paid it no heed. He talked; she was silent; the world was silent; and the hours passed, as if in a feverish dream.

She would not walk: whether it was because she could not, or would not, even she could not have said. She only knew that if William had set her down on the snow and walked away from her, she would not have moved again. She was sure of that. And it was clear that William understood that, too, because he carried her without discussion, on his back, over his shoulder, in his arms. When he became too tired to carry her farther, he set her on the ground and rested, lying against her with his feet in her armpit and hers in his and their bodies pressed side to side so that they might warm each other. He had no shoes, no jacket, and he had had no food since before he began his walk home. Donal Og had left him what food he had, but William had finished it all in the days Honora was in the cave.

Because William had to carry her, because he had been made weak by the hunger and was growing weaker, because it was becoming more

76

difficult by the hour to navigate in the blinding, disorientating snow, the way back took too long.

That early winter's night, years later, the man listening to her story stopped her as she told him of the journey back from the cave and said, If you had found food in time, everything would have been different, but to say that was to show that he had no understanding of anything at all, really. If anything had been different, everything would have been different. What was, was. Her world, William's world, was a fixed thing that they had no chance at shaping. They had to react to what they were faced with. There were no choices to be made, no regrets to be had, because regrets meant free will, choice. They walked for too long; they had no food; her baby did not live: these things were, and she, and William, fitted in around them.

There was no food: that was the immediate, pressing problem of every moment, the thing that colored all else. They had set out from home for food; they had failed to find it, and now they were hungrier than ever—this was what William did not mention in his flow of talk on the first day. There was no food, and so they had to eat snow and grass, and the grass gave William cramps, and the cramps loosened his bowels so that he began to pass black water. He had a terrible pain in his head, he told her. He had had the pain for some days now, but the glare from the snow was making it so bad that he felt sick to his stomach. Her bread was long gone; they had been hours away from the lake before she even remembered it. She hoped it had been Nell who had taken it, for her children, and then immediately she knew that that was something she herself might have done, but not Nell. Nell wouldn't have taken the bread. Honora found that she had no appetite for food, in any case; if she had been presented with the most fragrant of stews, she would have turned from it. She had eaten grass since she'd been a child: it had a curiously nutty taste to it, which was not unpleasant, and she didn't mind the cold crunchy snow on her tongue, either. The bleeding slowed, and though there was a foul-smelling discharge that ran from her still, she found that she could clean herself well enough with snow, and that the snow staunched it, even. She felt almost completely numb below the waist, so the cold did not touch her there, and, free from pain, she was lightened, detached, almost revived.

But William grew weaker.

On the evening of the second day of the way back, just before night fell, they came on an abandoned cottage. They had spent the first night in a ditch under some thorn trees, and she could not imagine them lasting another such night. They had slept only fitfully; the fire had burned low, weakly, and William had jumped at every shadow and noise in the darkness. By the time morning had come, he had looked different—paler, darker about the eyes and mouth, frailer. He was appalled, she knew, by the idea of himself as a person who had to sleep out in the fields like a tinker. In William's eyes, to be without land was to be no one, nameless, and that was the worst thing that could befall a person. He was frightened, and he was not a person who managed fear well. Fear fueled her, but William was frozen by it. He had always considered himself a person of some significance, rooted to a place, and now the world was presenting him with the vision of a future that unmoored him, and he was lost, adrift. Since rising that morning, he had been quiet and was getting quieter, and as the hours passed, he stumbled as much as walked and once had fallen onto his knees and had only risen with difficulty. He could not carry her for much longer. That was clear now to both of them.

Something was going to have to change. Something was going to have to happen soon, one way or another.

When he saw the cottage in the distance, he shouted out, "Our luck is turning, Honora!" and then he began to cry, keeping his face turned from her to hide his tears. Her heart leaped in her chest, and she thought, We are saved; we are saved, and the joy and the relief were like honey in her mouth. William almost ran the last steps to the cottage, and they fell in the open door; he set her on the ground and then lay down next to her with his hands crossed on his chest. He looked as if he had been stunned by some kind of blow to the head, and Honora closed her eyes and thought, over and again, We are saved.

"They must have gone to America," said William, eventually. He sat up. He looked rosy cheeked, almost revived. "By the looks of this place, they'd have had enough for the passage."

There was nothing left in the cottage but shadows. She could see where the bed had been, and the table, the chair by the hearth, the hook for the pot over it. The people who had lived here had picked up everything they owned and walked out and down the hill and away. They had gone with the intention of not coming back.

America, she thought. She liked the sound of the word, the way it started and finished with the same letter, so it made a circle of itself, and how the sound of it seemed to stretch out, open at the end. It was a word you could shout out from the top of a hill, and the echo of it would come back at you like a swallow swooping.

"You wouldn't get me going there," said William, guessing at what she was thinking. They had spoken before of America. "I'll tell you that much. Looking for something you know can't be found."

He looked across at her to gauge her reaction. He wasn't happy with whatever he read on her face, because he shook his head and said sullenly, "What?" Then he threw his hands in the air as if he were throwing something at her, and stood up and walked outside.

But you have to keep looking, she thought. If you don't keep looking, what is the point? Even if you're searching for something you know will never be found. It's the searching; it's the moving that's the thing.

America.

William was back inside in minutes.

"It's a well-built place, all right," he said. He had shaken off his bad temper already, and his face was burning with excitement, and he was speaking very quickly. "Whitewashed, and the roof is still thatched and all. The land's open to the valley below, but they banked it up the back to give a bit of protection from the winds. Those winds would cut the face off you even on a good day in this part of the country." He was walking around the room now, rubbing his hands together hard. "They even planted a flower of some kind, outside. They must have been delighted with themselves altogether when they first built this place," he said, and he gave a mean-sounding laugh. "Planting flowers and all. They thought they'd be here long enough to see roses up the wall." He spun around, almost theatrically, so that he was facing Honora. "And where did all their plans end up? In America." He rolled his tongue on the *r* of the word so that it sounded like *Amerrrrrica*.

He gave a sigh then, as if he were tired suddenly.

"We deserved this bit of luck, though," he said, more quietly. "Thatched, and all, by God. We can use the thatch to make a fine fire tonight."

He sat down very suddenly with his back against the wall.

"Do you remember our own place, Honora?" he said. "We never had time to make anything of it." He frowned, as if something had just struck him. "All gone now, by God."

It was very quiet in the cottage; the air itself was too quiet. She realized that she was holding her breath to listen to something that was trying to make itself heard. She put her hand up to William: stop. She crawled across the floor so that she was next to the hearth and put her hand on its cold black stones. She felt a strange tightening of the air around her.

We must not stay here, she understood.

She shook her head at William and made a noise in her throat.

"What's wrong with you?" he said, startled.

She pointed to the door. They should leave this place. Something had happened here, perhaps, or something was about to happen. She was not sure yet, but she knew that they should not stay. There was something here telling her that they should leave, keep going on.

"Go away and don't be annoying me," said William. He raised his hands, shaking them over his head, and crossed his eyes and made a noise, mimicking her. *"Hnn."*

He stood up, and walked to the door. "I'm pulling down that thatch and making a fire, and tonight I'll sleep warm and well. If you want to head off out into the snow and the dark, I won't stop you." He stood in the open doorway, facing out into the night. "I'm very tired, Honora," he said, without turning to look at her, "and I've pains in my bones." It was almost as if he were speaking to himself. His voice sounded strange, lighter than usual. "I have to sleep tonight."

A moment later, she heard him on the roof above her and then the sound of the thatch being torn.

She could crawl outside, perhaps. But she would not survive a night on her own in the snow. She put her face down on the ground. Be easy, Honora, she told herself. Maybe it just felt sad in this house, the natural sadness of an abandoned house; maybe she felt uncomfortable because it had always felt unnatural for her to be indoors, confined. She was fully at ease only when she was outside, under the sky. And after all, the worst that could happen had happened.

What more could happen?

~

"No one expected you to live," William said to her.

They had a great fire going in the hearth, and it was a violent, bright fire that was too big for the room they were in. She lay against the wall, as far from the fire as she could get, with her eyes closed. She had felt for some time that William was watching her across the room, but she kept her eyes closed and her face still. He had been unusually quiet all evening, since lighting the fire, and had hardly spoken at all for the last hour. Why does he not sleep? she thought. What is he waiting for? Usually, when he watched her, and he watched her often, his face was without expression. Many times, she had caught him looking at her and had expected, from the studied blankness of his face, a rebuke, only to be surprised when he said something like, "You are a very good-looking girl," in a voice that indicated the opposite. She kept her eyes closed now because she did not want to look at him, to have to read his face.

But a quiet William was not usual and demanded attention, and though she kept her eyes closed, she was alert; she waited.

"Not me, not Nell," he continued. "Though she only left you because her children were gone, and even then, she seemed unwilling to abandon you."

At the mention of Nell, she opened her eyes. He had his head on one side and was considering her.

"She was a good friend to you," he said. The forced surprise in his voice as he spoke was clear. "A good friend, and she not even related to us and from a family of donkey eaters by all accounts and the husband a wastrel lost to the drink in Galway. We must remember her, when all this is over. We must show our thanks, in some way, to her."

He was speaking more quickly than normal. She would have said, had she not known better, that he had drink taken. She had seen him in the early stages of drunkenness many times, and he had that same empty energy to him now. He gave a laugh and kicked his heel against the ground.

"Not a soul expected you to live, and yet here you are," he said. "Not a man in a hundred could have survived what you did. People always did say that you were marked different; your own father said it. Old Alice said things that I thought I could put out of my mind easy enough, but by God, that robin that went into your house the night you were born—I could have done with a robin myself, by the looks of things. It's well enough you're doing with the piseog on you, all the same."

It was the first time he had spoken so openly of the piseog. She sat up against the wall. His face seemed to be aflame with light, as

—

if burning from within. He put his hand to his forehead, tapping it, thrumming his fingers against his skin, a curious, almost girlish gesture for William.

He was tall and had wide-set shoulders and a barrel chest, and he could eat a pot of potatoes faster than anyone else she knew. He needed food; he could not continue for much longer on grass and snow. Something, she felt, was shifting in him.

"It's taking us too long to make our way back," he said to the fire. "One day should have done it. I thought we would meet the others on the way home, or that they would come looking for us. My father must be looking for us, surely. But in this snow, and with this pain in my head, I don't know if it's forward or backward I'm going." He gave her a strange, sour look. "Don't you worry, though. You keep on not talking, not walking." He gave a comical, extravagant shake of his arms, as if he were throwing out invisible reins. "On you go. Hup!"

He gave a half laugh then and lay down on his side, with his hands folded together under his face.

She watched him until his eyes closed, and he slept.

~

Whenever she smelled cold smoke again, for the rest of her days, she was taken back to that morning, that abandoned house. A long time after, she woke up late at night in the cabin on the prairie and the fire in the hearth was smoking, nearly dead, and the smell of it made her think for a moment, before she woke fully, that she was back in the cottage in the snow with William. The recollection was so strong in that moment that she thought she would be sick to her stomach. She was again starving, bleeding, freezing; she felt unclean, invaded, like she wanted to pull her skin off. She had to get out of the bed and walk to the door and open it, though she was in her thin shift and a wicked wind was blowing in from the dark prairie.

"I wish I hadn't told you all those things," she said, standing in the doorframe with the black sky at her back. "About Ireland, about the walk." She put her hand up over her mouth then, a thing she still did when she'd said too much, as if she would like to push words back into her mouth, back down her throat.

He was sitting at the table with a single candle in front of him, and he was busy cleaning the saddle when she spoke. He was always busy at something. She had never known him to pass an hour without doing, fixing. And he loved to clean the saddle: he liked to say that he rode better on a good-looking piece of equipment.

He said, "What?" and she knew why: he'd heard what she'd said well enough, but he wanted her to say it again, partly so he could gain some time to ready an answer, and partly because this was a conversation he didn't much care to get into, and he would have liked to have delayed its beginning for as long as possible. His "What?" was long, drawn out, amused sounding, and swinging up at the end; she would never tire of his way of speaking. She was used to his slow speech, his easy ways, by this point. He was steady and constant in his habits and tastes and considered in his responses. And he was used to her, too, she guessed: her late-night walks and her crying out in her sleep, her fitfulness, her diffidence, her silences.

"Ireland," she said. "I wish I hadn't told you."

"Seems a funny way to think about it," he said. He was regarding a stirrup strap with a frown. "Those things would still have happened even if they hadn't been told."

But the telling of it made it real, she wanted to say. It would be foolish to wish it hadn't happened; there's no point thinking about things like that. I could have better controlled, though, the telling of it.

Because that was the thing she wanted to express: stories were only real once they were told. All the other stories that weren't told, or heard, that had no teller, or listener—it was as if the thing had never happened at all. You could pretend it had never happened, or you could refashion events in your head to your own liking until you came to an ending you liked. Once you made the choice to tell a story, it went from being yours to the listener's, and then there was no way of managing things after that; the story belonged to other people, then. If she had never told the story of what had happened to her, to William, to the people on the walk—it could have been like it had never happened at all. It was too late now.

"Difference between wishing something hadn't happened, and wishing something that happened hadn't been told," he said. "I don't see that the telling of things is the worst of it."

She said nothing. Don't talk, she told herself. Keep your hand over your mouth if you have to. Let him talk his way out of it, away from it; he will.

He was rubbing oil into the leather now. He was using an old, clean bit of muslin and had fitted two fingers into a corner of the material and was working his way across the saddle in small, careful, overlapping circles. This was the part of the job, she knew, that he liked best. The saddle was beginning to glow richly under his hand. He would wash out the muslin with warm water when he was finished, hang it to dry by the fire. He did this every night: the saddle, the bridle. I have only one saddle, he would say, and I look after it, and it looks after me.

"The story you've told me—that is your side of events." He lifted his hand from the saddle, looked at his work. She could not tell if he was pleased with it or not. His face was in the shadows, and the candlelight was weak. "And I'm not saying it is not exactly as occurred, but it's how you remember things, and maybe your memory isn't so reliable, or maybe you choose to tell those things, and you left some things out, because it suited the story, suited you. I don't know, is what I'm saying. Seems like a lot of people died on that walk, when they didn't have so far to go, when it wasn't as cold as it gets here on a fall morning. I'm just saying. I have no way of knowing what lies beyond the edges of the story."

He looked up from the saddle and looked at her straight on.

I will never tell you about the baby, she thought, looking back at him hard. You will never know that.

"Guess I'd like to know what lies beyond the edges, Honora," he said, and then he dropped his head and continued cleaning his saddle.

~

She was stiff from lying on the hard ground, and it took her a moment to move herself up into a sitting position. William was still asleep. The door had swung open in the night, and the snow lay banked up the entrance to the cottage. The sky was a strip of brilliant blue above the snow: it had stopped snowing in the night, at least. But she could see the white winter sun, and it was too high in the sky; that meant that they had slept too long. She did not understand why William still slept; the hunger usually woke him at dawn.

She would have to stand, to walk, because she could not call to him. She put her hands on the ground and stood for a moment in an upside-down V, and then moved forward, in that ridiculous position, walking on her hands toward her stick. She took hold of the stick with both hands and pushed it into the ground and then pushed herself up against it like she was climbing up the stick, hand over hand, until she straightened up to standing. She was very weak—it was amazing to her how light she felt, as if she could blow away in a strong wind, as if her whole body were occupied purely by light and she was no longer flesh, blood, but something entirely less substantial. She fitted the stick under the crook of her arm and began to walk. She had to drag her feet along the ground, with her toes curled underneath; she could not yet flatten her feet out. She went around the fire to William and folded over him again into a V and put her hand down on his shoulder. She shook him. He did not stir. She saw that he was breathing, but the breath was coming too quickly and with a noise like a rusty whistle. She moved her hand onto his forehead. His skin was burning; his hair was wet with sweat.

He had the fever.

She sat down on the ground as quickly as if she had been pushed and put her hand to her heart, and then she opened her mouth to say his name, and all that came out was *ahn*. She kneeled on the earth and beat her fists on it out of frustration and anger and despair.

William, she said in her head, *William*.

He needed food. She had to get him food. They had a pot that William had carried with him on a string over his shoulder—she had laughed at him for bringing that pot!—and in his shirt pocket he had a slingshot, which he carried with him everywhere but rarely used because he said it was poorly made and not worth the trouble. He had never let Honora use the slingshot—respectable married women shouldn't be going around shooting at things with stones, he'd told her, more than once. Well, you can't stop me now, William, she thought, and you didn't want me to use it because I'm a better shot than you, and lucky for you that I am. She had used a slingshot since she was a child and had always had luck with it, and though the countryside was picked clean even of birds, if she could get something, she could cook it in the pot over the fire with snow and make William some kind of soup. And if she made the fire big enough and then the soup hot enough, she could perhaps break the fever.

She put all the dry thatch they had left in the room on the fire. For a terrible moment, she thought she had done it too quickly and roughly and had killed the fire in the process, and she almost wept with relief when the fire took. She had no skill with the flint—she could not make wood take fire, and without the fire, she could not make a soup. There was too much smoke: the thatch was not dry enough, she feared, and it spat and hissed terribly, but the fire came, eventually, and she clapped her hands at the green flames.

She took the slingshot out of William's pocket—his heart under the pocket was beating as fast as if it were trying to work its way through his chest—and then stood back up and turned away from the fire, and William. She would not let herself think beyond what was happening right now. The fire was lighting; she had the slingshot in her hand; she would go and find food.

She had to climb up and over the bank of snow blocking the doorway on her hands and knees. The world outside was full of blinding light, and it took her eyes a minute to adjust after the darkness of the cottage. Still on her hands and knees, she crawled away from the cottage and up the hill behind it; it was easier and faster to crawl because the hill was very steep, but the snow was burning her hands and legs blue already; she would have to stand. When she was at the top of the hill, she pulled herself up on her stick. The land fell away below her, down to a valley. At the bottom of the valley was a small wood. It was not usual to see trees so low down in a valley, and there was water there, she suspected, a small river, maybe, and good enough cover in the trees.

She began to make her way down the field. The snow had settled in deep drifts behind the cottage, around it. The farther from the cottage she went, the deeper the snow was, and before long, she was forced to push and drag herself through it like she was wading through water. She made progress only because she had Alice's stick. *Is this the test, Alice?* she wanted to shout. *Or is this the trouble to come?* Stop thinking, Honora, she told herself, and keep moving. If you fall, you will not be able to right yourself again—you are too weak. But she did not fall, and the land was on such a steep decline that the way down was faster than she had expected.

The trees were no more than a copse, she realized soon enough, and certainly not a wood, and they were bare branched, but the ground beneath them was dry, almost soft, and smelled of living things. She had been right: a stream, nearly frozen, ran by the trees, and so the soil here, by its banks, was sandy. There was hardly any wind, so her scent would not carry, and the snow and the hunger were making any animals that were still alive behave unusually, recklessly. She went to the edge of the copse and lay down flat on her stomach. She had the slingshot in her hand, and in it she fixed a small sharp stone. She waited. She was prepared to wait for as long as it took.

When she saw the rabbit, she lifted the slingshot, took aim, and shot. The stone made an arc through the air and landed on the soft ground behind the rabbit. She'd shot too far. The rabbit lifted its head to the wind and froze perfectly still, listening, watching. If it runs, we are finished, she thought. I will not have this chance again. Very slowly she put her hand down to the earth and felt for a stone. She put it in the slingshot. She breathed in slowly, and on the slow release of her breath, she shot again. The rabbit fell. She went to it: it was still alive, just stunned. She kneeled next to it and hit it twice on the head with her stick and then picked it up by its rear legs and considered it: it was a fine big rabbit with good meat on it. All this she did without thinking. She knew what to do; the action needed no thought, and it flowed from her and through her, unbidden, unforced, like breath itself. She picked up a handful of earth and threw it away from her, over her shoulder, and into the wind. It was a habit she had of old: when she was successful in a hunt, she was accustomed to marking the passing of the life of the animal, to give thanks to the wind and the world around her for its sacrifice. She had seen animals killed for pleasure for as long as she could remember, and it was as strange a practice to her as any she could imagine. She had wondered at those people who laughed at her and her ways, when their own were as dark as a bad dream.

She went back up the hill to William. It was nearly too much for her, and she managed it only by lifting her legs very high like a mountain pony and stepping over and through the snow as if navigating her way over invisible ditches. But she had food; she would cook it; she would feed William; she would break the fever.

He slept by the fire still. She went to him and felt his face: he was hotter than before, and now there was a strange flowering rash blooming high across his cheeks, as if someone had dotted him faintly with little spots of paint, and under his eyes the skin was shining, almost black.

William, she wanted to say. She was on her knees now in front of him. *I have a rabbit. Look.*

She held the rabbit in front of his face and shook it at him. In her mind she was saying, *I did it, William. I caught a rabbit. If you would just look, you would see. Open your eyes and look. Help yourself.* But William did not even stir in acknowledgment.

He does not know, Honora, she told herself. You caught the rabbit with the slingshot that he said over and over was no good, and everything you have ever done or been he has not seen. She felt that if only she could, she would scream with frustration until she woke him and made him see her, at last. For a moment, she thought that she would hit him in the face with the rabbit. He did not deserve the meat, as he did not deserve the effort behind it.

She turned away from him, took the pot, and went out to the snow; she filled it and went back inside and put the pot on the fire. Her heart was beating very fast now, too fast, and too loudly, like a drum, bang, bang, bang, and it was becoming difficult to breathe fast enough to keep up with the speed of the beating, the banging. She had no knife to skin the rabbit—why did they not have a knife? She would not go anywhere again without a knife—so she did what she could, breaking the limbs and tearing at the fur with her hands. The rest of the fur she would try to pull off when the flesh was cooked and softer. She would need more firewood soon, enough to last them through the night and into the next day; she suspected it would take that long for the fever to recede. She would have to go up onto the roof to get the thatch. It would not be easy to pull it down, and she was weak now, and dizzy—her body was shaking from tiredness and from the effort of trying to breathe so fast. But she was afraid to lie down in case she fell asleep, so she sat down on her haunches and put her hands under her thighs, pinning them down so she didn't have to watch them shake. She would stay by the fire and watch William sleep, and wait. That's what the world makes me do: stay in one place, and wait, she thought, and when all this is over, I won't be stopped again. There'll be no more staying, waiting.

The snow was slow to melt. The rabbit, half-skinned, sat on top of it, the wound in its head bleeding into the snow. The fire was too low: she needed more wood now, and not later, she realized. At this rate, it would take hours for the snow to melt, for the water to begin to boil, and the rabbit would surely be frozen solid by then. The pot, the fire, the rabbit lying on top of it with its eyes open wide to her in astonishment: it all looked absurd, wretched, like something a child would put together. She had to stop herself from kicking the whole thing over. She began to rock backward and forward on her heels.

Don't cry, Honora, she warned herself. There's no use in crying.

Do something.

Standing up, she went to William and half lifted him so that he was settled onto her lap. She pushed his wet hair back from his burning forehead. In moving him, she woke him, and he turned up to look at her.

"Honora," he said.

He looked as if he were surprised and yet not unhappy to see her, and he gave her his old slow smile, the smile that used to make her stomach twist with desire. In their early days together, they used to swim in the river at night—it had been high summer, and those nights were lighter than the days almost, and she remembered how William's body had glistened in the water under that light, and how he would throw his head back when he came up from underneath the water to clear his hair from his face. She had loved that movement, the elegance and ease of it, and how the water made his hair as smooth as a blackbird's wing, and the curve, too, of his hair falling across his forehead.

Do something, Honora, she told herself now. Do something. Think harder, faster.

She took a handful of snow from the pot and put it to William's mouth. She wished she could say, *I caught a rabbit, and it is cooking in the pot, and all will be well, William; do not worry,* but of course she could not. She could say nothing at all because her stupid mouth would not work.

He took the snow into his mouth, as obedient as a shy child, and then he looked away from her, toward the fire, closing his eyes again.

"I'm tired," he said simply, after a long time.

I'm tired too! she thought, suddenly alive with fury. But only one of us can sleep, and speak, just as only one of us could carry the baby or kill the rabbit. Some of us have to sit here, mute, waiting for a frozen rabbit to cook and all the time wanting to scream loudly enough to make the hills ring. She wished that she could pick William up and shake him until his teeth rattled in his head, shake him enough to shake the fever out of him.

Don't you leave me here, William, she wanted to scream at him.

Don't you leave me here alone.

She was crying now, finally, but William did not notice. She put her head down so that her face rested against his, and for a while she listened to his breathing. It grew steadier; he was sleeping, she realized, and so she stayed perfectly still with his head on her legs, and because it was very important that she not fall asleep, too, she made herself deliberately uncomfortable by sitting up as straight as possible and not shifting under the weight of William on her legs.

Outside, the day was bright and windless, and the sun was a cold white flame in the sky.

When William woke, the snow had melted in the pot, and the half-broken rabbit was floating in the lukewarm water, uselessly. The fire was very low; she needed to get firewood, but she did not want to leave

William; she could not risk it, and she slowly closed her eyes against what this realization meant.

"When I was a small boy," he said, "my father took me to the market day in Galway." He looked up at her. "Did I ever tell you the story, Honora?" She shook her head. He had told her parts of the story, more than once, but she wanted him to talk. "It took us three days to get there, but we had the loan of the cart from the O'Learys, and we still had the old donkey then, and an easy way we had of it; the sun shone on us, and I slept for hours on the warm straw on the cart. It had a lovely sway to it that would send you straight off to sleep, and when I woke, I'd see the mountains in the distance and the blue of the sea beyond it, and, of course, there was the excitement of Westport to keep you going all the time. When we got to Westport, there seemed to be people everywhere, and it was very loud, and I was only a small fellow, I suppose, and I was frightened. I lost my father in the crowd; he moved away from me and let go of my hand, and I ran across the square in my fright and into the path of a cart, and didn't it go straight over me—the wheels of the cart rolled right across my back. I don't know who got the bigger fright, me or the cart driver. He jumped off and stood me up and he said to me, 'Are you all right?' and before I could answer, he went to the cart and got down a churn of milk, for it was milk he was carrying, and he lifted the thing up and started pouring the milk down my throat to revive me, and it seemed to me that I was drowning in milk. I couldn't catch my breath, and that's why, to this day, I can't abide the taste of milk, or the smell of it even." He gave a quiet laugh. "I'd drink a cup of milk now, though, if I had it." He held his hand up to her, as if he wanted to show her something cupped in his palm. She took hold of his hand. It felt very cold and very smooth and not like his hand at all. "The journey there was the best part of it, Honora. My father and I on the cart, and the dusty road under the old donkey's hooves, and the sun in the evening sky. I never had a day like it again."

He was holding her hand as he used to during those long summer nights in their cottage, in the river. She looked down at their hands knitted together; oh, how he used to kiss her on those nights, with his hands in her hair, and the hunger he'd had for her then, before a different kind of hunger had come for them both.

"I'll rest awhile now and gather my strength," he said. "I just need to build myself up again."

Are you afraid, William? she wanted to ask him. She was sorry that she had called him a coward; she wished she could tell him that. She had hurt him, and she wished that she hadn't. But it was too late now, for talking. All the things they had said to each other, the good things, and the bad, seemed suddenly not to matter anymore.

She sat with him then, holding his hand, until the fire burned out, and all that was left was the cold smoke.

PART II

America

1850

VII

Honora had a bunk under the eaves of the ship. Passengers had carved their names on the wooden ceiling above her, and dates, and someone had crossed the days of their voyage off by drawing lines through lines until the dark wood was full of X's like badly drawn stars. She could trace these carvings with the tip of her finger without even extending her arm. She had to be careful of her head when she sat up, but she preferred to be on top rather than underneath; it would be impossible for her to rest with people lying above her. She heard the girls below her say that you couldn't make them take the top bunk for love nor money: if you fell out in the night, they said, you'd crack your head open like a nut on the hard ground. They were surprised by her willingness to be on top.

This was only one of the things they were to find surprising about her.

"She can't speak," said the tall one to the two others.

They had called her down from her bunk on the first evening at sea, and the tall girl had said to her, "What is your name?" Honora had her hand to her throat and tapped it and shook her head in a no. Then she waited for understanding to spread across the girl's face. Some people understood her quickly; others took an age and had to have it explained to them in different ways. This girl was fast to take her meaning.

"What are you saying to her, Mary?" said one of the other girls, pretending at exasperation.

"She can't talk," said Mary, without taking her eyes away from Honora's.

Honora looked back at the tall girl, meeting her gaze steadily.

"And her going to America all on her own," said the other girl. She had come to stand directly in front of Honora and was regarding her with naked interest. "Are you going all on your own to America?" she shouted.

"She's not deaf, Elizabeth," said Mary. "She can hear you. She understands what you're saying." She looked at Honora. "Don't you?"

Honora nodded.

"See?" said Mary to the others, and to Honora she gave a sudden, brilliant smile. "I told you so."

"She doesn't have a scrap with her," said Elizabeth to a third girl, out of the corner of her mouth. "Apart from the old blanket. How did she get the money for the fare, and it so high a price and her dressed in rags and as barefoot as a pauper." Her words were heavy with fake concern. I take your meaning, thought Honora. You think me a stowaway, and you are right, and let's see now what you intend to do about it. Let's see what you are made of.

"Write your name," Elizabeth said to her. She pointed to the sawdust at their feet. "Write," she said too loudly.

I'm not deaf, and I'm not slow of understanding, either, though maybe you are, she wished she could say, but she crouched down and, in the dust, she wrote, with her finger, *Nell.*

The girls leaned over her, watching her write, and Elizabeth said, "Nell."

"She can't read," said the third girl, and she pointed at Mary. "That's why we have to read things out loud for her."

"Thanks, Annie," said Mary.

"She was never sent to school," said Annie. "It's not that there's anything wrong with her."

She and Elizabeth started to laugh.

"That came out wrong," said Annie, trying and failing to stop laughing.

"Again, thanks," said Mary. "Be sure to go around America introducing me like that."

"I'm only saying," said Annie, and she was laughing so hard now that she was nearly crying.

"Annie," said Elizabeth, sternly, "pull yourself together. It's no laughing matter, Mary's ignorance." She gave Annie a comical wiggle of her eyebrows, and then she turned back to Honora.

"Where do you come from?" she said.

The third girl had moved toward Honora now, and she put her hand on her hair, stroked it, picked up a handful. It was very hard not to hit the girl's hand away.

"She has lovely hair," she said to the others, almost dreamily.

"Stop, Annie," said Elizabeth. "You're being unusual."

The girl started and stepped back from Honora.

"Annie is easily distracted by things she finds attractive," said Elizabeth. "Like Colm O'Riordan. Isn't that right, Annie?"

Mary gave a snort, and the color rose high on Annie's face.

"Where do you come from, we asked you," Annie said to Honora as angrily as if Honora had been the one to laugh at her.

She could turn from these girls and their questions and games, but they had weeks ahead of them together on this ship, and she had to be careful.

So she kneeled and she wrote in the dust, *Doolough*.

No one said anything for what felt like a long time.

"Doolough," said Annie, but quietly, as if embarrassed by the word.

Honora put her hand out and brushed away the word. It was gone now, *Doolough*. She must remember that.

"Where are your people?" said Elizabeth eventually.

"We've all heard about Doolough," said Mary. "We know what happened there." She put her hand out to Honora and pulled her to her feet. "Leave her be."

"Nell," said Elizabeth, and she made the word a question. She put her head on its side and regarded Honora as a bird might look at a worm, looked at her feet, her poor dress, her face, and Honora waited while she was considered, watched Elizabeth make her decision.

"We have a dress we can give you," she said, and she spoke in a high, bright voice now. "You can't stay in those rags."

I am safe, Honora thought. For now, at least.

She nodded at Elizabeth. She would not smile a thank-you at this pointy-faced girl. Let her think her sour, or simple. Elizabeth lifted her chin at her and said, "Do you have a position to go to in America?"

Honora shook her head, no.

"She'll struggle," said Elizabeth, to the others, but still looking at Honora. "With the not being able to talk, and all."

"Will she, though," said Annie. "Many is the mistress would prefer, I'd say, a nice quiet girl who can't answer back or tell tales. And she's strong enough looking, though she's small; I'd say she'd be able for a day's work."

"I don't know," said Elizabeth. "To me she looks like she wouldn't be able to take the skin off custard for you."

There were few things that she would be less suited to, and was less inclined to pursue, Honora wished she could tell Elizabeth, than life as a domestic servant. She knew that with as much certainty as she had ever known anything. But as a reply she made her face a blank. She would have to be careful, she realized, to say things only in her head now and not out loud, for though she hadn't spoken to anyone for a long time, it was not because she couldn't—the ability to speak had come back quickly enough.

She didn't speak now because she didn't want to.

~

On the long walk after William had died, back to the empty village and then afterward on what she always thought as the walk out of Ireland, she had not spoken. She had spoken only to herself. She talked to herself almost constantly, but quietly, as if she were trying not to be overheard by someone who was standing very close to her and was overly interested in what she had to say. The childhood habit she'd had, of narrating her life to herself out loud, she deliberately picked up again: Go on, Honora, she told herself. Talk away. There was a small, unacknowledged part of her that worried that she might lose the ability to speak at all if she did not use her voice at least occasionally, so she partly spoke for practice. But mostly she spoke to herself as she walked because she was very lonely, and it was too quiet. She had grown up in noise: during the day, the village had been full of people and talking and laughing, and at night, there was singing and shouting, and now all was silence, and it was hard to bear. Often, as she walked, she felt dizzy and distanced from herself, as if she weren't properly in her own body because she was being erased by the weight of the silence. She walked past houses empty of people, past fields empty of animals, over land that was without color, and past trees that were black sticks against the sky, and it was as if instead of walking through space, she were walking her way through time, tramping across the minutes and on the hours and the days. Sometimes she felt that she was a ghost, and sometimes she felt that the country was inhabited by ghosts and she was the only one left alive, and more and more, she knew that she was something between the two, and that the place she inhabited was neither of this world nor the next. No change there for you, Honora, she said, for isn't that where you've been from the day you were born?

She had been surprised, every day, to find herself still walking. But the walking kept her alive. As long as she could walk, she could walk out of one story and into another. She drank water from the rivers, and she ate grass, the flowers in the fields. Once she had the great good luck of finding a nest of duck eggs; those kept her going for days. She chased a fox from the carcass of a hare and cleaned its bones of meat. You just keep going on, Honora, someone said to her years later, and she thought, I always have, even when I didn't want to—especially when I didn't want to.

~

At first, she had walked to get away from Doolough. But soon enough, she realized that if she were to keep going, she needed to be walking toward something. She decided to go to America as easily as she'd ever decided anything. She would walk to a port, get on a ship, and go to America. She would work out what to do once she had arrived. America, she thought, is the solution to the problem that is Ireland.

And then the trouble began of how to get there.

Everywhere there were roads that led nowhere, the relief roads that started suddenly and ended in the middle of a field, and that, she and herself agreed out loud, told you all you needed to know about the state of the country. So the first thing she had to work out when she started walking was what direction to go in. She could not afford to walk in the wrong direction; she had no time to spend on roads that led to nothing. She knew in the quick of her that she had to get out of Ireland as fast as possible, while she still had it in her to go.

She started by walking toward the setting sun, because she had learned in school that the sun rose in the east and set in the west, and she knew that America was west and that was where she was heading, she supposed. Then she met a man on the road who was walking toward her, and because he was going past her and not in the same direction—she would not have stopped him if he'd been going in the same direction; she did not want to walk with someone—she put her hand up to him. When he stopped, she drew a ship with her stick on the dirty snow on the road; he looked at her and then looked down at her bare feet and then back up at her face, and he shook his head and sighed.

Westport is three days' walk, he said, but four for you, probably. Keep the sea on your left and the mountains behind you. When you get to Westport, look for the ship. It's up to you then how you get on it. I'd say you'll need all the luck you've never had to get on that ship. If I had food, I would give it to you, he said, or money, but I've nothing. She had started to walk away from him after he had given her directions, and she kept walking as he called down the road after her, I've nothing, nothing at all, and it's to the workhouse I'm going, and you'd be better off going there yourself, for you won't make it to America, and the not making it will be even worse than the not trying.

The whole point was to move toward something, to go more forward than back. If she allowed herself to stop or be stopped, she would disappear. She might as well already have disappeared, as far as the world was concerned, for there was no one in it who knew where she was, or even if she was alive or dead or cared either way. It was a startling thought, really, and one that was beyond her full comprehension: that she could not wake up one day and no one would know and there would be no record of her left, at all. It would be as if she had never walked the earth. As long as she kept walking, though, she was walking away from that possibility. And so she'd kept walking, and she would walk, she had determined, until she walked off the land and onto the ship, onto the sea, and to America.

She would walk herself into being.

~

The quay, when she first saw it, was black with people. There were people sleeping, fighting, crying, eating, and she'd felt like shouting out, *This is where all the people are! The country is empty because they all are here, falling off the edge of the land!*

She arrived at the quay as a mute, a small-boned, pale-eyed, dumb girl. Everyone she met was surprised by her. Be quick, Honora, she told herself, to turn that surprise to sympathy. From sympathy it was only a short step to succor. This she realized so fast that she nearly couldn't remember not ever knowing it.

It was more than useful to be thought of as someone who could not speak. People expected less of her and helped her more; their pity was only to her advantage. They spoke freely around her, as if, in accepting her to be incapable of speech, they believed her to be less able in other ways, too: less able to understand, less able to act on what she heard. They were emboldened, at least, by what they perceived to be her powerlessness to repeat what they said or tell of what they did. Their ease around her opened doors. Her silence bought her information, helped her avoid danger, and overhear secrets that she hoarded like money.

Her refusal to speak, others' belief in her inability to speak, and her ability to inhabit the space between the two was a power. It's lucky I am to have it, she thought. She would never forget, she knew, the feeling of not being able to speak. Even the memory of the words being stuck in her throat like stones made her feel cold with fear. But you can speak now, Honora, she told herself, And you are alive still; you have survived, and you have a chance here that you won't have again, and you should take it.

So do what you must to get on that ship.

The time she spent on the quay, trying to get on the ship to America, was the easiest she had spent since she was first married, and it would be the easiest, she felt, for a long time to come. At one point, she thought that maybe she would stay forever on the quay, and maybe it wouldn't be the worst thing that could have happened to her, all in all. She slept under the barrels by the loading spot, and it was warm and dry there, and she had enough to eat, which was a thing she had never, she realized, been able to say to herself before. People offered her food; what they had, they wanted to share. They were panicked into a generosity born out of grief and fear and relief at having made it so far: Eat, girl, eat, they said to her as they pressed food upon her, and their sadness was writ clear across their face when she and they discovered together that she could hardly eat anything, because her stomach was too small now to hold much. An old man gave her a blanket. It had been his wife's, he said, and she had not made it to Westport; she had died on the road in his arms, and now he was going to America on his own. His wife would have wanted her to have the blanket, he said, as though Honora were going to refuse it. It was a fine wool, gray, cross-stitched, and it smelled of sweet heather. He patted her on the head when she took the blanket from him, as if she were a child; when she turned back after she'd moved away through the crowd, he was standing up on his toes and searching for her. Everyone on that quay was looking for someone, it seemed to her, and not for the first time she thought that she was alone, but at least she was free. Maybe one leads to the other, Honora, and maybe they are the same thing, in the end, or at least parts of the same thing.

She settled quickly enough on a plan on how to board the ship; that part was easy. She would pretend to be with a family with many children; if anyone at all stopped her, she would not speak, and pretend not to understand, either. It was simply a question of waiting until there was enough confusion and upset and then moving quickly and quietly, of doing the right thing at the right time.

What she did not expect was her own unwillingness to get on the ship when the moment came. As it had been easier than she had expected to be on the quay, getting on the ship was harder than she could have imagined. Nothing important is ever going to be easy for you, Honora, she thought when she realized how she was going to struggle. You should know that by now, for nothing ever has been, nor will it, and the sooner you get over it, the smoother a way you're going to have going down the road.

The ship was black as a crow; its sails beat terribly in the wind, and it groaned like a live thing in pain. She watched the people climb into it, like they were ascending a terrible mountain. She did not like the ship, and she did not like the sea it sat on top of, not the look of it, nor the smell of it, nor the sound, nor the size of it. It was not right to leave the land for the sea, surely; it was not right for her, at least, and it was an exchange she wanted no part in. Standing in the line to get on the ship, she saw this now, quite clearly, too late. She was from a people who had no business with the sea. She belonged to the world of mountains and trees and fresh, sweet water. Nothing about the sea seemed right to her: not the cold creatures who lived in it, nor the wicked too-big birds flying over it, watching her with their hungry eyes. She was not of the sea, and it was not right to leave the place that held the body of her baby; it was against nature. She did not want to leave the baby. She should at least stay near her; she should not abandon her to the black lake. William was dead, and Nell was gone. There was no one left who knew the baby had existed, apart from her. She had held her in her arms, and now the baby would fade into the earth, and it would be as if she had never even been a dream. She was such a beautiful baby—she suddenly wanted to cry, and she put her hands up to her face and to her mouth in alarm because she felt then that she might cry out loud.

A woman standing near her was watching her too closely.

"Are you unwell, dear?" she said. "What is the matter with you?"

Don't make a sound, Honora, she told herself. Put your hands down, and make your face empty. She stood up straight and looked back at the woman with such an expression that made the woman shake her head at her and look away. Now, she said to herself, you had a lucky miss there, and if you're not careful, you'll land yourself in trouble, and do you want to get on that ship, Honora, do you?

She was afraid to get on the ship, and that was the hard truth of it. I want to turn around and go home, she thought. *Slan abhaile*, the schoolmaster would call to her at the end of every day when she left the schoolhouse. That was how you said goodbye in Irish: safe home. She wanted to go home now; she wanted to go back to the baby; she wanted to go back to the black lake and dig at the earth with her hands until she found her. That was what she should have done as soon as she'd woken up in the cave and realized the baby was gone. She should never have allowed William to take her away from there; she should have fought him until they both bled to make him leave her by the lake with the baby. She would go back now and find the baby, and then she would find a priest and have a mass said for the baby. She would have the baby named, recorded. Then she would find a graveyard on a hill, and in it a spot by a tree, and she would rest the baby there on the soft, kind grass and around her head plant pale flowers that would bloom in the spring. She would have a fine headstone, too, in gray limestone, and on it she would put the baby's name and her date and place of birth, carved out in letters more beautiful than any even the schoolmaster could make. She could pick another name for her! She did not like the name Aine. It sounded like a yawn. There was time, yet, before the funeral mass to pick a better name.

She was nearing the gangplank now. She had the gray blanket over her head and her stick in her hand, and she kept her eyes down. The line of people moved forward, and it was carrying her forward with it, as she'd planned. There was a ship clerk, and he was calling for tickets and shouting for people to get in line and trying to count heads as people pushed past him, but his face was creased with worry, and he looked like he was ready to give up, or start crying, or both. She had been watching this clerk for days and had been depending on him making a poor job of things. She'd been right. You don't need to second-guess yourself, Honora, she told herself, almost as an aside as she stepped up onto the gangplank. You're reliable. If you think something is, it usually is. You only slow yourself down by questioning yourself. Remember that. Stop slowing yourself down, and trust yourself more. She had pressed herself against the back of a girl of about ten who was with her family, and together as a group they were moving along very quickly now, too quickly.

She needed to think about what to do. If she tried to get out of this line, even for a moment, she would attract attention. If she stayed in the line, she would end up on the ship. I need time to think, she realized. This is happening too fast for me. She lifted her face up to the sky to breathe; it was becoming hard to catch her breath. But the sky above was already a strange sky to her. Its colors were all wrong; the wind that blew across it was unreadable, discordant.

Get on the ship, Honora, she told herself. If you get out of this line, you are finished. There is nothing to go back to. You never had a home, really—certainly not as a child, and not with William. The baby, and William, the life you knew in the woods and Alice and the song of the robin by the door—all these things are gone now. Get on the ship. Even if you stay, you cannot go back. You can't get the baby back. And you cannot stay here on this dock, between the land and the sea, doing nothing. You can only go forward. Go forward, Honora. Keep moving.

People were crying now and calling out to each other and to the people on the dock, and then it seemed as if all the voices joined as one into one great cry, each to each, and it was a final terrible cry of farewell, and then there was a surge forward, and she was on the ship. I should have taken a handful of earth from Ireland with me, she thought. How could I not have thought of that? She pushed through the people to get to the side of the ship and leaned over as far as she could, tipping so far, indeed, over the edge of the ship that she thought for a moment that she might fall into the water below. If I fall, I fall, she thought wildly. It will be a choice taken away from me, at least. She stretched her arms out and tried to grab at the air with both hands as if it were the earth itself, but the ship rocked, and she fell backward and away from the side. She couldn't hold on.

She fell facedown onto the deck and hit her chest, hard. She sat up and put her hand to her heart to steady it. Then she felt that there was something against her breast. She put her hand down her dress, feeling beneath her breast, and when her fingers found the feather, her heart gave a great jump. Alice's feather. All this time it had lain against her skin, and she had not even felt it there. All these days that she had not washed or changed her clothes, and the feather had been there, waiting to be found. She took the feather out and held it up in front of her. She felt, suddenly, like laughing, without knowing why. *Is this the test, Alice? Or is this the trouble? Where are you now, Alice? Where are all my people? Why am I here alone?*

She looked at the feather. I feel nothing, she thought. I begin to forget the details of parts of my life and remember only how I felt when I lived them. I don't remember the color of William's eyes. I can't picture my father's cottage. This feather means—nothing. She put the feather to her lips, and then, without thinking, held her dress out and put it back under her breast, above her heart.

A man standing above her was shouting, Goodbye, goodbye, and another man near her said, more to himself than anyone else, That's it, now. Honora put her hand up to her mouth, to stop herself saying anything at all. Don't speak and don't think and don't feel, she told herself.

Just hold on.

~

Elizabeth and Annie had letters. They were very keen to impress this on her. Annie had an older sister who had made the journey to New York two years before. Elizabeth had an aunt who'd been settled there for even longer. These relatives had sent home money for the girls' passage, and more important even than the money were the letters they'd sent full of names and addresses and information. The letters had been folded over and over until they were tiny squares, and they were kept in carefully stitched bags of fine cotton. The girls opened these bags as if they were revealing a great treasure to her, took out the letters, and smoothed them flat on their trunks, and smiled and nodded encouragement as they watched her read, their hands hovering nearby, like pale moths, ready to snatch the papers back.

Mary, they told her sadly, had no letters. The girls had grown up together in Galway, and they had raised Mary's fare between them. The New York relatives had arranged positions in service for all three, and God, they couldn't wait to get to America and for their lives to start; they'd had enough to last them an eternity of the hunger and rain and the gloom of Ireland, and, Jesus, Annie added, half laughing and half crying, I never want to even think about the whole place ever again.

Mary was quiet, and Elizabeth was sharp-tongued and quick, and Annie was dull-witted, she suspected, but the girls were not unkind to her from the start, and as time passed, they grew warmer, and then even affectionate, and she was surprised and suspicious of this until it struck her that they didn't know about the piseog, and maybe this was how life was if you were not marked out from birth. They understood that she did not want to be seen as much as she could not be heard, and they hid her whenever someone official came below deck. They gave her food—they seemed to have an endless supply of oatcakes, and they fed her on a mush that they cooked every night on a fire on the foredeck into a kind of warm porridge. The promised dress was too big for her, but warm and clean, and they gave her a pair of woolen socks, and a white cap for her hair. She had never been given such gifts—her father had given her nothing, and William had only talked of the things he would one day give her. She was amazed that the girls gave so easily, but they only gave what they could spare, they said, and Elizabeth said it would make her feel melancholy if she had to look at Honora's rags and her dirty bare feet for any longer than necessary. They brushed her hair and showed her how to plait it into fishtails and how to dress it in a neat bun on the top of her head. She would need tidy hair, they said, when she was in service; she was doing herself no favors going around looking like an escaped lunatic from a mental asylum. The shoes and the shawl and the undergarments she would need could be had, they said, with help from the relatives once they were in New York.

Her presence gave them a purpose, she suspected, distracted them from the tedium of the days. Annie had left a boy behind—Colm O'Riordan—and she suffered without him, and she suffered at the hands of Elizabeth, too, who delighted in making fun of her loneliness. Annie liked to brush Honora's hair every morning, and always as she brushed, she talked, of Colm's glowing character, of their time together, of their plans for the future.

"As soon as he can," Annie said to Honora one day, "he will join me in America. He's working for his awful old uncle on the farm and trying to put aside the money for the fare."

"That's the story he's given you, anyway," said Elizabeth.

"How do you mean?" said Annie. "And it's not nice to come up like that on people when they're having a private conversation. You gave me a fright."

"You're hardly having a conservation," said Elizabeth. "That would take two people. And Colm O'Riordan is as slippery as an eel," she said to Honora. "He's made promises to every girl he's ever met."

"He's very good-looking," said Annie sulkily.

"No one's saying he's not," said Elizabeth, "if you like that kind of look. But that's neither here nor there, and we've told you that until we're blue in the face." She rolled her eyes at Honora. "Blue in the face," she repeated. "And, Annie," she said, "leave poor Nell alone. Just because she can't talk doesn't mean she has to listen to you all day."

She had never had such companionship from other girls, known such banter. Annie and Elizabeth were full of information about New York, all gleaned from the letters, and they shared their knowledge with her as willingly as they shared their food. There were organizations in New York to help the Irish, they told her, because the main thing was to stay with your own people, to fit in and to be helped and then to help, but those organizations were for people who didn't have letters. If you had a letter, you could skip all of that and take up a position straightaway and no messing about. It was your lucky day the day you met us, Nell, they told her, and before too long, Honora began to believe that yes, she had been lucky to meet these girls. You stay with us, they said, and we'll look after you, and such was the force of their enthusiasm that she began to think herself that there were worse things that could happen to her than being a maid in New York.

She would have a bed in a clean room in a fine house, food every day, maybe more than once a day even, clothes, shoes—two pairs, the girls said: boots for the winter and lighter shoes for the summer. She would be paid for the work. Annie and Elizabeth said that there were dances to go to on your free days; the relatives had said that these were not to be missed. They planned to save their earnings and buy themselves new clothes—a fur muffler, said Annie, was the first thing she was going to get, and silk ribbons for her hair—and they would wear these new things to the dances. Just think, Nell, of the time we'll have! and they squeezed her hands as they spoke, and their eyes shone with excitement, and sometimes even they kissed her on the cheek when she laughed with them. You are our friend, now, Nell, they told her, and as they talked to her, they touched her cheek, and this delighted her, and at the same time she was frightened by the strength of her delight and full of an awful loathing for herself for being so easily pleased, for being so hungry for such a meaningless love.

They like Nell, she warned herself, over and over. They want to be friends with Nell, who is silent and mild of manner and makes herself small and still and smiles on demand. They would not be so keen, she knew, on Honora.

Remember that, Honora, she tried to tell herself. Remember who you are, but every day it got harder to stay fixed on exactly who she was. The farther they got from Ireland, the farther she was getting from Honora, she felt, and maybe by the time she got to America, she would be all Nell, and Honora would be lost to memory like the baby, and maybe that was the way it was meant to be, after all. To stay as Nell would be the easier road to take, and she had been on a hard road for a long time now, and no one would argue that. She began to be convinced that she should stay as Nell. And after she had been in America for a while, she could recover her voice. She would say it was thanks to the kindness the girls had shown her and wasn't it a miracle, and this would endear her and bind her to them even more, and she could work, and go to the dances, and have food, and there was nothing wrong with such a life, surely; it was a life many she had known would have welcomed.

In her father's village, there had lived an old man who had questioned the fight against paying the rent to the landlord. If we don't pay it to him, then who are we to pay it to? he used to ask. It took her a long time to understand what he had meant. Only now, really, did she see that he could not understand that the argument was against paying any rent at all, and not to whom. His mind could not go that far. It was the same for Annie and Elizabeth: they could not understand why anyone would not want to be part of a tested, tried system that worked, and perhaps, she began to think, they were not wrong. Why would you not want to be a maid in a nice warm house? she asked herself. Why not, Honora?

"My worry," said Annie to Elizabeth one evening, "is that we won't be able to find her a position because of the not being able to talk, and what will we do with her then?"

This was a conversation Annie and Elizabeth often fell into, in one form or another. They would not give voice to any fears they had for themselves; it would erode their courage if they gave light to them, Honora knew. It was safer to talk about the problem that was Nell, and over and again they talked about their plans for her until one day Mary turned to them and said, "Leave her be! Maybe she doesn't want to go into service with you two! Maybe she'll go out West and be free!"

"All right, Mary," said Elizabeth. "There's no need to shout."

"You haven't asked her if she wants to go with you," said Mary.

Mary was careful around Annie and Elizabeth, because of the letters, because of the fare they'd raised for her, Honora supposed, but they'd been many days on the ship in uncomfortably close quarters by now, and she was growing less careful by the day.

"In case you haven't noticed, Mary, Nell can't talk," said Elizabeth. "But she seems happy with the idea of coming along with us, and why wouldn't she? Why wouldn't she, Mary?"

"Mary," said Annie to Honora, "is a dark horse. We think she doesn't want to stay in New York. She has a beau who went out West, and we think she wants to join him out there. Don't we, Elizabeth?"

"A beau," said Elizabeth, with a snort. "Ignatius O'Herlihy. I wouldn't cross a small room to see Ignatius O'Herlihy, never mind the wilds of America." She turned to look at Mary. "The problem is," she said, "that Mary thinks she's too good to be a maid." She smiled at Mary, encouragingly. "Don't you, Mary?"

"I never said that," said Mary quietly.

"You don't need to," said Elizabeth.

"Anyone who would even think about going out West is simple," said Annie, "or at the very least slightly touched. Aren't they, Elizabeth? You'd want to be simple to go somewhere with raving madmen all over the place and not a mark of civilization as far as the eye can see."

"No dances out West," agreed Elizabeth, very coolly, in what Honora knew now to be a dangerous voice.

"No fur mufflers," said Annie.

"It's far from a fur muffler you were raised," said Mary.

"All I'm saying," said Annie, affronted, "is that I don't plan on crossing this ocean to go somewhere even worse than the place I've left behind. That's all I'm saying."

"Well, Annie," said Elizabeth, "that's reasonable." She was standing in front of Mary now; her head was on one side. She was a small, neat, compact person, considered in dress and behavior, and yet there was something about her that made Honora feel that she was always one moment away from doing something dangerous. "What wouldn't be reasonable, on the other hand, is having your friends help with the cost of your passage and having your friends' relatives arrange a job for you, and all the time to have a different, secret plan of your own. That wouldn't be the thing to do at all. That's the kind of thing that would result in trouble."

"I think," said Mary, "that we all agree with Annie. We're all crossing this ocean to go to a better place than the place we've come from."

Elizabeth kept her head on one side; she was looking at Mary, and everyone waited.

"And as long as we're all in agreement about where that place is," she said, "we're grand."

∼

What is the West like? Honora wanted to ask Mary, and at the same time she wanted to say to her, *I will go west.* It sounded right. It felt right. You cannot be a maid in a city, she said to herself. You cannot be in a house with locked doors, in a uniform, living under someone else's rules. Even if you want to, you cannot. You have been playing with the idea of it, as you have been playing at being Nell. Who would not want to be free, she thought, and why would you not want to go to the place that promised it? I will go west, she thought, and it felt like realizing something that she had known all along to be true: the words sounded easy, clear, light.

The girls had said that New York was a city with buildings so tall, they blocked out the sky, as if that were a good thing. She didn't want to be somewhere she couldn't even see the sky, she wanted to say to them. And New York was next to this cold sea they were crossing, and once she got off this ship, she wanted to get as far away from the sea as she could manage and never have to look at it again or smell it or feel it under her. She certainly didn't want to have to be reminded, every time she looked at it, that across it was Ireland, and the baby, and all the parts of the life she had once known. She would turn her back on the sea, she determined, and face in the opposite direction, and the opposite direction was west. She wanted to be in a place where the wind had room to blow free, where the birds threw shadows on the land from a great height. *Is that the West?* she wanted to know. But how could Mary know? She knew no more than Honora, surely; she was coming from the same place as she was, and she was on the same ship.

You'll have to find out for yourself, so, Honora, she thought. Go and see.

~

There was something over her face. She couldn't breathe; she felt that she must be under the water and drowning. She tried to sit up, and she was pushed back down. There was a hand over her mouth and another hand on her chest.

"Stop fighting." She couldn't see who was speaking. She opened her mouth and tried to bite at the hand, and it was pulled away. "Stop," hissed the voice. "It's me, Mary."

Mary was leaning over her; she could just now make out her outline in the darkness. Honora grabbed at her. If she had to fight, she would.

"Stop," whispered Mary urgently. She pushed Honora away. "Jesus. You're talking in your sleep."

Honora sat up. She shook her head at Mary.

"You are," said Mary very quietly. "You can talk."

Without waiting for Honora to respond, Mary took hold of the edge of the bunk and climbed up and sat so that she was facing Honora.

"What I want to know is, is this as much of a surprise to you as it is to me?"

Honora put her hand to her throat, tapped it, and shook her head.

"No," said Mary. "Stop that. You can talk."

116

Think, Honora, think. Don't go down a road here that leads nowhere.

She nodded.

"Talk, so," said Mary.

She opened her mouth. Nothing came out. Her hand went up to her throat like a bird flying against the bars of its cage and rested there.

"Talk," said Mary.

I am trying, she wanted to say, *and I am afraid now that I am mute after all, and I fooled no one more than myself.* Talk, Honora, she said to herself. Push the words out.

"I lost the ability to talk for a long time," she said. Her voice sounded thin and strange. "I was sick. Then I lost the desire." She opened her mouth to the dark air, opened and closed it.

She could hear Mary's steady breathing in the darkness.

"You lied to us," said Mary.

"I didn't tell you the truth," said Honora. Her voice was too quiet, without strength. It didn't sound like her voice at all. "I didn't know you. I didn't owe you the truth."

The truth has to be earned, like trust, like love, she thought, and it's hard earned and easily lost.

Mary leaned against the wall at the end of the bunk, pulled her knees up to her chest, and let her head fall back. For a while, she said nothing. Honora waited.

"Annie and Elizabeth will be disappointed," Mary said. She was perhaps half smiling, thought Honora. It was hard to be sure in the darkness. "They were looking forward to introducing you to the relatives. You're their little pet." She moved to watch her across the bunk. Honora could feel her eyes on her. "There'll be letters written home about this."

Mary had told her that once Elizabeth had cut a girl's hair to the bone in a fight over a perceived slight. Now that she knew more of Elizabeth, it seemed like the least of things that she might do.

Mary had heard her talking in her sleep and had woken her. She had not rushed to tell Annie and Elizabeth what was happening. She wanted answers, an explanation. She was looking for something; Honora could feel it. She did not, Honora was nearly sure, want to be a maid in New York. No one had sent her to school; no one had paid for her voyage; no one was waiting for her on the other side of the sea. She had no letters; her clothes were poorer than Annie's and Elizabeth's; she had less food than they did. The only friends Mary had, it seemed, were Annie and Elizabeth, but she was different from them, and she knew it, and they knew it and used it against her when they wanted to.

"What do you know about going west in America?" she said to Mary.

"Why?" said Mary.

"I'm collecting information," she said.

"Boys I grew up with went looking for work out there," said Mary. "They welcome the Irish, it's said."

They welcome the Irish in Boston, too, Honora thought, so that's not the only reason to go there. There's more. She's not telling me all that she knows, and I don't blame her, thought Honora. I'd do the same. She's careful; she's guarded—that's good.

"Do you have an address?" she said.

"I do," said Mary.

In her mind? thought Honora. Has she memorized it? Does she have it written down somewhere? She can't read it, if she does. She doesn't know for sure what it says.

"Is it hard to get there?" said Honora.

"I suppose it is," said Mary. "Everything's hard."

"And harder still when you can't read the address of where you want to go, or follow directions on how to get there," said Honora.

It was risky to say this. She let the words settle. She was holding her breath, she realized. She kept holding it.

"Annie and Elizabeth," said Mary slowly, "will want back their dress and their socks and their bonnet, and they'll begrudge the food they gave you and the offers of help when they learn that all this time you led them a fine dance. No one likes to be made a fool of, and we're only halfway through our time on this ship."

"We could go west together," said Honora. "I stay mute; we get off the ship together in New York; we go west together."

Mary said nothing.

"Show me the address," said Honora. She must have it written down somewhere; someone must have written it down for her.

She couldn't see Mary's eyes in the dark, but she could hear her breathing, still steadily, evenly.

"Why do you carry that stick with you?"

"A woman I knew gave it to me," said Honora. "She said it would help me."

"Has it?"

"I'm here," said Honora. "I'm alive. I've made it this far. I hope to make it farther."

"Why?" said Mary.

"Because I can," she said, "and all those I knew can't. And I can't go back, and the farther I can get from where I've come from, the better. I want to go somewhere that doesn't remind me of where I've come from. I want to forget. Don't you?"

"Yes," said Mary, and the word was an exhalation, a release. "Was it very bad," she said, too quickly, "in Doolough? What did you see?"

"Show me the address," said Honora.

"Was it bad?" repeated Mary.

The address for information: Mary wanted an exchange.

"It was as bad as you can imagine," said Honora.

"What happened to you there?" said Mary. "You cry in the night, most nights. Sometimes I turn you onto your side, and you stop then.

Or I shake you or pinch your nose. You never wake, but you stop crying."

Honora put her hand up to her face. She was crying now, silently at least, and Mary couldn't see her in the darkness. *But you cannot be like this, Honora,* she said to herself. *It is dangerous to cry as easily as this. You'll weaken yourself. Stop crying, stop talking, sit up, and tell Mary she can keep her address.*

She could feel Mary waiting.

Then she heard skirts being lifted and the rustle of paper.

"It's written down here," said Mary.

She could hear Mary moving toward her.

"It's a letter," said Mary. "It's from a boy I knew from a townland near mine. He was keen on me since we were children. He wrote me the one letter, two years ago."

"What does it say?" said Honora quietly.

It was suddenly hard to care about Mary and her letter, about America and its West. It was hard to care about anything when she remembered what she had left behind. Even the sound of the word *Doolough* made her feel like she was drowning in the black waters of the black lake.

"I don't know," said Mary. "I've never given it to anyone to look at, until now. He said he would write to me when he got to America, and tell me where he was, and how to join him."

Two years she had had this letter, and she had never tried to have it read. Was she simple? Was she a coward? How did she even know it contained an address?

Honora put her hand out in the dark.

"Give me the letter," she said.

Something was pushed into her hand, and she closed her fist around it.

"We'll go up on deck and find a light to read by," said Honora.

"No," said Mary. "No."

"No what?" said Honora. "What's wrong with you?"

She is afraid, thought Honora, of what is in the letter. It was easier to carry it against her breast like a promise that couldn't be broken than to read it and find out what it said. It was easier to talk of going west and all the time to be resigned to staying a maid in New York because the alternative was too frightening, to believe that you might have done something different, braver, better, if circumstances had been more in your favor. But things didn't work like that. You had to make things happen or stop pretending to yourself about what it was that you wanted.

You had to keep on going on.

"Come on," she said to Mary. "We're reading this letter."

She never went up on the foredeck at night. There were gangs of men up there, drinking, and women, too, cooking at the braziers, shouting to each other and at the men, and she didn't like the smell of the sea at night, not the endlessness of it, nor the way it mixed with the darkness of the sky and made a closing circle about her. But she put her head down now and pushed through the people until she was next to the light of a brazier in a corner that burned low and had no one around it because its fire always burned badly. Mary was at her elbow. It was very cold up on deck, and the smell of the smoke from the fire would stay in her hair and on her skin after this, and she could not bear that smell, the smell of cold smoke. Without thinking, she stepped back from the fire and its smell.

She was holding the letter in her hand. I should throw this letter on the fire, she thought, and I should stay in New York and be a maid, and that will be fine. I will be safe and warm and fed, and that's more than I've ever had.

She looked down at the paper in her hand. *Don't read it, Honora,* she said to herself. *Don't make trouble for yourself.*

There was an address on the front of the envelope. It was hard to make out: she had to hold the paper up to the light of the fire. *Mary*

Kerrigan. Then, *The Reverend Father Healy, Ross, Galway, Ireland*. There was a mark in the corner of the envelope where the stamp had been. She turned the envelope over; it had been opened, carefully. She took out the sheet of paper; it was full of writing, on both sides.

Dear Mary, she read, to herself.

The handwriting was neat, well formed, better than she would have expected. *Peannaireachta*: the master had set great store by it. You cannot get on in the world, he would tell them, if you can't write a good letter. You'll never get anywhere if you write like a dirt digger. She could hear him now, roaring at poor Frank Whelan: *Ta do chuid peannaireachta go hainis*. Your handwriting is shocking. But this handwriting was careful; this writer had made it out into the world by writing such a letter. The master would have approved. Peannaireachta. She wondered when she would begin to forget the Irish, when she would stop translating everything from Irish to English and back again in her head. It was as if she were always looking at an object from two different directions, and it was tiring. It was a waste of time. And as long as she remembered the Irish, she could not forget Ireland. She would welcome the letting go of the language, the being free of it. The sooner she began the business of forgetting, the better. She had enough of being weighed down by remembering; if she could, she would burn every memory she had on the fire in front of her.

She looked up from the letter to Mary.

"Will I read it out loud?"

She spoke very quietly; she could not be heard speaking.

Mary nodded. She was ghostly white in the firelight. She moved to stand closer to Honora so that their arms were touching. It felt odd to be so close to someone. Mary was taller than she was, broad, and she had thick shins and a distinctive dry, woody smell to her that was not unpleasant and an unusually husky voice that seemed to fit her smell. Mary had her eyes fixed on the page; she was frowning at the words, as if she would read them herself.

"I'll read it through, so, without stopping," said Honora. She felt unaccountably nervous. Her voice would not hold up, she feared, to the strain of whispering; it had been too long since it had been so used.

"Dear Mary,

I know you will think me neglectfull for not writing sooner which I intended doing but things have been hard and it is only now I find the time to write. I write to you from the town of Bolt which is in the Oregon Territory and is the place out West where we have come for work. The journey here was very dificult. We had thought the boat would be the worst part of it but the journey across America was a trial. I was glad that I had good traveling companons in Jim O'Sullivan and Tom Moore, we are together here and it is a blessing to have compiny from home though my heart is ever in Ireland."

She paused and looked up at Mary, who had turned to look out at the sea, as if distracted by something very interesting and far away.

"I still hold dear the promises we made to each other, and I wish I could offer you proof of my fidility but I believe you know Mary that I am true. Be sure to do all you can to make haste to join me here. A note from you telling me how your plans proceed would be highly prized. You can write to me care of the trading post, Bolt. Have you spoken with your uncle about your fare for the crossing, as you said you would? What are your plans? Be sure that you make arrangements to have money enough and a good companon to travel the road with. It may be that I am selfish in asking you to make such a journey as the one to Bolt but I long to see you Mary and to make good the promises I made you which were made in ernist and are not easily forgotten by me nor are your own promises to me. There is land to be had out here, and good prospects all round. The mines are Irish, and all who work in them, and there are fortuns to be made. Mary, come as soon as you can and God speed you and save you from Ireland and its misfortuns.

Don't forget me I have a great deal more news to send you but I will have to send it another time.
With love I remain same old
Ignatius.
Excuse all the mispeeled words, should you find any."

~

She folded the paper over and put it back in the envelope and handed it to Mary. Neither of them said anything, and then they both spoke at once.

"Ignatius . . . ," began Honora. She meant to try to make a joke of things, to say that Ignatius sounded very earnest, altogether.

"My uncle . . . ," began Mary.

"Go on," said Honora.

"I've no uncle with money," said Mary. She was looking down at the letter in her hand, so Honora could not see her face. "I made the story up, to impress Ignatius. I said my mother's brother had gone years since to Dublin and made a fortune." She looked out to sea. "No one in my family ever even owned a pig."

"Why did you tell him that, so?" said Honora.

The wind picked up Mary's hair and blew it across her face; sparks flew about them from the brazier.

"Ah, I don't know," said Mary. "So he'd like me. So I'd be different from the other girls."

"Well, he liked you all right," said Honora. "I'd say you can be sure of that."

"The strange thing is," said Mary, "I never even liked him that much. He was a skinny, serious little fecker, and he was always trying to put his hand up my dress and then getting annoyed with himself for wanting to. But I knew he would go to America, and I wanted to tell him a story so he'd remember me once he got there. I said I had a rich uncle, that I could get the fare and I'd come out to him, and then he started making plans, and I went along with the plans. It was exciting. It was something to do."

She looked at Honora. "Isn't that mad?"

"I've known madder things," said Honora.

Mary gave a laugh. "I'd say you have, all right."

"Do you want to go to Bolt, to Ignatius?" said Honora.

"Hmm, I'm not desperate to see Ignatius again," said Mary. "But—" She stopped.

Honora waited. Then she said impatiently, "Go on."

"Say he's given up waiting for me and found someone else," said Mary. "He was that type, the settling-down kind. And say I turned up and acted affronted to find that he had broken his promise, and he was made to feel that he had to compensate me, as it were." She held up the letter to Honora. "I have proof of promises made; I know that now."

"It's a risk," said Honora. "He might be waiting for you still. You're stuck then."

She looked at Mary. There was something else here. She was missing something. Think, Honora, she told herself. Think.

"His traveling companions," she said. "Do you know them?"

"Tom Moore, I know," said Mary. "Well enough." Her face was unreadable, a studied blank.

She wants to go to Bolt because of this boy, maybe, Honora thought. That would make sense: that is why she told Ignatius she had a rich uncle. She planned it so that he would ask her to join him. She lied to Ignatius and yet will have satisfaction from him and will use him to be with Tom Moore; she lied to me not one minute since about her motive for lying to Ignatius. She has lied to Annie and Elizabeth.

"Sure I'd never make it all that way, anyway," cried Mary suddenly. "Even if I tried. And why do you want to go there so much? What's it to you?"

"Stop shouting," said Honora. "You'd get there if you were with me. I can read; I can understand maps; I can hunt. We'd be safer together on the road than alone."

"Ha," said Mary. "Says you."

What I say is true, thought Honora. The question now is, Do I want to go with Mary? I could stay in New York, or I could head out on my own. I don't need an address. And I don't need a traveling companion like Mary Kerrigan.

Mary was looking at Honora like she was seeing her for the first time. She is clever, thought Honora. She can see that I am judging her.

"You didn't answer my question," she said. "Why do you want to go west? What is it that you want, Nell?"

"I'll let you know when I get there," said Honora, but she thought without hesitation, I want to be free; I want to live; I want my own land, and I never want to be hungry again, and how can I have not seen this before now?

Mary was watching her, and then, when she saw that she wouldn't say more, she threw her head back and laughed.

"Jesus, you're tricky," she said then, but she sounded jubilant, and she gave Honora her brilliant, wide smile, and she said, "Ahhh," and the exhalation was a release. She turned back toward the sea. Mary had wild hair the color of the fire, and it streamed out from her head into the wind, likes flames. She said that her hair was her cross to bear in life, because it was too thick and grew out from her head in the shape of a triangle and was the color of a fox's back, and everyone knew that that meant it was tinker hair. Annie had said once that Mary had enough hair for two people, and Elizabeth had said, Yes, twice the trouble, and none of the gain.

Mary was humming now under her breath. This was something she did sometimes, Honora had learned, when she was thinking. *You already know what you want to do,* she wanted to say to Mary. *Everyone always does. You're only going around your answer and looking at it from a different point of view.*

"Do you have any other secrets you'd like to let me in on?" said Mary to the wind. "Apart from the not being mute? Anything else pressing you'd like to tell me now, like your name isn't Nell, or you're actually a man?"

"Do you?" said Honora. "Any more Ignatiuses or Toms or made-up rich relations?"

Mary turned and faced her and blew at her, very deliberately, pursing her lips together and blowing like she was blowing out a candle. It was such an unexpected gesture that Honora put out her hand and pushed at Mary, and Mary grabbed at her hand and swung it high into the air, and they stood there like that, frozen, facing each other.

"I liked you more when you were mute," said Mary.

"What do I say in my sleep?" said Honora.

Mary was still holding her hand, and they stood in front of each other as if they were about to break into some kind of dance, and they were waiting for the music to start up.

"Ah," said Mary, and she smiled. "Nothing I can understand."

I don't know if that's true, thought Honora. I don't know what she knows, and I don't know who she is.

"I'm sorry I pinched your nose," said Mary. She let go of Honora's hand and leaned forward and touched the tip of her nose, very gently. "I never did it too hard. Will we go west?"

Honora started to put her hand up to her throat, but she stopped herself and put her hands down in front of her and made one hold on to the other. She felt weak, suddenly, worn out. She was not used to being touched; it was not a comfortable thing for her. And her mouth felt dry; her voice felt like it might fade away. She was tired of talking. It was easier to be silent, and she missed the silence already and the peace in it.

"Unless something else reveals itself that makes it seem like even more of a bad idea than it already does," she said, "I might."

It was important that she seemed in control here, that Mary understood how things would be between them. But it was an effort to speak. *I am very tired,* she wanted to say. *I wish I could rest and cast this tiredness off, but every morning I wake tired from my dreams, and I need someone to travel the road with, at least for a while. I have to acknowledge that, at least to myself.* Mary's face was calm, open, intelligent. She had big hands, big feet; she moved through the world with an easy determination, occupying her place in it without apology. Mary was strong, able.

The air smelled of smoke and the sea and night and possibility.

Bolt. Oregon Territory.

"All right, Mary," said Honora.

"All right, Nell," said Mary. "If that's really your name. Let's shake on it, so."

And so they did.

VIII

She had not thought it would be cold in America, and certainly not so cold that the air in the room where they slept at the top of the house shimmered with cold, or so cold that they had to dress under their blankets, pulling layer on top of layer and then undressing every evening by peeling the layers off bit by bit so that bare skin was never left exposed to the air. It was so cold that Mary's hands swelled, and her fingers turned thick and slow, and it became impossible for her even to tie the strings of her cap under her chin. Honora had to do it for her and tie her apron and do the buttons up the back of her dress too. Honora did not feel the cold as Mary did, and when Mary began to be sick from the cold and the work and then found that she could not move from her bed, and when she sweated cold and cried out in the night, Honora covered her with her own blanket, and fed her, and began to do her work in the kitchen as well as her own.

It is too cold, Mary would say to Honora at night. How are you not cold, Nell? *Because I lived out in the woods,* Honora didn't say, *because I raised myself, because I walked through the snow after having a baby in a cave and we are in a warm house now. We have food and clothes and shoes, and I did not expect you to be so weak, Mary. I thought you would be more like me, and I begin to understand that you are not; you are easily broken.*

Now, in the mornings, Honora did not stop to ask Mary if she planned to get up for work. Mary was eating less all the time, and when

Honora had brought up her dinner today, she had found Mary lying on her side but with her eyes open, looking at the wall, and when she had finally turned to look at Honora, there had been something in the dark emptiness of her eyes that was not right. It was nighttime now, hours since dinner, but the plate was on the stool next to Mary's bed, still untouched.

"Will you lie with me, Nell?"

It was dark in the room, because Mary had burned through their allowance of candles, but Honora didn't mind the dark; there was light enough from the small window.

"I can't sleep anymore," said Mary. "I'm too cold for sleep."

Honora got out of her narrow bed. She went across the room and got into Mary's bed. Mary was curled on her side with her hands between her knees, facing the wall, and Honora lay against her, and they fitted together as one.

"You're wearing all your clothes," said Mary, without turning around.

You have my blanket, Honora wanted to say. *I have to.*

"You should be wearing yours," said Honora.

Mary was wearing only her nightgown; even her feet were bare.

"That's the strange thing," said Mary. "I'm hot and cold at the same time. And I can't sleep, and I can't think clearly, Nell; my mind is muddled."

Honora said nothing, but she thought, This is what I saw in her eyes before.

"Do they ask for me downstairs?" said Mary.

"They know you are sick," said Honora.

"Lazy Irish," the cook said to anyone who was listening when Honora told her, every day, that Mary was still too sick for work. The cook, Mrs. Bentley, was from Dublin, but she was English, she said, because she had been born under the Crown, and proud she was of it too. Last week, Honora had asked if they could call a doctor for Mary, and Mrs. Bentley had looked at her and said, "Ha!" and then she had turned to the kitchen maid, and said, in a tone of exaggerated astonishment, "A doctor for a scullery maid, Grace—did you ever hear the likes of it?"

That night, though, when Honora had made to leave the kitchen, Mrs. Bentley had followed her to the door and had pressed a bundle against her. "Boiled chicken," she had said quietly. "And mashed vegetables, bread soaked in tea. Tomorrow I'll try to get you a tonic for her."

Honora had looked at her. *Why?* her face had said.

"They don't like it when the Irish stick together," the cook had said, without looking at her. "And the mistress likes to tell her friends that she has an English cook." She'd kept her eyes down on her hands and worked them around each other. "I'm from Cork," she had said, very quietly, and before Honora could say anything, she'd turned back into the kitchen without another word.

"Thank you," Honora had said then, in a whisper, but only to the shadows in the darkness.

~

"How many days am I here now?" said Mary.

"Over a week." It had been much longer than a week, too long. We cannot continue like this, Honora thought. "Don't think about that now," she said as much to herself as to Mary.

"Can you manage the work?" said Mary.

"I can," said Honora, and it was true, she could, though it was hard enough doing her own work without having to do Mary's as well, and more and more often now she had to sit down on the stairs before she was able to climb back up them. "It keeps me warm, at least."

She put her hand on Mary's back and began to rub in slow circles.

"Sleep now," she said. "I have to go and talk to Miss Foster early tomorrow, so I have to get up while it's still dark to do the fires. I won't see you in the morning."

"What does she want with you?" said Mary. She sounded drowsy already—Honora could feel that she was growing warmer under her hand.

"We'll find out tomorrow," said Honora.

That night, sleeping next to Mary, she dreamed of William. She hadn't been able to imagine his face since she had left Ireland, though she could remember her father clearly enough, and Old Alice, and Donal Og. But she couldn't see William. Sometimes she tried to remember him eating, or turning toward or away from her, or laughing, and then she would have a glancing impression of him, but it was like looking out the window and trying to understand if it was raining: you could only see the rain against something else, and never the thing itself, clearly.

In the dream, she put her hand out to William and said, I miss you, and he took her hand and said, I miss you too, and when she had woken in the cold moonlit room, the memory of him had been so strong still that she had felt like she was under some kind of spell. She'd washed her face and fixed her hair and dressed in the darkness and had gone down to the kitchen to drink her milk and eat her bread and start the fires, and all the while it was as if William were with her: she could smell him; she could see him as clearly as if he were standing next to her. *William,* she wanted to say, *why did you leave me?* and as she was thinking of him, she was thinking, too, Soon the memory of this dream will begin to fade. I can't stop it going away from me, and I won't be able to see William anymore, and then it did, too quickly, and she felt its loss as keenly as pain.

By the time she went up the stairs to Miss Foster's office, all that was left of the dream was the lonely feeling of its leaving.

"Like ghosts, girls," the housekeeper had said to them on the day they had arrived. "That's what we want you to be like. Ghosts."

Miss Foster was from the north of England, and she had narrow lips and narrow eyes that narrowed even more when she spoke. To be invisible: for a scullery maid, that was the most important rule of the house, said Miss Foster. Servants of their class were not to be seen and not to be heard by the upper orders, and by *the upper orders*, Miss Foster meant the other servants, for their employers were figures as distant as the landlord had been to Honora in Ireland. Her and Mary's world was to be ruled by the housekeeper, and then the cook, and then the kitchen maids, and their place in that world was so insignificant that they were required to leave no mark on it. She and Mary were to stay to the back stairs, always. They were not allowed to eat with the other servants; Mrs. Bentley said they had to watch that the range was burning properly, while the others ate. They were to be present only after and before the other servants had used the kitchen.

It was always cold in the scullery, and cold in the coal hole, and Honora was not allowed to sit by the fire in the kitchen because the fire was for the cook and the kitchen girls, and she and Mary were only scullery maids, and all day she worked, at laying fires she couldn't sit by, at cleaning pots with lye that stripped her hands raw, at emptying chamber pots, at scrubbing stone floors, but it wasn't the work that she minded. It was the invisibility it required that she couldn't abide.

The great gray house, that in the beginning had seemed huge, unknowable, now felt as if it consisted of a series of boxes fitting inside each other, with the house itself the biggest box of all, and she and Mary existed in the smallest box, the tiny room at the top of the top of the house. It was too cold to go outside—everyone agreed on that, for the wicked wind crept up the street from the iced-over river like an assassin—and so there was no opportunity to leave the house, to see something outside, to see the sky.

They were trapped inside, like birds in a cage.

Every day she thought, I came to America to be free, and this is not freedom. I have never been less free in my life.

∼

She stood before Miss Foster's desk and waited while the housekeeper wrote out long columns of numbers in her ledger. You could have finished this before I came, Honora thought. You do this only to look important. When Miss Foster finally put down her pen, she looked up but not at Honora; she fixed her gaze on a spot to Honora's right, and kept it there. I am invisible to her, perhaps, Honora thought, and she wished she could ask, *Do you not see me, Miss Foster? Why do you look at the wall?*

"Well, Bridget," she said then.

My name is Honora, she wanted to say. *I don't know why you call us all Bridget; I don't know if you think it's funny or affectionate or proper, but I know you know what my name is, and yet you never say it.*

"It's a year now since you came to us," said Miss Foster, "and I like to have a talk with a girl once she's been with us for so long." She blinked slowly, and then turned her eyes to Honora, and frowned, as if she were surprised and unhappy to see her standing there. "I am happy to report that Mrs. Bentley finds you to be a good worker," she said, though she sounded as if she meant the opposite. "You have an unusual manner, she says, very quiet, but your work is good. She speaks very highly of you." She looked down at her rows of numbers and blinked again, slowly, heavily. "If you work even harder, Mrs. Bentley says, and always pay attention so that you make no mistakes at all, and if Mrs. Bentley agrees, one day, in perhaps two years, or three, you might well be made kitchen maid." She looked up. Her lips were one thin line now. "You will do well in service, Bridget," she said grimly, "as long as you continue to give no trouble."

She picked up her pen, let it hover in the air above the paper.

"Now," she said, "as to the matter of your wages."

"I have five dollars a month, and room and board," said Honora.

"I know that, Bridget!" Miss Foster cried suddenly, unexpectedly. "I did not ask you for information!"

She put her long fingers to her white collar; her hands danced across it like moths.

"I know that you are owed payment. Three months, by my calculation. However."

She blinked at her ledger.

"It has been a long winter. Heating costs, because of the inclement weather, have been a great burden. Food has become shockingly expensive. You are kept warm here; you are well fed and dressed; and moreover, you are being taught to work. You are being given valuable training, and at the same time, the cost of keeping you here, Bridget, the cost of you, as it were, has risen to such a level that I have been instructed to keep back your salary for these last three months, and to put it toward your keep."

There was a silence in the room, as if the walls themselves waited for Honora to say something.

"I don't understand," she said.

"Your wages," said Miss Foster, "will be kept. You will not have them."

"I have worked for that money," said Honora. Her voice sounded flat to her, and then she realized, I have been trained in hardship, and disappointment, and this is no great surprise to me. Some part of me anticipated this.

"You have worked for your keep," said Miss Foster, and then she gestured upward, as if to the sky, "and for the keep, let us not forget, of your companion upstairs, who is unfit for work, and yet is still with us, as if we were running some kind of hospital, which we are not, Bridget, which we are most decidedly not."

"She has worked too," said Honora. "And she will be well again for work soon enough. She has earned her keep, and her wages, as well."

She was afraid to speak to Miss Foster like this, and she hated herself for being afraid.

"Bridget," said Miss Foster, "you're a long way from Ireland now. I don't know how you carry on over there, but here, in this house, you do not answer back. Here you nod, and say, 'Yes, Miss Foster,' when you are spoken to, and you do as you are bid."

Miss Foster stood up, and her hands holding on to the edge of her desk were like birds' white claws, and her face was white and pinched looking.

"I am sorry," she said, "that you have chosen to take such a tone. Our talk is over now, Bridget. Go back to your work. In some months, we can review matters again, and perhaps adjustments can be made then." She blinked, rapidly now, as if trying to clear something from her eye, and then Honora watched as she put her pen into its wooden box and snapped it shut, watched as she closed her ledgers, stepped away from her desk.

"Am I not to be paid, going forward?" said Honora, and she had to make herself say the words without thinking first.

"Our talk is over now, Bridget," repeated Miss Foster, and she went quickly to the door and opened it to Honora, without looking at her.

Don't catch her eye, Honora told herself, and don't say any more. Just get out of this room now.

She went past Miss Foster, through the open door, and down the narrow corridor to the top of the kitchen stairs. Stop, Honora, she told herself, and she put her hand against the wall to steady herself.

She closed her eyes.

This will not stand, she thought. I will not let it.

～

She worked through the cold and the silence of the day, and then she went up to the bedroom in the attic and got into bed next to Mary, without saying anything, without, even, taking her shoes off. She lay on her back with her arms crossed on her chest and looked up at the ceiling.

I've had enough taken from me, she thought. The land in Ireland, our language, our life, and still, here people take from me what is mine.

If you stay here, Honora, she told herself, you will become a kitchen maid and rise no higher than that, for Miss Foster will never allow it. And it is possible that they will not pay you again, or they will pay you less, or they will ask you to pay for your board; you have no way of knowing what they will do now. What will become of you, if you stay here? And what will become of Mary? Every day you stay here, you grow duller, more stupefied, and when you think at all, it is only to remember Ireland and to go over and over what happened there, and those memories are like nets that you're caught up in, drowning in.

You will not stay here, Honora, she told herself, because this is not America. The realization was so strong that she sat straight up in the bed from the shock of it. *I haven't found America yet,* she wanted to say, out loud. I must get out of this house, and keep looking for America.

She leaned over Mary and put her hand on her cheek.

Mary was sweating and then shivering as the sweat turned cold on her body.

"You look like a delicate little bird, Nell," Mary said, speaking to the wall, "and not fit for circumstances like these, and yet you are warm to the touch."

She put her hand on top of Honora's hand.

"So warm," she said.

"You're frozen," Honora said. "If I pinched your nose now as you used to pinch mine, it would snap off in my hand like a little piece of ice."

Mary laughed, a small thin-sounding laugh.

"Yes," she said.

"Do you think you are getting better, Mary?" she said.

Mary's hair was stuck to her head, and dark with sweat. There was a curious smell rising up from her body that was sweet and stale at the same time.

"I don't know," she said quietly. "I feel very weak."

Honora lay back down next to Mary. She put her hand on her shoulder.

"Mary," she said. "Turn around and look at me."

Mary turned, slowly, and looked at Honora. Their faces were very close together, in the dark.

"We can't stay here," said Honora.

"We have nowhere else to go," said Mary.

We should never have taken these positions, she would have said to Mary if Mary had had the strength for the argument. *We should have walked off that ship and kept on walking, as I wanted to.* But it had been very cold and dark when they had landed in New York, and they had been frightened by the size of the buildings and by the people everywhere. New York was darkness and dirt and the terrible cold and narrow streets that bore down upon them. I am not meant for this place, Honora had thought as soon as she stepped into it. I cannot be here. It is like being in a bad dream. But Annie and Elizabeth had taken them by the arm and led them from the ship, and they had gone along with them, like obedient children. We need time to think, Mary had said when Honora had protested against taking positions. We can't just head off into the night and hope for the best. Let us settle ourselves. Let us earn some money, and then we can see how best to move forward. And now they were in this house, boxed in, and it seemed to her more likely with every hour that passed that unless she took action and took it now, she would never be free again.

"We did not come across the sea for this, Mary," she said. "This was not the plan."

It is a long way to come for nothing, she wanted to add, and then she thought, And it is because your courage failed you at the precise moment you most needed it that you are here, now, Honora, and though no one knows about the piseog, it is upon you still. It sits on the windowsill in this room, like a squat dark bird, and it watches you. It will not let you be free.

Her heart was beating very hard against her chest now. Mary, without saying anything, let go of Honora's hand and turned back toward the wall.

"The plan was to go west," said Honora, but she whispered the words to herself, and then she thought, And I need to do whatever it takes to get us out of here and get us there.

~

"We're going now, Mary," Honora said.

She had propped Mary up in bed by setting her back against the wall, and she was dressing her like she was a doll. She had already pulled Mary's wool dress on over her night shift; it was bunching at her waist, and she had to work to get it down to her knees by lifting her and pulling the dress under her. She was making a noise like huh that seemed to come from somewhere deep inside her, and she was sweating from the effort. Mary was watching herself being dressed like it was something that was happening to someone else, entirely. She did nothing to help, or resist; she could not, Honora thought. When the dress was finally on, Honora stood up. She pushed her hair away from her face with the back of her arm and regarded Mary.

"Well, you're dressed," she said. "So that's something."

She took her hat from her head and put it on Mary's, pulling it down over her ears. Then she started on the fingerless gloves.

"We're not staying here anymore," said Honora.

It was not easy to work Mary's fingers through the glove holes; her fingers were so swollen and twisted that they looked like fat raw sausages. Mary was silent, slumped over, and she was so different from the Mary she knew that Honora felt that she might begin to laugh out loud. I am in a dream, she thought. This is not happening, and maybe I am still in Ireland; maybe I am still in the cave, and all of this is as unreal as it feels.

She moved to kneel at Mary's feet. She pulled Mary's socks on easily enough because they were too big for her, but the boots were difficult because she needed Mary to push her feet down and into them, and Mary just sat there, doing nothing. Mary had to wear her boots—she couldn't go out in the snow and the wind in just her socks. Honora got them on, finally, by putting the boot on loosely over the foot and then leaning on Mary's knee and forcing the foot all the way in, toe first. She had to do it roughly, and still Mary didn't react, and she felt then like she would like to shake her, and slap her, too, and the urge was so strong that she could feel herself growing red in the face, and she had to steady herself by starting on lacing the boots up. She'd put on her own boots already. They had come from a kitchen maid who had worn them through several winters already and had this year bought herself a new pair, and though they were old and fitted Honora badly, she had been glad to have them; she had never had boots before, and the shoes she wore every day for work were too small for her and cut her feet cruelly.

She tied the laces on the boot on Mary's left foot tight, too tightly, and Mary shifted then, and said, "What are you doing?"

"We're going west," said Honora. As she spoke, she was testing the laces to be sure that they would not come undone. They would have to run, she suspected, and she didn't want Mary's boot falling off her. Mary was clumsy and fell easily, and she would need tightly done-up boots.

"I can't," said Mary.

Honora looked up at her. She was holding Mary's right foot in her hands now.

"You can and you will," she said. "Mary. They will not give us our wages for the last three months. I have told you this more than once. They may never pay us again. So we go."

"Nell, I cannot," said Mary in a whisper.

"You can," said Honora. "I think that as soon as you leave here, you will begin to be better, very quickly." She began to undo the top lace on the boot; it was too loose, and she needed to redo it. "You're getting weaker. You look like you're half-dead. All day you lie on that bed, facing the wall. At night you cry. You don't eat. I'm doing the work for the two of us, and I don't mind, but it's work I'm not being paid for, and sooner or later if you don't go back to work, you'll be out on the street. I'm not waiting for them to tell us when we have to go."

"We don't have any money," said Mary. "Or not enough, anyway."

The money they had earned over their first months in service had been spent on repaying Mary's ship fare to Annie and Elizabeth and then on uniforms and underclothes, and hairbrushes and ribbons, and on a tea set that Mary had been determined to buy. If we had kept the money we'd earned, Honora wanted to say, instead of spending it on what you owed and on fripperies that you wanted, we would be in a much better position now.

She dropped Mary's foot hard on the floor and stood up.

"Do you recognize this coat?" she said.

"What?" said Mary again.

"This coat, Mary, the one I'm wearing," said Honora. She had to grit her teeth as she spoke. It was hard to practice patience when what she wanted to do, what she was ready to do, was run. "Where have you seen it before?"

She watched Mary's face, waited for the recognition to come.

"It's Mrs. Bentley's," said Mary.

"I took it," said Honora. "She leaves it hanging in the hallway outside the kitchen, and I took it last night, after everyone had gone to bed."

The coat was too big for her; it hung off her shoulders, and below her knees, and she knew she looked ridiculous in it. She had been sorry to steal from Mrs. Bentley, who had done all she could for them, but there was no other way. They had to be free. And Mrs. Bentley, she thought, would not begrudge them her old winter coat. There had been something in the looks she had given Honora recently that had made her think the cook suspected she was planning something. *Go,* Mrs. Bentley would have told her, she believed. *Go while you still can.*

She put her hand in her pocket and took out a small brown paper bag. "And I took this too," she said. "It's money."

It sounded unbelievable, said out loud. I am a thief now, she thought. I have committed a crime.

"Nell," said Mary.

She stood up from the bed. Her legs were shaking so badly that it seemed to Honora that she would fall over; she had to put her hand on the wall to hold herself up.

"From the other girls," said Honora. It was important that Mary understand exactly what she had done, so that there could be no argument made for staying. "A little at first, so they didn't notice, then tonight, the rest of it. And I stole from Miss Foster—she keeps her money down the back of the piano. I've a coat for you, too, that I took from Miss Foster as well, and we're going now, before the morning comes."

She had had to go into Miss Foster's bedroom to take her coat; it was her good Sunday one, and she kept it in her wardrobe. She would not tell Mary that.

"What have you done?" said Mary.

"What needed to be done," said Honora.

All my life, she felt like saying, *I have done as I was told. I have always been a good girl, and for what, Mary, for what? Obedience,* she wanted to shout, *is overrated, and I've had enough of it, and let's go.*

"You're mad," said Mary.

"What would be mad would be to stay here," said Honora. "They took our money, Mary. Do you hear what I am saying to you? They stole from us, and now I'm taking back what is ours."

"You have stolen," said Mary "and no one will take our side over theirs. You have put a stain on us, and now we have to go in the night, as thieves, and they will come after us, surely. I did not ask for this. You did not have the right to do this to me."

"I had a baby," said Honora, "and she died."

Mary's mouth fell open and stayed hanging open, as if someone had slapped her.

"In Doolough," she said. "And I had a husband; his name was William. We walked with the people from our townland to get relief from the landlord, but he wouldn't see us when he said he would, and afterward we had to walk back across the mountain in the snow, and everyone died on the walk, the baby, and William, too; William died too. There was no one left in our village after, not William's father, not any of our people, so I started walking on my own, and I walked to the ship. I didn't survive all of that to finish here, lighting fires for other people. I can't stay here, Mary. And my name isn't Nell. It's Honora."

"Jesus Christ," said Mary, "I knew there was something unusual about you," but she looked more awake, Honora thought, more alert, more alive.

"You asked me what it was like in Doolough," said Honora. "When we were on the boat, you asked me. Well, now you know. Do you see now, Mary? Do you see now why I won't stay here, why I can't?"

Mary was looking down at the ground as she listened, and then she lifted her face, and Honora saw that she had made a decision, and she knew what that decision was without Mary having to say a word.

"Can I take my tea set?" said Mary.

Honora gave her a look that she hoped said, *No, Mary, you can't.*

She pointed at a bag by her feet.

"I stole this too," she said. "We have food, a knife, a pot."

"You've been planning this for a while," said Mary.

"I have," said Honora. "Seeing as you haven't been great company recently, I had to do something to keep myself entertained. We'll never be more ready than we are now. You know that."

She bent down and picked up her stick.

"Let's go," she said, and they did.

IX

"This is Nell," Mary had said, pushing her toward Ignatius.

They had agreed that she should stay as Nell for Ignatius. Ignatius might not respond well to the name Honora, Mary had said one night, when they were on the road, and when she'd asked her what that meant, Mary had answered, You'll see. The more I hear about Ignatius, the less I like him, Honora had said in response, and Mary had said nothing at all to that, and that was a bad sign, she knew, because Mary now was rarely without a retort. Afterward, she was glad that she had been known as Nell in Bolt. It helped her to think of the things that happened to her there as happening to Nell, only. I was never Honora there, she thought. I was never myself, and there is a saving grace in that.

Ignatius was waiting for them at the trading post in the middle of the town, as they'd arranged. Mary had sent him a telegram from the East to tell him that she had arrived in America, and that she was on her way with a friend from Ireland, but they found themselves short of funds; they did not have the money for the coach journey to Oregon, she wrote. Please send money, the telegram said, and Ignatius had, and now they stepped off the coach, and he stepped out of the shadows. This cannot be him, Honora thought. This cannot be Ignatius.

He was no taller than she was; he came up only to Mary's shoulder. He was small boned, too, with sloping shoulders and a narrow face and narrow lips and long, sand-colored hair that he wore oiled and parted in the middle and swept behind over his ears and down to his collar. She had expected someone big, strong, loud, but Ignatius was almost refined looking, and he spoke quietly, and with a slight lisp that sounded affected to her. He wore a gentleman's jacket that he stroked fondly like it was a pet, though it was ill-fitting and shiny with grease and smelled terribly stale, and rolled-up trousers and shoes that looked too tight for him and curled up at the toes, which were strange shoes for a man who worked in a mine to be wearing, she thought.

This is Ignatius? she wanted to say to Mary, and she turned to her and gave her a hard stare, but Mary wouldn't meet her eye. Instead, she grabbed at Honora's arm and pulled her back from Ignatius and linked her so that they were standing facing him together.

"Well, girls," he said, smiling and nodding at them both, "here you are." He had a paper in his hand, and he was waving it at them. It is our telegram to him, perhaps, thought Honora. Why is he waving it like it is a bill, or a proof of purchase?

She had been ready to smile, to greet him nicely. First impressions are important, Mary had warned her on the coach. Try to be less Honora and more like a normal person when you meet him. What does that mean? Honora had said, and Mary had answered her, Don't be so serious. Smile more, be lighter.

But she could not smile at this person. She could not speak.

"Here we are," said Mary. "We had a hard-enough way of it, but luck was on our side, for the most part."

"I had started to think," he said, and he was speaking only to Mary now, "that you were not going to come at all. I was starting to get worried that you'd taken the money I had sent you for the fare and run, as it were. The telegram you sent me was some months ago now, some months, and it was not an insubstantial sum, the fare for two of you. I was most surprised to get word that you were on today's coach."

"We sent the telegram two months ago," said Mary sharply. She muttered, so only Honora could hear her, "Not many. Two." Her face changed then; Honora recognized the shift, knew what it cost her to make it. "I said I would come, and I have," she said, and she gave Ignatius a bright smile and a shake of her shoulders. "Here I am."

Mary took hold of Honora's hand so tightly that her nails cut into her skin, and Honora almost laughed from the shock of the pain; she had to stop herself from shouting, *You're hurting my hand, Mary; get away from me.* It would be hard to remember that they were not alone anymore, that they were in the company of other people now and would have to behave accordingly.

They had been alone together for a long time, on the road.

Honora pulled her hand from Mary. Mary looked at her, and the look Honora gave her back in response made Mary empty her face and stand up taller.

"Where are the boys?" she said. "Jim O'Sullivan? Tom Moore?"

"Tom Moore, is it?" said Ignatius. "Oh, he headed out months ago, a year ago. We had a disagreement, I suppose you could call it, some unpleasantness, over money. I haven't heard a word from that quarter since, and I don't expect to again." He smiled, but it was a fleeting smile that moved across his face like the shadow from the wings of a moth. "Good job you didn't come all this way to see Tom Moore."

He thinks, realized Honora, that Mary is sweet on Tom Moore. I thought the same thing, once. She has let him think this. She knew it would be useful to her, one day.

Mary let go of her arm and took a step toward Ignatius. She put her arm around his neck and kissed him hard on the mouth. She drew back and looked at him.

"Isn't it," she said.

~

Ignatius said he had a friend, a highly respectable Irish woman, who ran an establishment in the town. Indeed, she was both the owner and the manager of this establishment, and because she was a great friend of his, as soon as she had heard of the girls' impending arrival, she had offered them lodgings. She had insisted, in fact, that they stay with her, and would hear no argument against the idea. She was a highly respectable woman, he repeated, well known in the town, and she honored them with such an invitation, and they were to be sure to express their gratitude to her by smiling and being agreeable. This invitation was a great honor, and he hoped they knew how lucky they were to receive it, them being two girls just off the boat with their hands hanging to them.

They were in front of a sign that said GENERAL STORE, and night was falling on the town now. There were a few people hurrying along the dusty street; they did not even seem to see Honora and Mary standing there, with their bag in their hands and their skirts in the dirt. They must be on their way home, Honora thought, those people, and though it had been a long time since she had thought of that word, *home*, she felt no longing at the memory of it. The darkness was heavy, soft: I could scoop this darkness up in my hand, she thought, put it in my mouth, and eat it, almost. The evening was warm, and there was a restless wind blowing that had a smell to it that she couldn't name. She closed her eyes and put her face up to the wind. There was something out there, beyond the small town, that was pulsing, throbbing. She turned so that she was facing the direction the wind was coming from, and she put her hand out and opened her fingers wide, and she felt then that there was a center and she was in it, that things were gathering, concentrating in her. I know this feeling, she thought. Something that calls to me is nearby. She opened her eyes. Ignatius was watching her, and there was an expression on his face that she could not name.

"Are you all right, Nell?" he said. He turned to Mary. "Is she all right?" he said. "Does she talk?"

"She can read the wind," said Mary. "And climb trees like you wouldn't believe and outrun a fast dog."

"Those are qualities more fitted to a tinker from Galway, and she'll have little use of them here," said Ignatius. "Can she talk, I said?"

"She can talk," said Mary. "She talks when she has something to say."

Ignatius looked at Honora, assessing her. He had small dark eyes like a river creature, too dark to read.

"Come on," he said.

He moved quickly down the street, with his head down.

"Stay close behind me, and don't be drawing attention to yourselves," he had warned them, and when Mary shouted out at the sight of a man riding a mule sideways, he turned, and before he could rearrange his face, Honora saw the anger writ plain there.

"Mary," he said, "you're not in Galway now, and I'll thank you to keep your voice low. Try to remember you're in America." He gave them a tight smile. "One of you mute and the other with a voice like a foghorn. God help us," and before Mary could answer, he was off down the street again at high speed, and now they were forced to run to keep up with him.

He took a sharp left turn before the end of the street and stopped outside a flat-roofed building on the corner. It was a hotel, perhaps, thought Honora; there were different-colored curtains at all the windows, and there seemed to be a great deal of noise coming from within, shouting, and laughing, too, and there were men standing around on the street next to the building who were more than drunk, and they cheered at Honora and Mary when they saw them. Ignatius knocked on the door, and it swung open under his fist. He was holding onto Honora and Mary now, and now he was pushing them through the open door. Why does he push us so? thought Honora. We go willingly enough. Then the golden evening light was behind them, and they were in a dark room full of gold-colored lamps and chairs covered with too many cushions and small tables piled high with newspapers and colored glasses. There was a window, but it was shuttered, and it was stiflingly hot in the room from the lamps and from the fire that burned in the grate. Over the fire was a large gold-framed mirror, and the frame was decorated with carved flowers and leaves. They remind me of something, thought Honora, those flowers, and then she realized, They are like the flowers on the gates outside the landlord's lodge. Her blood began to bang. Trouble coming, trouble here, she thought.

Because the room was poorly lit and crowded with objects, it took her a moment to see that next to the fire was a very fat woman who was seated in a small, lavishly upholstered red wingback chair, watching them. Her bare arms were heavy, pale, like slabs of meat. How did a person become so fat? Honora had never seen such rolls of flesh before.

The woman was dressed in crackling silks, her dark hair piled high on her head in a stiff, elaborate arrangement. She had a big shiny red mouth and enormously dark, heavy eyebrows, and she seemed to Honora to be not so much a person as a piece of furniture, like the chair or the mirror in this overstuffed, overheated room. Certainly, she looked like no one Honora had ever seen before, and now, as she began to stir, she seemed not so much like a person at all but a huge furry caterpillar.

"Girls," said Ignatius, "this is Mrs. Egan, of whom I have spoken to you, and who has offered you rooms so kindly. Mrs. Egan, here are the two girls from Ireland who I explained to you would be arriving, presently, on account of the duly received telegram they sent me. Here they are."

He will choke on his words if he says more, thought Honora. He was flushing dark red and bending over Mrs. Egan's outstretched hand. Is he to kiss her ring like they say a bishop's ring is kissed? Mary was leaning forward to understand what was happening, but Honora stood back, and she could feel Mrs. Egan's eyes on her as she let Ignatius take her hand and pull her up out of the chair with a pop. For a moment, it seemed to Honora that she was stuck in the chair and that she would have to stand with it still attached to her.

"It's not often we have girls straight out of Ireland," said Mrs. Egan. She had a deep voice and a strong accent: she rolled her *r*'s as she spoke. "And such fine-looking girls too."

"I told you, Mrs. Egan," said Ignatius. "I spoke to you most truthfully of Mary's height and her impressive growth of hair, and I was not incorrect in assuming her friend would be a pretty girl."

"You were not, Ignatius," said Mrs. Egan. "You were not incorrect."

She moved closer to Mary and Honora and then put her hand out to touch Honora's cheek and made a noise, *mmm*, as if she had eaten something that tasted good.

"Stop," said Honora before she could think. It was the first word she had spoken in Bolt. She took a step back. Her face was hot, and she was light-headed, because she had been very close to striking Mrs. Egan—so close it felt like she had.

Mrs. Egan smiled.

"You have fight in you," she said to Honora, "and that is no bad thing. And this one"—she turned to Mary—"is beef to the heel and would carry a churn for you, as they say in the kingdom of Kerry."

"Mrs. Egan is a Kerrywoman," said Ignatius, with a low bow to her.

"You can take the girls to their room, Ignatius," said Mrs. Egan. "I am very pleased."

~

Ignatius had closed the door behind them and stood now with his back against it. Honora looked around the room. There was one bed against the wall, a wardrobe in one corner, and a dressing table with a cracked mirror in the other, and around the dressing table were pinned pictures of naked women with men, and with other women. There was a damp, unpleasant smell coming from the papered walls, from the dirty curtains at the window. She could hear a banging sound coming from the room next door, and laughter, and muffled talking, from the rooms above and below them.

"We will not stay here," said Honora, and she made herself turn to face Ignatius.

"The room is small, I agree," said Ignatius, "and not well appointed, but you won't be spending too much time in it. You are here to work, girls."

"At what kind of work?" said Honora.

Why did Mary not speak? Why did she stand there dumbly?

"You are to entertain gentlemen callers."

He has rehearsed this, she thought. He is enjoying himself now, the power he feels.

He came toward them then, smiling and with his arms held out— she thought that he meant to embrace them—and at the last moment, he went up on his toes and swerved past them, as if he were dancing. Still on his toes, he swirled around and toward the bed and sat on it; then he began to bounce up and down, as if testing it out.

She looked at Mary. What did he mean, entertain? She did not understand. Did Mary? But Mary would not meet her eye; she was watching Ignatius. There was an energy coming from her that Honora recognized; if she looked down at her hands, they would be held in tight fists, she knew. She was readying herself for action.

"Last year," he said, "I found myself in some financial difficulty. I owed a debt to Tom Moore, which he most unreasonably demanded I settle forthwith. Things became unpleasant, and Tom Moore revealed himself to be a brute of the lowest kind. Threats were made. Had Mrs. Egan not come to my assistance with a generous loan, I might not be here now with you, girls. Think of that. Mrs. Egan made Tom Moore leave town with his tail between his legs and took me on as her business partner, and now here we are." He stopped bouncing, put his hand on the bedcover, and began to smooth out its creases. "Mrs. Egan loaned me the money for your fare, Mary, on top of the other monies she gave me, and now the money must be repaid, in kind, as it were, the money Mrs. Egan gave me, the money I gave you, the money all being from the same source, and to the same source it must return, as it were."

He leaped up and went to the window and, looking out, stretched his arms up toward the ceiling, his fingers wiggling above his head. It was the kind of stretch someone might give in the morning, when they awoke: easy, unhurried. Then he turned abruptly on his heel and made for Mary. He took a fistful of her hair and too quickly and roughly began to coil it round and round his hand, and as he twisted her hair, he spoke, but he sounded distracted, harried, as if he were in some kind of dream and what he was saying hardly came from him at all.

"So you are to work here until the debt is repaid. There are two of you; a year should do it. Maybe two."

"What is the work?" said Honora.

It was important to establish this, she thought. The coach fare had not been so much, surely—how could Ignatius pretend it would take so long to pay back? She did not understand what he wanted of them, and how could she agree to something when she didn't even know what it was? How did he know either of them could do the job? He knew nothing of her and her abilities or her limitations, certainly.

Ignatius began to laugh, but it was a false laugh. She watched him and waited.

"Wasn't it a great day when Mary met you," he said, "and you so innocent of the ways of the world and all the more desirable for it."

He stopped laughing.

"This is a whorehouse, Nell," he said. "Do you know what that is? The men of Bolt work in the mines, and it's hard, dirty work, and when they are paid at the end of their shift, they need relief, and this is the place for it. These men will come to you, and there are plenty of them, and they will be here every day, and you will lift your skirts for them and let them do to you as they wish."

He held his hand out to her, palms facing upward, fingers outstretched.

"Is that clear enough for you?"

"I will not do it," said Honora.

"You will," said Ignatius. "Something tells me you will not go to the law. I know Mary and her ways of old, her stories of rich uncles and other untruths. She is someone who has been walking the wrong road for a long time, and no one is going to believe the word of a girl like her, or a girl like you." He put his head on one side, considering her, and then he smiled. "And there is nowhere for you to go from here. Beyond Bolt, it's open prairie. The prairie crows would have your eyes out in a day. Mrs. Egan is a powerful force in this town, and no one will cross her to help you. So you are here and here you will stay and you will work and you will do what I say, and that is the end of it."

He was still holding Mary's hair and he used it now as a rope to yank her toward him. He pulled her face down to his, and he kissed her, and the kiss was too hard: Honora saw his mouth bang against Mary's mouth. Mary tried to twist her face away from him; she raised her hand to strike him, and he hit her arm away and bit down on her lower lip, drawing blood. He stood back from her then, still holding her by the hair so that she couldn't move, and he wiped her blood from his mouth.

"Mary, Mary, quite contrary," he said with a slow smile. "You will find that I have learned some things since we were last together."

Honora had put their bag on the ground by the bed, her stick next to it. Mary was crying, and Ignatius was pulling her to him again, fighting her as she fought him ineffectually, uselessly, almost as if she were embarrassed to fight him now, and he did not see as Honora bent and picked up the stick. She moved behind him, silently, and raised the stick and brought it down on his head. There were knots on the stick, and thorns, nearly smoothed now but still powerful, and she hit his head on the top, and the back, at its weakest point, and watched as it cracked open before her, like an egg. Blood began to pump from the crack, to run down the back of Ignatius's head, down his face. He fell to his knees as if his legs had been cut from under him.

I have killed him, she thought. I am not sorry.

Mary opened her mouth and began to scream. Ignatius was on all fours now; there was blood all about him, in a pool.

She was standing over Ignatius, the stick still raised in her hand.

"Stop it, Mary," she said. She could not afford to look up at Mary; she had to keep her eye on Ignatius.

She should hit him again. She raised the stick back, up higher, and paused to gather herself, and in that moment, Ignatius reared up like a roaring beast, like a bull. He came up at her and hit her so hard across the face that the stick flew from her hand, and she was knocked against the wall, headfirst. She heard her head hit the wall with a solid thump and felt her neck give a snap, and then she slid down the wall and landed on the ground. She could hear noises coming from somewhere in the room; it was hard to understand what was happening, because she could not see clearly, but Mary was crying, and Ignatius was shouting, and then she saw Ignatius throw Mary on the bed, and the last thing she saw before her eyes closed was Mary's eyes looking at her from the bed, her face turned away from Ignatius and toward her, and his hand over Mary's mouth, and his other hand at her dress, tearing it from her.

X

They were always to walk ahead of the gentleman up the stairs, said Mrs. Egan, and they were to be sure to walk nice and slowly, too, and with a good swing to the hips so the customer could appreciate what lay in store for him. It was small tricks like this, she said, that helped things run smoothly, and the sooner they learned such tricks and even thought up a few of their own, the better it would be for all involved. For more advice, and for tips on matters like hairstyles, or dress, or general toilet, she recommended they make the acquaintance of the girls who had been in the house for some time. These girls, she said, experienced as they were, were treasure troves of information and good fun into the bargain, and when they were not engaged in their work, they enjoyed a tipple together, and this was only to be encouraged, for what was life if not for enjoying; a glass or two of an evening or on a morning after a long night was the least a working girl could expect. Ignatius might be in charge of their finances, but that did not mean they had to go without fun, completely. And a glass of something strong before entertaining a gentleman, she said with a wink, was often not a bad idea, either, particularly if you were faced with a troublesome customer, and some of them were, some of them were. Troubled. For this reason, there was always a bottle of whiskey and two glasses on a tray in the room, and it was encouraged that they offer the gentleman a generous glass before proceedings got underway and that they have one themselves, and then the cost of both glasses was to be added to the customer's bill at the end. Finances, said Mrs. Egan often, and with relish, are our master around here, and a hard master they are too.

It was difficult to know how old Mrs. Egan was. It was impossible to imagine her outside of the house, out in the world, in Ireland, in Kerry. She spoke to them, every day, all day, it felt, sometimes, because they were the only Irish girls in the house, and there was nothing like your own kind, she said, over and over, but she never asked them a question. She talked; they listened. She knew not the first thing about them. She could not even have described what they looked like, thought Honora, if pressed.

They were nothing to her.

～

Ignatius came to the house every evening. He was in charge of all of Mrs. Egan's business affairs, one of the girls told Honora. He collected the money; he distributed and loaned it, and Mrs. Egan managed the house and all within it. That is a dangerous man, the girl said of Ignatius to Honora. I seen his kind before. He likes to be wicked, just for the sake of it.

Sometimes, after he'd concluded business, Ignatius took tea with Mrs. Egan, and sometimes he sent for Mary and had her in the front room where he took tea. He never speaks to me, and he never looks me in the face, Mary told Honora one evening. Not when I come in the room, not when he turns me around and puts me over the back of a chair so that he can lift up my dress from behind, not after he's finished. Especially, she said, not after he's finished. He goes to the window then or busies himself with the books on the desk while I fix myself; anything to not look at me. He doesn't look at me, and he hardly touches me, she had said. He doesn't put his hands on my skin. The only contact is— She had stopped talking then and turned to the wall. When I walk into that room, she said to the wall, I look at that fine mark you left on his head, and it's the only thing that keeps me going. He'll have that for life, I'd say, she said. Something to remember you by always, and she turned and smiled at Honora, who saw a flash of the old Mary then, but it was only for a moment, and only a fleeting flash.

~

From the moment she had woken up that first morning at Mrs. Egan's, with a broken face and the sour taste of blood in her mouth, and remembered what had happened, and what was to happen, it was as if everything she was gathered itself into a ball inside her, concentrating her, purifying her. It was the same feeling she had in Ireland when she was out by the wall of the cottage, listening to the cry of the high wind, or the feeling she had when she hunted, when she felt herself simplified, unified. She was occupied now by one thing: the determination to escape from the house, and to destroy Ignatius in the process. I have not survived this long to be brought down by such a man, she told herself. I survived the hunger, losing the baby, losing Ireland, New York, and I will survive this. This is just another thing to be survived, but gloriously, this time. This time I will take pleasure in surviving.

That morning, she melted down two candles and made from the wax a tiny figure of a man. On the wooden floor, under the bed, with the black pencil she and Mary used to ring their eyes, she drew the star that she had seen Old Alice draw more than once in the earth. It was a simple star, a cross, with another cross laid over it. She put the wax figure down in the middle of the star. She took a pin from her coat and stuck the pin in the little wax man's chest and pulled it out and stuck it back in again, and again, and again. Then she leaned back on her haunches and looked at the pin, the wax figure, the star. It is time, she thought, that I began to use the strength of the piseog that I was born under, to call upon all it means. I have been afraid, all this time, of what Alice saw in me. I am afraid no more.

From that day on, every evening, as soon as she was alone, she took out the little wax man from under the bed and stuck the pin in him, and as she did, she closed her eyes and called up in her mind the sound of the wind in the trees in Doolough and the sound of the voices of her people, calling to her.

~

Because there was only one narrow bed in the room, and because Honora was often troubled by nightmares that led to her crying out in the night and even to sleepwalking and to being a generally unsatisfactory, restless sleeping companion, she and Mary had agreed that they should work different shifts. She would work during the day, and Mary would work in the evening and sleep during the day; this way, they would each have the bed to themselves for a few hours.

As she and Mary shared a bed, so they shared the one dress they had between them. All the girls had to buy a dress from Mrs. Egan before they started work, and sharing the dress meant they could halve the cost of it. Along with the dress, they bought two cheap, brightly colored shawls, and the trick was to wear the dress with a different shawl or to turn the same shawl a different way to cover the dress. We won't be here long enough to need two dresses, Honora had said. We'd be spending money we don't have getting more than one. She came to bitterly regret, to curse that statement and the optimism with which she'd delivered it, the sheer brazenness of it. You'd have thought, Honora, she said to herself afterward, that you'd have learned enough to know that you were going to need two dresses. Surely life has taught you that much, at least. The dress, high necked and made from a stiff material that felt like hard paper, was dark green, trimmed with a coal-black fringe. It was too small for Mary and too big for her, and it was bad luck to wear green, Mary had said when they first saw the dress, lying on the bed like it had been assassinated. They had looked at each other then, and neither of them had said, *We are beyond bad luck now*, though the words had hung in the air, and if one of them had spoken them, she thought, they could have both laughed the idea off and tried to break that bad luck. But they had stayed silent and had only looked at the dress, and Mary had sighed a deep sigh that spoke for both.

The sharing of the bed and the dress meant that they only ever saw each other at dusk, in that narrow window when they were both free, and in time, their meetings grew to have the curious character of something separated, distanced from their everyday existence. Afterward, when she thought of those days, she thought of a color—indigo blue— and when she remembered the two of them together in that small, quiet room, it was as if she were looking at a series of paintings, washed over with the same blue: a painting of her and Mary sitting facing each other on the bed, a painting of one of them taking off the dress and the other standing behind, waiting to put it on, a painting of Mary at the mirror and her looking out the window. Her life in that room had been suspended in a space somewhere between a beginning and an end, and there had been a strange peace in that, even as outside the room was chaos, and fear, and violence.

All that was missing from the paintings in her mind was the sound of the two of them talking, talking themselves out of the day and into the night as they slowly, almost languidly, got into and out of the dress, prepared for bed or rose from it, washed at the bowl under the mirror, fixed their hair, pulled on their stockings or rolled them off, and all the time both of them talking, talking. What had they talked about? she wondered afterward. She had never talked so much again.

~

Being together only at that particular time, in that peculiar mote-filled light, had colored things between them. When they had first set out from New York, they had been often suspicious of each other, competitive and impatient and sometimes even harsh, unkind. She had been embarrassed by Mary and her way of speaking, of her illiteracy, of her rough ways. Mary was a thief, and a liar, she told herself, and she should regret her very association with her, for she saw that people did not distinguish between them, and judged them with equal harshness. *I am better than Mary,* she often wanted to shout. *I can read! My husband was the son of Donal Og!* But to everyone they met, she and Mary were just two poor Irish girls running away from something, and they were right to think that, she told herself. She was no better than Mary in any of the ways that mattered, and though she was ashamed of Mary, she was more ashamed of herself, still.

On one night at the start of the journey to the Territory, they had slept on their coats in a ditch and eaten grass, and although they had already been traveling by then for some days, they were only beginning to understand how many days were still ahead of them, and how difficult those days would be. It is possible, Honora had thought that night, that we will not make it. Certainly, she had thought, it is very unlikely that we both will. Everything is against us. We are fugitives, so we cannot seek help. Mary is sick still, and weak. We don't have enough money. Half the time we can't understand what people are saying to us because we can't understand the English that is spoken here, which is like a foreign language to us, and I thought English was English, and the English in Ireland was hard enough to learn. Everything is frightening—we are both afraid and cold and hungry all the time.

Mary had cried that night in the ditch, more out of anger and frustration than anything else, Honora knew, and had said she wished she had stayed in Ireland, where at least you expected to have to eat grass, and she had shouted, too, that she wished that she had never met Honora, and though Honora had said nothing in response, in her head, she had let herself acknowledge that she had perhaps made a grave mistake by not staying in New York, and that heading out, instead, with Mary, like this, as a pair of thieves, had been the work of a prideful fool. That evening in the ditch, all the world had lain open ahead of them, and yet the sheer scale of its unknowability had made her feel like she was being shut up again in a box.

And now, in the small bedroom in this house in the Territory, she could not imagine being without Mary.

It felt that they had been so long together that sometimes she didn't know where she stopped and Mary started, and more and more, she didn't even know if that was a good or bad thing or neither, or both. On the days they didn't see each other, when she was late back to the room because a man wanted to go again, or couldn't and wanted to keep trying, or wanted to talk to her or do any of the other too many things she knew now that men liked to do when on their own in a room with a woman they had paid for, or when Mary had to start early because a regular wanted her, or Ignatius called for her, and she had to go in her thin cotton slip, with one of the shawls wrapped over her to hide the lack of the dress—it felt like a door had been left open in the day and time was made unnatural.

It was unnatural now for them to be apart.

~

She lifted the dress so that it was above her knees, and then she ran down the stairs and down the corridor to their bedroom. She hoped that today, of all days, was not one of the days when she did not see Mary, and on thinking that, she broke into an even faster run, and by the time she arrived at the bedroom door, she could barely catch her breath. She opened the door; Mary was standing in front of the mirror, fixing her hair.

Honora was so relieved to see her that she blurted straight out what she had meant to reveal slowly.

"He asked me to marry him," she said. "The cowboy who comes every Friday. Prosper Gould."

Mary did not turn around, and she had stopped moving. Her hand was suspended in the air, above her hair, as if it were frozen in ice.

Honora went to stand behind Mary so that they were both facing the mirror, with their faces laid one over the other in the glass so that it was nearly impossible to distinguish between them. Still, Mary did not turn. There were two long narrow windows in the room that gave out onto the street, and the light from these windows was warm and heavy, and the light in the room was golden, sweet.

"Take the dress off," said Mary. "I'm here waiting."

The mirror was mottled and warped with age, and their reflections were distorted, fragmented in the glass. It was to their reflections that Mary spoke, one laid over the other. She had let her hands drop to her sides when Honora had come into the room, and her hair was already starting to slip down her back, out of its pins.

She was looking for her hairpins now and sticking them, savagely, into the violent mass of her hair.

"Are you taking that dress off or not?" she said to their reflections. "I don't have all night."

Honora began to pull at the buttons on the back of the dress. The whole dress was a horror, from its fabric to its unfortunate color to the line of impossible buttons with their too-small buttonholes that ran from the back of the neck to the top of the bustle. It was a dress that required two people to get you in it and two people to get you out of it, and they were in the wrong place for that kind of assistance, for unbuttoning and unbuttoning took time that the clients of the house would rather spend in other ways. I would burn this dress if I thought it would burn, Honora thought suddenly as she tore at it. I will burn it on the day I leave here, if I can; I will laugh at its green flames.

"Am I to guess at what your answer was?" said Mary.

Honora looked up. Mary was watching her in the mirror.

"I said yes," she said.

Mary closed her eyes.

"You know why," said Honora.

Mary was looking down at the ground now; she would not meet her eyes.

"We cannot stay here," she said. "Every day you are getting bigger. Soon you won't fit into the dress, even. When he discovers this and realizes that you did not tell him in time, you will have his rage down upon you, Mary. We have to go before he finds out. You are useless to him, to her, like this. Do you know what that means?"

"Ha," said Mary. She began to hum wildly. "He will not let us go. He will never let us go."

"We are not asking permission from him," said Honora. "He does not own us. We are free."

"Oh!" cried Mary. "Free! Free to do nothing and go nowhere! He will kill you before he lets you go."

"He will kill me if I stay," said Honora.

She was as sure of this as she had ever been of anything. Ignatius had not spoken to her, had not looked at her since she had attacked him with the stick on that first night, but this did not mean, she knew, that he was never not thinking of her, and waiting, planning for the right moment to have his revenge. She was useful to him now, and he enjoyed keeping her where he wanted her and having her do as he pleased, but sooner or later he would tire of her, and then she was finished.

"He's not interested enough in you to kill you," said Mary suddenly, bitterly. "Don't get above yourself."

The bigger her stomach grew, the more Mary had seemed diminished by it; she had been trying, Honora had thought, to make herself into a smaller, quieter person, to compensate for her frantically growing, uncontrollable body. Now, in her anger, she seemed to fill the room.

"I told Prosper my name wasn't Nell," said Honora.

"Oh well, Jesus, we're fine so," shouted Mary to the sky. "That solves everything."

"I haven't told him yet about you," she continued. She had to shout over Mary, who was moving around the room now and still saying "Oh, oh well," very loudly.

"I thought I'd let the idea of marrying take root first. He's a good man, Mary," she said. "We need not worry," but as she spoke, she realized she had no way of knowing if what she said was true. She did not know Prosper Gould outside of this house, and in this house, it all was strange and unnatural, and perhaps out in the world, he would be a different person entirely.

She would not tell him about Mary before they left, she decided suddenly. She would not give him the time to think about saying no.

Mary sat down heavily on the bed. She leaned forward, holding on to the side of it, as if bracing herself against some strain. She closed her eyes and hummed quietly, almost to herself. She looked very tired; even her hair seemed deflated, dulled. Honora had often wondered at how Mary's hair seemed to change color to capture her mood. She had known it to be the pure red of fire; now it was brown, dirty looking.

"You wouldn't be marrying him if you didn't have to, if you had other choices," said Mary.

Well, thought Honora, all my life, I've done things because I didn't have any other choice, so there's no change there. She was surprised that the notion of choice was something Mary even considered worth mentioning.

"That's neither here nor there," she said.

"It's too much," said Mary. "You cannot do this."

"You would do it for me," said Honora.

Mary looked up at her.

"You would," said Honora.

She went to stand in front of Mary, and she put her hand on her shoulder and squeezed it. She was too shy to do more.

"I never did anything for anyone before I met you," said Mary, and she was looking toward the window when she spoke, and her face looked strange, almost as if the planes in it had been rearranged. She didn't look like herself.

"This is good news," said Honora.

"It is good news for you, perhaps," said Mary. "But I don't want you to marry!" She put her hands over her face, across her mouth. "I don't see where I fit in. And in my condition—what will he say about that? And does he know you are barren? Did you tell him of the baby you lost?"

It was wrong of Mary to use that word. Fields were barren; animals were. She had been careful when she spoke of Mary's situation. She had been considerate, generous, even, while all along thinking and planning and hardly sleeping from the worry of it all, hardly eating and barely speaking to anyone outside this room in case she gave something away, and now Mary should not think that she had the advantage, that she could say what she wanted because of the trouble she was in. Just because you are full of life, thrumming and bursting with life, and because soon you will have a baby to hold does not mean that you can say what you want, Mary, and get away with it. That is not right.

She went to the window. She had unbuttoned the dress, and it felt good to have the warm air on her bare back. She put her hand against the window and looked out. The line of the prairie lay against the sky, always out of reach, too far away, and she traced the line of it along the glass with her fingertip.

"That's not sure," she said, making the words low and slow so they followed the movement of her finger along its line.

She didn't want to talk to Mary now. She wanted to be silent; she was tired of words. It was time to go; they had a chance to go; there was no more need of talk. It was quiet on the street outside. It would be night soon, and darkness would fall like a blanket drawn, and then the men would come under its cover. No more, she thought. I will do it no more, and neither will Mary. It is as simple as that. One way or another, we leave here tonight.

She put her face against the window. It would be something, she thought, to be out on the prairie in the darkness. It had been a long time since she had slept out under the open sky.

"The doctor said—" said Mary.

"How do we know the doctor was right?" she said, without turning.

"I was here in this room when he examined you," said Mary. "He said you were barren, and he seemed sure enough all right of what he was saying."

~

She could feel now the doctor's cold instruments and smooth cold hands against her skin. Mrs. Egan arranged for a doctor to examine new girls before they started work to be sure they were clear of private diseases, for she was a businesswoman, she said, and she couldn't afford to engage girls who didn't have the cleanest bills of health; her reputation depended upon it.

"Bad scarring from a serious infection here," the doctor had said as he examined her, sounding interested. "No chance of pregnancy. Barren, most likely, from such an infection. No monthly bleed, either, I'd warrant. Hmm?"

She had not answered him. She had closed her eyes when she lay down on the bed and had lifted and opened her legs, and she kept her eyes closed as he spoke. She did not want to look at him; she did not want to have a memory of his face in her mind.

Mrs. Egan had answered, though, with a whoop of triumph.

"Well, Nell," she said. "I knew the first time I laid eyes on you that you were a lucky one. Aren't you the fortunate girl, who can look forward now to a future free of worry, and us the lucky ones to have found you."

~

"A person can be sure and still be wrong," she said to Mary. "That doctor was old and half-blind. And Prosper Gould asked me if I wanted to marry. Not if I could have a child. I gave an answer to the question he asked."

"You were careful," said Mary, "with the truth, as you'd say yourself."

Mary could say what she wanted, thought Honora, but she wasn't going to start listening to her. Mary would have kept them in New York. Mary would keep them here until they had nowhere left to go. It was up to her now, Honora, to keep them going on. The reason they had bought only one dress still stood.

She opened the window. The sky was a gathering of dark blues. Above the town, a single swallow dipped and dived. The only bird that flies for pleasure, she remembered the schoolmaster saying. The most wondrous of birds, children, he had said, for every winter it flies all the way far south to countries we don't even know about, and then in the spring, it comes back to the exact point it departed from, never loses its way, and is as brave and as swift as it is small. She put her hand out and traced the line of the bird's rise, its fall and rise. Oh, sweet bird, she thought, set me free.

"What are you doing?" said Mary.

Honora stood back from the window and moved into the center of the room.

"You're looking at birds again," said Mary, and her voice was low with anger now, and tight with frustration. "I see you. Every evening you watch those birds like you're looking for some kind of sign. What are you looking for?"

Honora said nothing. She pulled the dress down and stepped out of it. Mary still had to unpin the bottom hem, because the dress was too long for Honora and too short for her, and it was a job that took too much time every day, twice a day.

"Are you going to answer me?" said Mary. "Have the birds told you what to do? Have they sent you a message in bird language? You and your birds and your silences, and now your plan with this cowboy." She stopped.

Honora waited, standing in her white shift with the window at her back and the green dress at her feet. In her mind, she saw the perfect simplicity of the bird's black forked tail against the blue sky and the flash of its silver-and-red back against the dying sun, and she was no longer in the small dank bedroom but already gone away as she'd gone into the woods as a child, as she would go from here, tomorrow.

"Jesus," said Mary. "Of course you say nothing."

Mary stood up, heavily. Honora watched her steady herself. Her chest was rising and falling like she was trying to catch her breath. Then she bent to pick the dress up from the ground, pulling at it roughly. Honora moved to help her, and Mary said no. But it was difficult for her to get the dress: she couldn't bend from the knees and had to hinge forward from the waist with one hand on her waist for balance and the other hand on her stomach, holding it up and in. She straightened up and pulled the dress over her head, trying not to touch her hair, and then she began to work at easing it down over her body. The dress stuck on her stomach, caught over her hips.

It was clear to both of them that it could not be buttoned up the back.

"Don't say anything," said Mary to Honora. "Your face says it all."

She sat back down on the bed, with her feet sticking out in front of her and the dress hanging from her shoulders. She had a bright red spot high on each cheek, and her hair was energetically freeing itself from its pins.

It was nearly dark now: Mary was already late for her shift, and she hadn't even begun to unpin the dress's hem. There would be trouble if she didn't hurry.

"All right," said Mary to the ceiling.

She had always liked the way that Mary said *all right*: she went up on the first half of the word and down on the second half and gave it a sweet swing. "Let's go."

Honora did not reply. She could not forget the expression on Mary's face when she had said that word *barren*. More than once she had thought that there was not much she would not do for Mary, and now she did not know; she was not sure of her anymore, and this was a feeling that frightened her. She did not understand Mary's anger, or why Mary had wanted to hurt her so. But Mary should not have used that word. *Barren*. It was a word like a stone in the mouth.

"Put the shawl on to cover the dress at the back," said Honora. "Start unpinning the hem. We can't afford to draw attention to ourselves by your being late. Everything we do from now on has to be as normal as possible. I will get word to Prosper to come tomorrow night."

"That's too soon," said Mary. "And how are you going to get word to Prosper? What are you going to do, write him a letter?"

"The sooner we go, the better," said Honora. "The longer we wait, the more chance there is of something going wrong."

She would not answer Mary's question about contacting Prosper because she didn't have the answer yet. She would find a solution, tonight. The important thing was not to delay on action just because she didn't have all the answers at hand. Mary would disagree if she told her this; Mary was always slow to action, and getting slower as her belly got bigger.

"We will not see Ignatius again," said Mary, and she sounded as if she were speaking from out of a dream.

"I think we've seen enough of him," said Honora.

"Ha," said Mary, and she laughed. Then she said, "I never laughed with anyone like I laugh with you. You're funny, and you don't even know it. And that's only part of what you don't know about yourself."

It was a strange thing for Mary to say, but still Honora did not look at her. She went to the mirror and looked at herself, instead. Her face was broken into pieces in the mottled glass. Her father had told her once that she had a bad heart, meaning that she did not forgive or forget. Though she had cried in the woods that night when she thought of what he had said, he had been right, she thought now. There was a door in her heart, and when it closed against someone, it could not be opened again.

When others looked at her face, did they see her closed black heart?

"Honora."

The sound of her name made her heart drop down in her chest like a stone falling down a well. At Mrs. Egan's, she was Nell.

She turned.

"You know why I want to come with you," Mary said. Her voice sounded odd, as if the words were too big for her throat, and choking her.

"You know," said Mary. She threw her head back, defiantly. "You know that I—that I want to stay with you. Do you understand me, Honora?"

"Yes," said Honora, and she did, very suddenly she did. The way Mary looked at her, when she thought Honora was not aware of it, the way Mary wanted to share the bed for company, the way Mary smiled at her and spoke to her, and Mary's anger now, at the thought of her marrying: everything was at once clear and terrible and too much to bear.

Mary was looking at her, and her face was a stranger's face, and Honora was seeing her for the first time, all at once.

"I wanted to tell you," she said, "before tomorrow."

She went to the door, and then she turned and said what they always said to each other when they parted in the bedroom at dusk, but there was a sadness, this time, in Mary's voice that she would never forget, she knew, and the sound of that sadness was a color, indigo blue.

"Sleep now," said Mary.

"I will see you in the morning," said Honora. She could say no more.

Mary closed the door behind her. Honora put her back to the wall and let herself slide so that she was sitting on the ground, and she stayed there until darkness came. Then she lit a candle and went to the bed. She kneeled down and lifted the wax man from the star, and then, very carefully and slowly, she put the flame from the candle to the pale wax.

XI

"There you are now," said Mary quietly, and she turned away from her.

Honora's hands had been shaking so badly that she hadn't been able to fix her hair, and Mary, watching her, had said, "I'll do it."

They were the first words spoken since Honora had come into the room. Honora was in front of the mirror, and Mary had come to stand behind her and had brushed out her hair. Honora had kept her eyes down and on her hands in her lap as Mary had worked. She did not want to look at Mary in the mirror; she could not. Her hair had been done up in the curls and whorls that Mrs. Egan liked, and it took Mary time to take out the pins and brush it straight. When she finished brushing, she plaited the hair tightly so that it lay smooth and flat against Honora's head and hung down her back in one thick braid. Usually when Mary did her hair, they talked about the day that had passed and the night that was to come, and sometimes they laughed; Honora knew that they were both thinking now of those times, and the whole feeling that had been between them then. That ease between us is gone now, Honora thought, and no point thinking about it, nor regretting its passing. Now we go on, away from here.

She put the washcloth in the bowl and soaked it, squeezed it out, and then held it over her face. When she lifted it away, it was heavy with rouge and the black paint she had to put around her eyes. She had to soak and squeeze the cloth and press it to her face again, and again, before her skin was clean. She looked in the broken mirror. Her face looked naked now, and ridiculous sitting on top of the green dress, like she had been put together from two different people. She stood up. Her stays were undone, and the dress was unbuttoned; she had deliberately not done it up when she left the upstairs bedroom. Such sloppiness was frowned upon by Mrs. Egan and likely to be reported to Ignatius if spotted. The girls in the house looked out eagerly for infractions; she and Mary were not popular, because they kept their own company, and because, Honora knew, they were Irish, like Mrs. Egan, like Ignatius. I am beyond your control, your promised punishments, now, Ignatius, Honora had thought as she came down the stairs from the upstairs bedroom for the last time.

Whatever happens tonight, it will at least be an end of something, and an end is a beginning.

She shrugged the dress off her shoulders and let it fall to the ground, then stepped out of and away from it. *No more dress,* she would have said to Mary, any other day before today. From the shelf on the wall, she took the dress she had been wearing on the day she arrived in Bolt and put it on. It was too hot to need the heavy winter coat, but she put it on anyway, because she did not want to carry it. One day winter would come again, and she did not predict many coat-buying opportunities in her future. She would need this coat. And it had big pockets, into which she'd put the lump of wax, her hat, and bread folded over potatoes and meat and a closed can with milk in it. She did not know if Prosper would have food with him, or where he planned to find food, and she would not go out into the night without food or the prospect of it. At the thought of Prosper and what he might or might not have planned, she felt almost sick to her stomach. Don't *think* about that now, Honora, she told herself. Just keep going; just keep moving on.

She sat down on the bed and put on her woolen stockings and boots. Her feet felt strange, lumpen, in the boots, and her body felt insubstantial and light under the loose dress. She stood up. Mary was already dressed. They looked at each other. Ignatius had taken their bag and Honora's stick. They would walk out of this room with less than they'd had when they walked into it all those months ago. She had thought of taking the white bedcover from the bedroom upstairs with her, and then she had told herself, Leave it there, Honora. Take nothing of this place with you.

The thin curtain rose and fell on the warm wind from the open window.

Outside was America.

She went to the door, but Mary went to the dress on the floor, and, leaning down, picked it up and put it on the bed.

"For the next girl," she said, looking at Honora, and her face was lit as if from the inside out, and her eyes were bright, unreadable.

They went out the door and down the corridor, down the back stairs and left at the bottom and past the kitchen. There was laughter coming from somewhere in the house, and shouting, too, and she was glad of the noise; it would cover any sound they made. She was to meet Prosper on the corner of the passage behind the house and the main street. He would have two horses, three if he could manage it, he had said, and she was to be ready to ride. She had never been on a horse before and doubted her ability to stay on one to even the end of the street. Could she and Mary fit on one horse? What would he say when he saw Mary? What if he did not even come? Where would they go? What would become of them?

She opened the door next to the kitchen and stepped out into the dark passage at the back. Mary was behind her, at her shoulder. She heard the door close behind Mary, and she turned to look. As she turned, someone came forward at her from out of the shadows and threw himself against her so that she was pinned against the wall. This all happened in a moment, and she was so shocked that she struggled to understand that someone had not fallen against her and she was not being attacked by a stranger; Ignatius was upon her, and it was no accident.

"Now," he said.

He had his face next to hers, and he was leaning against her, pushing his body against hers, and he was smiling, nearly laughing with excitement. He smelled stale, unwashed, unclean, and she thought she would be sick then, from the terrible smell of him, from the shock. He took one of her hands and put it above her head, twisting her arm against the wall, and despite herself, she cried out in pain. He laughed and she kicked at him, but he sidestepped neatly, lifting his legs high like he was at a dance. He twisted her arm higher, tighter.

Where was Mary? If they fought him together, they might have some chance.

"Mary," she shouted.

"Come here, Mary," shouted Ignatius, in a high voice, mimicking her, mocking her. "Your friend is calling you."

Mary came forward, so that she was standing behind Ignatius, in his shadow. She kept her head down, her eyes on the ground.

"Look up at your friend," Ignatius said to Mary. "Tell her."

"We have known each other a long time," said Mary, but she spoke to Ignatius only, and looked only at him as she spoke, and it was as if she were reading something rehearsed, learned from a script. "We have been acquainted since Ireland."

"We have," said Ignatius. "Old friends. Old debts. Things not so easily cast aside."

She had told him that they meant to escape; she had betrayed her, them.

He had Honora's arm pinned still above her head, and he put his other hand on her face, and there was something cold against her skin then, cold as a stone and sharp as the smell of blood, and he was pressing the cold thing into her. He has a knife, she realized. Of course he has a knife, and he will cut me with it, mark me with it as his own. She tried to move her face away from under the point of the knife without even understanding what she was doing—it was as if her body itself revulsed at the feeling of the metal and what that feeling meant—but Ignatius just pressed the blade harder against her face and then ran its tip carefully across her cheek, down under her chin. She could sense how perfectly soft, how much like velvet her skin must feel under the knife, how easy and satisfying it would be to sink the blade deep into her, how difficult it must be to resist doing so. He will kill me, she thought. I have survived so much, and this man means to kill me here, now, in this alley, like this.

Ignatius's fingernails were cutting into her skin now. He is holding himself back from cutting me, she realized. He is waiting, though it is not easy, for prolonging the wait will only increase the pleasure anticipated, and there is pleasure even in the anticipation itself. He waits, though the easiest thing in the world would be to slice me open.

"What do you mean to do with her?" said Mary. "You promised me—"

"Well, Mary," said Ignatius, "it's only now really that I'm considering my options. Isn't your friend like a little doll? She's my little doll. I'm going to play with her."

He put his head on one side and considered her. Her hair had come loose from its plait, and with the hand still holding the knife, he smoothed it back from her face, slowly, carefully.

"Oh, my dolly," he said quietly. "Let's make you nice and tidy."

He stroked her hair with the flat of the knife and tutted, "Now, now," and frowned as he fixed her, and he was looking anywhere, she realized, but at her eyes, as he spoke.

"Your friend here told me everything, Nell," he said. "Told me all about your plans, told me about your witch's star under the bed and your little wax man and all. I always took her for a good sensible girl, and right I was proved, and indeed she has gone up in my estimation now that she has delivered you to me like a present. You, on the other hand, have no sense, and no manners, either, running off in the night like a thief, like the whore you are."

She closed her eyes.

"I'll put manners on you, by God," he said in a whisper.

He caught her face by the chin and twisted it so that she and Mary were facing each other. Close your eyes now, Honora, she told herself, and take yourself away out of your body if you can to save your strength, rise up out of yourself and set yourself free. Ignatius was moving himself against her. He means to have me here, in front of Mary, she thought, and hasn't it always been so; hasn't my body always been used in the service of others, and I tethered to it and it the weakest, the most useless part of me.

Then Ignatius began to shake her face so hard that she wanted to cry out, Stop, you will kill me. In her time at Mrs. Egan's house, she had often been treated roughly: she had been pushed, slapped more than once, on her body, her face, but she had never felt, until now, that she was in the hands of someone who would see her dead. I was wrong to think he wanted to have me, she realized. He means to kill me, and I must do something, and do it now, or he will kill me here in this alley in the dark; this will be the end of the road for me, and I have to do something to stop it, now, and think, Honora, think and act and save yourself.

He stopped shaking her, and she made herself open her eyes. Look at him, Honora, she told herself. He was breathless, sweating, from the effort.

"Tell her," he said to Mary, without taking his eyes from Honora.

"I had no choice," said Mary, dully, in the darkness, and then she cried out, "I'm having a baby, for God's sake, Honora. Ignatius is going to take care of me and the baby. We are going to marry."

Honora turned to look at Mary then. She wanted to see what she looked like after saying those words, whether she still looked like Mary, or if she had been changed in some fundamental way from thinking, from saying, such things. We were together on the boat, and in New York, and on the road, and I have been a fool to have thought you someone so far from who you are, for I never read you for a coward, weak hearted, and a traitor too.

"Did you not guess about me and Ignatius?" said Mary, suddenly. "How could you not have known?"

There is more here, she realized suddenly. She has been planning this for some time, and I will never know for how long. The stories she told me about what Ignatius did to her in Mrs. Egan's room—I do not know if any of that is true. I don't know if a word she ever said to me was really true, and it doesn't matter now, because even if everything she has done up to this moment she has done truthfully, honestly, it is all destroyed now; it is as if it never happened at all, anything between us.

"She's gone mute again, Mary," said Ignatius. "No matter. Better off." He gave his shoulders a little shake. "So now so. It is all settled and agreed between me and Mary, as you can see. The only problem outstanding now is you yourself, Honora, Nell."

"We have known each other a long time," said Mary again.

He had both of his hands around Honora's neck now, and the knife was against her neck, nicking at her skin. If she moved, if she breathed, it would prick her. Ignatius kept the knife steady, but he moved his face toward hers, then laid his cheek against her hair and whispered in her ear.

"Small little thing you are," he said very quietly. "Little bird bones. Easy little bones to cut, to break."

There was a click then, behind them, in the darkness. Ignatius understood what it meant before she did; his hands stopped moving on her neck; his breath stilled.

"I figure you don't have a gun."

Ignatius did not move the knife from her neck, but he moved his head back from her, and she saw his mouth tighten into a line.

"Leave her go now, nice and easy."

"It's the cowboy," said Ignatius to her, to himself, and he sounded disappointed, like he'd discovered his dinner had gone cold. "Well." He looked at her, as if looking for an answer.

"I have a knife," he called to Prosper then. He winked at Honora, like they were sharing a great joke together. He was still facing her; the knife was still against her neck. "I can cut her as easy as you can breathe."

"Knife's no good against a gun," shouted Prosper back.

Ignatius sighed. He moved the knife up her throat until it sat in the place just below her jawline, slid it back down again, and then just in the moment when she sensed him tense and she stopped her breath against the inevitable blade, he pulled back from her, took his hands from her neck, and then put them out to either side of him and flapped them, like he was a bird trying to fly.

"Come here, Honora," said Prosper. She could not see his face; he was a figure standing in the passageway, stepping toward her out of the darkness.

"Come here, Honora," repeated Ignatius, in a voice like a girl. "Fly away now, little bird."

She moved away from Ignatius, slowly went around him until she was standing next to Prosper. He did not look at her. He was holding the gun up so that it was level with his shoulders and pointing it at Ignatius. His arm was shaking all along the length of it, from his hand, down to his shoulder; she wanted to put her hand out to hold his arm and steady it. *Lower the gun,* she wanted to say. *You hold it too high; your target is not so far away that you need it lifted so. And the gun is not so heavy—why do you shake like this? I have held that gun many times, and it is just the right weight, well balanced, and neat against your hand.* When Prosper came to see her in the upstairs bedroom, he would leave his gun on top of his folded pants on the chair, and one day she had asked him to show her how he used it. He had laughed at her, but he had showed her, all the same, and every time he came for weeks after, she made him show her again and again, until she had learned how to load and unload the barrel, how to aim, how to fire. She liked to hold the gun because she liked the feeling of the cool metal against her skin, and because she liked how she looked holding it, she had told him, because she knew that was something he would like to hear, but it was not the truth. There is trouble coming down the road, she told herself, for I am never far from it nor it from me, and I need to be able to use a gun, and I need to learn how to ride a horse, too, and the list of things I need to be able to do to just survive grows longer by the day, it seems.

She watched Prosper's shaking hand now, and she thought, If I had that gun, I would not shake so.

"You're not going to shoot me," said Ignatius. "We all know that. You couldn't shoot a chicken. So what's the plan?"

"You're going to throw that knife on the ground and kick it toward me. Then me and Honora are going to leave together," said Prosper. "That's the plan."

"Well," said Ignatius. "I don't think so. Honora Nell is in my employ, and I will be out of pocket without her, and you're just a cowboy who can't even aim straight, so I think she will be staying here, and you we will be dealing with separately."

He took a step toward Prosper, and Prosper, in response, raised the gun higher.

"I've decided that I'm going to take that gun from you," said Ignatius, calmly, reflectively. He took another step toward Prosper. He still held his hands out to either side, like he was walking a tightrope, balancing on a line.

Shoot him, Prosper. The words were clear and shining in her mind, like small sharp stars. *What are you waiting for? Shoot him.*

The gun gave another click, gently this time, like it was rolling over trouble, setting something wrong, right, and then Ignatius leaped forward, up like a cat. He held the knife out in front of him, pointing down, and he seemed to land on Prosper from a great height. He has stabbed him now, she thought, and we are all done for, for Prosper cannot have escaped that knife. Ignatius and Prosper both swung through the air before her, slowly, and as one, and then in a great curve, the gun flew from Prosper's hand. Out of the corner of her eye, she saw Mary move toward her.

Now, Honora, she thought.

The gun was flying, then spinning in the dirt, shining silver. Mary was coming at her, and not for the gun. And that's a mistake, Mary, she thought, and not the first mistake you've made tonight. Mary was slow and heavy, and Honora was as fast as light, and she knew what to do. She put her head down and ran, threw herself at the gun, and grabbed at it as it spun toward her. The ground was wet—they emptied chamber pots out of the windows at the back of the hotel, onto this passage—and it smelled terribly, and she was covered now in a dark, sticky mud; there was mud in her mouth, in her eyes. Mary had hold of her dress, and Honora twisted herself around violently, wrenching her skirts from Mary's hands, and Mary fell then, heavily, onto her belly. I am going to fall too, Honora thought, and so she bent her knees and arched back and then forward like she was on a thin rope over a river to steady herself. Holding the gun balances me, as Alice's stick did, for it has the same feeling to it, and then she realized the stick was only an idea. Alice meant me to understand that I should prepare myself for a world that wants to fight me, and that I must fight back; I must arm myself. That is what she wanted me to learn, but I knew that already, Alice. I knew that from the moment I was told about the robin flying into my father's house as my mother lay dying.

She looked down at her hand. The gun fitted nicely into her palm, like it belonged there, and she put her empty hand under her wrist so that her arms, sitting against each other, made one line that led her eye straight down to the gun and beyond it, to Ignatius. Prosper and Ignatius were whirling, tumbling in front of her in the mud, and she could see the flash of the knife between them. Mary was trying to stand, and as she got onto her knees, she lifted her head and looked up at Honora. Her face was black from lying on the ground, but she didn't cry, and her face was as empty and unreadable as it had been at dusk in the bedroom.

Honora looked down on her. *If I were you, Mary,* she wanted to say, *I'd get on my feet and I'd run, and I wouldn't look back.*

Mary looked up at Honora, and whatever she saw in her face made her stop trying to stand. She put her arms down, so that she was on all fours, and let her head drop between her arms. Good, thought Honora. Stay there, so.

She went toward the men. They were on the ground, rolling over and over. Ignatius still had the knife—she could see its glint in his hand. The important thing now was to pick the right moment, and not wait for the moment to come to you; she knew this from hunting in the woods. Then she was back there again, in the trees, under the high sky; she could smell the damp earth, and she wanted to cry out, *Mary, Ireland! It's like I'm back there!* and then she raised the gun and breathed in and squeezed the trigger, and as she breathed out, she released it, and all of this came to her as easily as if she'd been born to it.

After she'd fired the gun, all was silence for a moment.

Then Mary began to cry, and Honora turned and pointed the gun at her.

"I will shoot you, too, if you don't stop," she said.

The gun had jumped in her hand when it had fired, and she was aware now of a pain beginning to move up from her hand, up her arm. She went toward the men on the ground. Ignatius was lying on top of Prosper—she had shot him through the top of his thigh, and already the ground beneath them was darkening with Ignatius's blood. Prosper pushed himself up and rolled Ignatius away from him, and Ignatius was making noises now and spluttering up something wet. He is not dead, she thought. I have not killed him. She stepped back, and Prosper stood up.

"He is still alive," she said, more to herself than to Prosper. Shoot him again, Honora, she told herself. You have not destroyed him as you meant to, as you promised yourself that you would.

Prosper bent and picked up his hat and put it on. He wiped his face with his sleeve.

"Give me the gun," he said, and he put his hand out to her.

"No," she said. He had not used it when he should have; she didn't know if he had ever used it at the right time, in the right place. She didn't know what he intended to do with it now. "No," she said again, more loudly.

There was only one way out of the alley. The horses, she guessed, were tied on the corner by the main street. The noise from the gunshot was still quivering in the air like light, and in a moment, Mrs. Egan would be here and the girls from the house, and that was only the start of who was coming, and she still had the gun in her hand.

She had never told Mary about the piseog; she had been too ashamed. She wished now that she had, so that Mary would fear her, would see that betraying Honora as she had was a grave mistake. In Ireland, she had been alone because she had been feared; she was alone now again, and fear was her due. She walked to Mary and stood over her.

"I hope he lives," she said, "and that you have to live with him."

Then she picked up her coat and dress and swung them over her arm so she could move fast. Prosper was next to her now and now ahead of her; she could hear the horses whinny at his approach. She let the hand holding the gun fall by her side, so that it was hidden in the folds of her dress, and then she began to run.

XII

The most beautiful thing she had ever seen was an Indian pony, colored tan and white, grazing in the long grass under young trees in the morning sunshine. She and Prosper had slept in the grass, and she woke before him and stood and walked to the horses. The piebald raised its head and watched her as she came near him. He had a curious dark circle about his eye, as if someone had painted a ring there, and four white legs, like he had been dipped in cream. She put her hand out, and he took a step toward her and smelled her and then moved away from her and into the trees. They were in a low spot by the river, and the trees grew over the water, and their branches trailed into it. The grass was as high as her hips, and walking through it felt like moving through water. The day was very still, and the grass shivered golden under her hand. She didn't know the name of the trees or of the birds in the high sky above her or of the small yellow flowers that grew on the riverbank, but they seemed familiar to her, and it had been such a long time since anything had felt other than strange and wrong that she was almost light-headed with relief. She sat in the grass by the horses and watched the piebald move between the trees, in and out of the light. If nothing good ever happens to me again, she thought, I will at least have seen this.

~

They had ridden almost without stopping since they had left Bolt, all through that first night and since late morning the day after, through until evening, and Prosper had said then that they would have to rest the horses, and maybe the next day they could ride a few more hours once the sun had set. It's good to keep them out of the heat of the day, he'd said, and we're going to have to slow down too. The horses can't keep up such a pace, and we have many days ahead of us and no horses to waste. We'll keep them to an easy lope.

Prosper said he was tired from the long ride and she must be, too, because it was no easy thing to go hard on horses through strange country for hours on end, and he was surprised that she hadn't clean fallen off the saddle, since it was her first time on a horse and all, but she was a good rider, no denying that, and so good it looked to him almost like it was not the first time she had ridden. He had looked at her then out of the side of his eyes. They were sitting by the low fire he had made, eating what was left of her bread and meat and drinking the milk she had brought. He had not brought food, and there was no discussion about where he might have found any. The horses were under the trees, grazing. Two of them were hobbled, but the third one, the piebald, was free. That horse can barely be ridden, but he's near as clever as any person I ever met, Prosper said. He knows what's what, and he's not about to go off in the night. He doesn't need to be tied up. Those other two would spook at a squirrel, but not that Indian pony. He sleeps standing up with one eye open.

"Is it?" he said.

The Indian pony shifted in the shadows.

"Is it the first time you've been on a horse?"

"Yes," she said.

He had long, narrow, heavily lidded eyes, and she was growing used to the way he moved his gaze down and across when he wanted to watch her.

"Well, you can ride," he said. "Shoulders like a soldier, hips like a whore."

He grinned at her.

She stood up, walked away from the light of the fire, and stood with her back to him, facing the prairie. One day, she thought, I will ride out onto that prairie, and I won't come back. No matter what happens between this day and that, I won't forget this promise to myself, and I won't forget that he used that word and then looked at me to see if I'd laugh, to check what kind of person I was.

I'm not the kind of person he thinks I am, and he'll find that out, soon enough.

"Sometimes even if you haven't done a thing before, it is in the blood anyway," he said to her back, "and it comes to you easy then. Did your people keep horses, back home?"

She turned around. In her time at Mrs. Egan's, she had learned to keep her face empty when a man said something unexpected. She had learned to wait to react, to store up what had been said so she could use it to her advantage another day. Be glad he used that word, she told herself. It is revelatory, and it frees you. It would not be wise to be too much in a man's debt, or to believe him better than he is. She looked across the fire at Prosper: he was watching her, waiting to see how she answered, and there was a tension in his face that was easy enough to read. He had been startled by her standing and walking away.

That's good, Honora, she told herself. Now, fix your face and walk back to him, sit down, and answer his question.

"No," she said. "We didn't have horses."

Where I come from, she wanted to say, *horses are ridden only by the people who own the land they ride on. The people who own the land own the horses on it and everything else, too, and when I was a child, I thought you had to be English to even sit on a horse; I thought that an Irish person wouldn't be able to do it.*

One night when she was very small and out in the woods, the landlord, had ridden up to her on his gray horse. She had had the impression of someone bigger than the night sky itself talking down to her, and the horse had seemed fearsome, enormous, as its eyes rolled terribly, and it spat white and yellow. The landlord had said to her, Why are you out here on your own, little girl? Go back where you belong, and as he spoke, the horse had seemed to rise up over her so that the landlord had to saw at its mouth, and at the same time, he put his heels to its sides so that the horse curved and leaped under him, sideways away from him. How skilled the landlord must be, she had marveled, to control such an animal, and yet she had felt sorry for the horse, who looked as if he were tied up in invisible ropes that burned him and caused him great pain. The horse and the landlord seemed to be engaged in a terrible fight, and it should not be so, she had thought. It should not, surely, be so difficult, to simply sit on a horse.

She thought of that now and said to herself, Well, Honora, you were right about that anyway; whatever that landlord was doing was all wrong.

My people are the people spoken down to from the rider up on a horse, she nearly said to Prosper then. *That you should think that we might have horses of our own shows that you have no picture in your head, at all, of how things are there. We have nothing. We own nothing. We eat grass by the road to live. If there were a horse about, it would be eaten: donkeys are; dogs are. We are as far from owning a horse as owning a palace in the sky.* She and Mary would have laughed about him thinking her people owned horses—not just one, he had suggested, but many!—and Mary would have made a good joke of it that would have pushed the memory of Ireland away. She realized then that for the first time since she had left Ireland, she was without a fellow Irish person by her side. When she was with Mary, she was with someone who sounded like her, who understood what she said, who saw the world from the same place. She was on her own now. If she told Prosper her father had owned a stable of fifteen horses, he would believe her. She had told him her name was Honora to give him something back in return for what he had offered her, but she could just as well have stayed Nell; he wouldn't have known. It wouldn't have made any difference to anything if he didn't know her real name. She could say what she wanted now, be who she wanted, without check.

Mary would have. Mary did.

The fire was throwing low shadows across Prosper's face now, making it hard to read.

"Do you think he is dead?" she said. "Ignatius. Do you think I killed him?"

They had ridden, slept, ridden again, and hardly spoken since Bolt, and she had barely thought about what she was riding from because it took all that she had to ride the horse. Her hand and arm hurt badly from the jump of the gun, so she had to hold the reins in her good hand and let her other arm hang by her side. That made it difficult to keep her balance, to stay upright in the saddle, and her face was swollen and sore from Ignatius's handling. It was not easy to ride as they needed to—Prosper was right about that—and she had feared in the beginning that she would not be able to manage it at all. They had two good horses and the Indian pony, which Prosper said he had got for nothing from a blacksmith because, though the pony was fast as the devil, he was too smart for his own good, and you'd need to be an Indian to make him do anything useful, and he was to be used only in an emergency. Let's hope, he had said, when they set out, that never happens, because any horse is better than no horse, but only just, in this case.

"There was a lot of blood," said Prosper. "But men like Ignatius die hard. I don't like to think a man like that dead until I see him in the ground."

"If he is alive, he will come for us," she said. "For me."

"That's why we got to keep riding," said Prosper. "We need to put as many miles as we can between us and him as fast as we can. But even if you had shot him in the head, we'd still be looking to get on. They have a sheriff in Bolt, and he's a regular at Mrs. Egan's, and he'll be on our trail, sure enough."

From the way he turned his face to the fire, she could tell that he didn't expect her to say anything in response.

"I'm sorry," she said, surprising them both. "You're caught up in a bad thing here."

She had shot Ignatius with Prosper's gun and then ridden away on Prosper's horse.

"No need to apologize," he said. "I reckon no one forced me to ask you to leave."

He looked almost embarrassed, and for a moment she saw what he must have been like as a young boy. He asked her questions about herself; he thought about her, she knew, but she had never asked him anything because she never talked. She knew nothing about him. She tried to think of something to ask him, but it felt ridiculous to start questioning Prosper now as if they had just met at a dance when, all this time, they had been doing things to each other that only a husband and wife could do, should do.

"I don't know anything about you," she said.

She had not meant to say that, but she was very tired, more tired than she had realized, even, and frightened, too, and it was hard to stop herself from saying what she was thinking. She had been pushing down the fear since they had left Bolt, and it was rising up in her now, and it began to be hard to breathe, suddenly, and she put her hand up to her throat, her mouth.

"What do you want to know?" said Prosper.

There was something about the way he spoke to her that settled her. He wanted nothing from her, it seemed, but to be with her. He was content to just be with her, in her presence. She did not have to shock him, impress him with her difference from others, defy him, just to hold his interest. William had been dissatisfied with her in every way possible, uneasy, unhappy when he was with her and unhappy and angry when he wasn't, when he didn't know where she was. Her father couldn't bear to be in the same room as her. Prosper does not know about the piseog, Honora, she told herself, and he does not know about where you came from and what you left behind. He doesn't know about William, about the baby. To him, you are a girl with strange-colored eyes and a way about you that he likes. If he knew more, he would not be so keen, perhaps. You need to think more on him to stop him thinking on you, Honora, because without him, you are out on this prairie alone, and alone in the world.

Ask him something about himself.

She tried to think. What did she want to know about Prosper? She had never seen him outside the upstairs bedroom in Mrs. Egan's house, and now that they were out on the prairie, it was hard to grasp that the two Prospers were one and the same and that she was the same Honora as the one in the bedroom or the Honora in Doolough; to conceive of even another Prosper, one who had existed in a different world before Bolt, was nearly impossible. She didn't know if she wanted to know more about Prosper: what she knew of him was enough. There was enough in her head of everything already; she felt she couldn't take in more.

"Why did you leave Tennessee?" she said.

She had to say something; he was waiting.

He gave a laugh.

"Oh," he said. "I lit out when I was thirteen. I had four brothers, and there wasn't enough of anything to go round, and I thought to get work on a cattle drive going up north. Once I started, I just kept going, I guess, and then after a while, it seemed like I'd been gone too long to go back. So I never did. It's been ten years since I left, and I reckon if I went back now they wouldn't know me."

"Do you think of it often?" she said. "Tennessee?"

This was one thing she wanted to know, she realized. Once you had been gone from a place for a while, for years, did the pain of going away leave you? Did the longing for it fade away?

"Well," he said slowly, "I guess I think of my mother. I can't remember her face, and sometimes I like to try to. But she was run out looking after my brothers; she never had much time for me." He rubbed his nose. "I've never given it much consideration, really. Tennessee. It all seems like a long time ago." He smiled at her. "And I like it out here in the Territory. I like ranching. All in all, I reckon I'm lucky. To be here, with you."

He was looking at her in a way she recognized. Mary would have asked him, *What is our arrangement to be now that we are no longer in Mrs. Egan's house, and you don't have to pay for me anymore?* It was useless, though, to think about what Mary might or might not have done, or said, when all she could say now for certain about Mary was that she hadn't known who she was at all, and that anything she said or suggested was as likely to be a lie as not. You're here, Honora, she told herself, in a strange place, with this man you barely know. Look to yourself now for answers.

He moved closer.

"I got something for you," he said.

He put his hand in the chest pocket of his shirt and took out something small, wrapped in a red kerchief. He unwrapped the kerchief very carefully and held out to her a small wooden bird.

She took it in her hand. It was the size of a robin, made from a smooth, light-colored wood, beautifully carved. Every feather had been carefully picked out; even the bird's eyes were perfectly done.

"You said once that you liked birds." He cleared his throat. "Maybe you don't remember that. It was some time ago. I asked you to tell me one thing you liked, and you said birds."

"I remember," she said.

"I wanted to give you this before, but there was never the right time," he said. "I made you other things as well. I was working on a new chair for you, before we lit out."

"You made this?" she said.

"Oh sure," he said. "I guess I can make most anything from wood. I can make you anything you want. Anything you need."

He gave a great exhalation, as if he had been holding his breath for a long time and was only now letting it go, and then put his arm across her shoulder and began to kiss her. William had kissed her only at the very beginning of their courtship, and there had been no kissing in Mrs. Egan's house apart from with Prosper. He had a short tongue that was too strong, and when he kissed her, she could feel his teeth press against hers. She didn't know if this was normal: she didn't like it, in any case, and was always eager for the kissing to be over as quickly as possible. What came after the kissing wasn't any better, but it was easier to pretend it wasn't happening; when she was being kissed by Prosper, she felt that she was being swallowed whole. It was impossible to breathe when he was working his mouth against hers, and she had to fight herself not to pull back from him, because breaking free would only have prolonged the whole business; it was better to let him kiss her, to get it over and done with. She held tight onto the little wooden bird and thought of Prosper working at making it perfect, the time he had spent on it, and all this for her, and that made the kissing easier. He was kissing her like it was a task he had to complete, and then he put his arm around the back of her head and began to maneuver her down onto the ground. He believed, she suspected, that this maneuvering was done without her realizing, that she was surprised to end up flat on her back so frequently, and not unpleasantly surprised, either.

She was on the ground now, and Prosper's arm was trapped under her head: with his free hand, he began to try to unbutton her dress from the neck down. *You can't do it with one hand,* she wanted to say. In Mrs. Egan's house, she had taken off her own clothes: Prosper had had no practice at buttons. He was red from the effort of it, but he persisted. He means to romance me, she thought, now that we are betrothed. He means to make an occasion of things.

You have two roads you can take here, Honora, she told herself. You have the winter coat underneath you, and the comfort of that is at least something; he will work away at the buttons, and then you can let him do his business while you lie on the coat and keep your eyes open and fixed on the stars behind his head. You used to watch the yellowed ceiling above the men's heads in the upstairs bedroom; you studied it like it was a map and learned so well the ways it changed in the light that you could have made a perfect painting of it; out here, the sky is a great, wondrous thing, and you can study on that now. Or you can do something different. You can change direction and use the surprise of that change to get ahead. Remember that you don't know Prosper, and anything you can do to protect yourself against surprises from others, especially so early on, is only to your favor.

She hooked her arm around Prosper's neck and began to kiss him back, hard, and at the same time, she pushed herself up from the ground with her free hand and moved so that she was next to him and then on top of him. She lifted her dress and pulled her drawers to one side. She had overheard the girls at Mrs. Egan's laughing about never taking their drawers off unless they had to, and she'd adopted the habit: it was quicker and easier to keep them on. Prosper began to fumble with his belt, but he was taking too long and trying to sit up to face her, and she feared that this meant more kissing, so she pushed his hands away and pushed him down and undid the belt herself, pulled his pants down to his hips, and took hold of him with her hand and put him inside her.

She felt Prosper take a breath, and his body ran hard with a tremor. She was surprised at how fast things were progressing. I should have tried this months ago, she thought, when I was counting out my hours like pennies; it would have made an easier job of things for me. She closed her eyes, but colors ran across the back of them like wild horses, so she opened them up again. Look at the sky behind him, Honora, she told herself. Look at the stars, and she did, and rocked, until she knew that he was nearly finished, and then she stopped and tightened herself up inside like a cat's cradle, as the girls at Mrs. Egan's had told her to do, and Prosper made a noise in his throat, and then it was over. She stood up, with one leg on either side of Prosper's waist, looking down at him. He pulled up his pants, did up his belt, and then he put his hand out to her, but she could not bear to be touched again once a man had finished; it made her want to pull her skin off. He thought, perhaps, that because they were to be married and no longer under Mrs. Egan's roof, he should be affectionate, considerate. *But it's all right, Prosper,* she wanted to say. *You can stop now.* She stepped over him, moved away, and began to make a show of fixing her dress and her hair. He let his hand fall back down, leaned back so that he was resting against his saddle.

"Did you like that?" he said shyly.

She looked at him and said nothing, but she thought, What does it matter if I did or not? Men always did what they wanted and then needed to know if they had done it well. William, and now Prosper—they were all the same, looking for their own way, and a way to justify it, too, and more than that to be praised for it. She put her head down and pretended at pulling her skirt into place.

"Well, I did," he said.

She could tell from his voice that he was smiling at her across the low fire; she hoped that he would not stand and try to kiss her or—worse—try to begin again. That had not been the plan. She had not meant to encourage him.

"Who was the girl in the alley?" he said.

This was unexpected. She looked up at him. Don't underestimate him, Honora, she told herself. You don't know him, as you didn't know Mary, and too much rests upon this to take chances, or to be careless.

"Her name was Mary," she said.

"Why was she there?"

"She is with Ignatius," she said.

He nodded. It was hard for her to say Mary's name out loud. I won't say it again, she thought, and I'll think of her as little as possible and less and less as time goes on, and soon, the memory of her face will fade away too.

Let the past have her.

XIII

There was a lone rider on the hills. She saw him first at dusk, on an evening at the start of the summer when the air was still sweet from spring and the nights were just beginning to grow longer. It was her second summer on the homestead, and she knew now that these days were the best of the year. The terrible snows of the winter still seemed far away; the great heat of high summer was yet to come. This was the right time of year for a traveler to undertake a journey, and she stood outside the low door of the cabin and looked out at the rider outlined against the sky and told herself, He is on the road to somewhere. He has not come here for you, Honora; he is passing on by. It is all right. Still, she turned and went into the cabin.

"There's a rider out on the hills," she said to Prosper as she walked past him.

Soon, they would eat. Prosper was washing the dirt from his arms in the bowl at the table.

"Just one?" said Prosper.

Water was running down his arms; he pushed his hair back from his face with his wet hands.

"Yes," she said.

She went to the wall where the long rifle hung and put her hand on its stock.

"Wait," said Prosper.

He dried his hands and arms on a rag and went out of the cabin. When he came back inside, she had taken the rifle down from the wall and was standing by the window, holding it across her chest.

"Whoever was there is gone," he said. "Let's hope they get going on."

~

The next day, at the same time, the rider came back. She heard the horses whinnying in the corral, and she knew instantly, before even thinking, what the noise meant. Horses made that sound when they saw a strange horse; it was their call to each other and to the other horse. She went to the door. The rider was in the same place, at the highest point of the hill, and he was watching the cabin. Something on his horse was glinting silver in the slanting light—his rifle, she guessed. She stepped forward so that she was standing on the flat dirt in front of the cabin. Stay where you are this time, Honora, she told herself. Don't run back inside. Stand your ground.

The rider turned his horse to one side, and it danced backward and forward, and she thought then that he meant to ride down to her. It was very hard not to turn and run, and she remembered then running down the hill away from Alice and turning back and shouting at her, and oh, that had been a different world, and she a different person in it. At the thought of Alice, a rising feeling came over her of peace and great energy, and before she knew what she was doing, she had raised her hand high in greeting to the rider, and the rider, after a moment, raised a hand back.

"Likelihood is it's a lone traveler," Prosper said, "out on his own and looking to see what we have that he can take." They had spent two months on the trail from Bolt and come far into the Territory, far enough to be given free land—and no one could track them all this way, Prosper had said, over and again, or want to, surely. Honora had Prosper's name now—they'd been married at the land claims office, because married couples were given more land, though that was not the reason he wanted to marry her, and he hoped it was the same for her, he'd said, and he had put the words as a question that she didn't answer.

Standing in the claims office, she had asked, instead, "This land that we are getting, who does it belong to?"

"What do you mean?" said Prosper.

"The land," Honora had repeated. "Who does it belong to?" *All land belongs to someone,* she had wanted to say. *Whose is this? And why are they giving it to us?*

"It's no one's," Prosper had answered, looking confused.

"There's Indians on the land, miss," the claims officer had said. "But don't you worry yourself about them. They're being cleared out as fast as we can manage. Soon as you sign here, this land is yours."

And it would be hers, Prosper had told her: the land he signed for would be in his name; her land would be in her name. They would combine their land together and have a great parcel of it, so much land that it would stretch farther than the eye could see. But my name is yours, now, Prosper, she thought, and how can it be our land if it is to be taken from these Indians? The English took our land and said it was theirs, but saying something doesn't make it so, doesn't make it right.

Prosper had smiled at her, in an encouraging and kind of fixed way that made her nervous, and had nodded at the paper on the countertop in front of them. She wanted to ask, *These Indians, if they are on the land, why is it not theirs? Why can it be taken from them and given to us so easily? Where are they to go, once they leave this land?* But Prosper had kept on smiling and nodding at her, and the claims officer had been holding out the pen to her, and there had been a long line of couples waiting behind them, and so she had taken the pen and signed, Honora Gould.

"You are safe now, Honora," Prosper had said to her as they left the claims office, "for who is looking for an Honora Gould? No one, is who. Honora Gould didn't even exist when we left Bolt, and Honora O'Neill, Honora O'Donoghue, Nell O'Donoghue, Honora Gould—a man would give up the search in the face of such a confusion, if he was searching at all, which he isn't." Her days of tribulation were behind her, he'd assured her. "Everyone in this country is running away from something or toward something," Prosper had said, "everyone I ever met, anyway, and you shouldn't worry so, Honora, for it will do you no good, and you are safe now, and your worries are over."

Though she'd said nothing when Prosper had said these things, she had thought, Not everyone is running away from or toward something. Some are doing both at once.

And: your name was known at Mrs. Egan's. They need only ask on the trail about Prosper Gould, headed west.

And you did not know Ignatius as I did. He is a man who would follow you to the ends of this earth to have his revenge. She could not imagine Ignatius spending months riding across the country to find her, but he would pay, certainly, for someone to do it. He would enjoy the idea of paying for her capture, of buying her, owning her again.

Now, she watched the rider on the hill, and she thought, Ignatius has employed a scout to find me, the best scout that money can buy, and it was worth the expenditure, as Ignatius himself would say, because it has paid off.

I have been found.

That night, she waited until Prosper slept, and then she rose from their bed and took the rifle down from the wall. She put on her boots and fixed her hair into two tight plaits.

She got back into bed and lay there as still as a grave, with the rifle on top of her, running down the length of her body from the top of her chest to below her knees. It was wooden, oiled, scented, and smooth to the touch, and she was a good shot with it: she could pick a prairie chicken off from a distance better than Prosper. You sure are a fast study, he used to say to her when they'd first arrived on the homestead. He'd been amused then by how quickly she learned, and proud of her quickness too. He was quieter about such things these days. Now, in her weaker moments, if she wanted an achievement marked, she had to call attention to it herself: Look, Prosper, she would say. Look how fast I can load this gun. Did you see how I took the ditch on that horse? I wasn't bad, was I, at chopping the wood for the fire? She needed him to notice what she could do, and not think about what she couldn't. I am here, she was trying to say. See me, and not what's missing. I am not enough for Prosper, and at the same time I am too much, she thought to herself, and it was the same with William, and the same, probably, with Mary. Too much and too little, all at the same time.

How could Prosper lie in bed now, sleeping soundly, unseeing? She knew what he would answer if she woke him and put the question to him. I am tired, Honora, he would say. I'm tired from the work. He was tired, always, and keeping the homestead going was bone-wearying work that made a young man old; she knew that, yet every day she wanted to say to him, *But you own this land, and ownership of the land is freedom, and freedom is happiness; surely, that is what we have always believed to be true. You have food to eat and no one to tell you what to do, where to go, how to speak or be or think. You are free, Prosper; you are free.* Her father and Donal Og and William had worked the land as Prosper did, but that land wasn't theirs—all their work had been for someone else. So you should not be so tired, Prosper, she thought. You aren't entitled to it. Wake up. If someone is going to come, they will come in the night, surely, and why are you not awake, readying yourself? Why didn't we go farther into the Territory, all the way over the mountains and into California? Why didn't we change our names, as so many did? Why didn't I shoot Ignatius in the head when he was facedown in the alley? Why did I leave him alive?

Lying in the darkness, she closed her eyes tight against all the things she could have done, and should have done, and she exhaled, hard, as if she'd been holding her breath for a long time and was only now letting it go.

The rider had raised his hand in a salute to her. If he meant you harm, he would not have held his hand up to you like that, she told herself. And he did not ride down to you, even though he saw you clearly, twice. He had come, gone, and come again, and there was something about the way he had sat on the horse, and the look of the horse itself and the way they had moved together that was different from anything she had seen before. There is something coming here, Honora, something you need to ready yourself for.

Hold on to that gun, she told herself, and the words in her head sounded like they were being said to her by Alice, in Alice's voice. Get ready, girl, the voice said. You're a better shot than Prosper, better than any man you've ever met, even.

You look out for yourself now.

~

The next day passed in a slow, tortuous unfolding toward dusk, and she went about her work, the work that repeated itself every day and was never finished—cleaning the cabin, trying to bake the bread, trying to make the butter, seeing to the pigs and the cow and the horses, tending the vegetable garden, and then out in the field with Prosper—all the while feeling that she was standing in a circle and the circle was getting smaller and smaller as the sun moved lower, and by the time the sun touched the top of the hill, the circle felt like a rope about her head, in her head.

He will come, she thought, and he did, and this time, she was waiting for him.

The sun was ready to tip below the highest point of the hill. She went out of the cabin and stood in front of the door with her feet well apart so that she was balanced, steady, and she held the rifle in her hands, lying straight and low along the line of her hips. Prosper stood in her long narrow shadow behind her, in the doorframe. "Come in,

Honora," he said. "Why do you do this?" But before he could even finish speaking, she was moving away from him and into the front yard, and then she was walking, walking away from the cabin and toward the foot of the hill. "Honora," called Prosper after her, and it seemed like he was already a long way behind her. She kept walking, and then the rider was on the slope of the hill, and she was walking up toward him, and he was riding down to her.

The horse held its head tucked in toward its chest, picked its hooves up carefully and with great delicacy, and carried its legs high as it moved. *That's a good horse,* she almost said out loud, and then she understood that she was having that strange feeling of detachment, of leaving her body, that she had known before—in the cave as the baby was about to be born, in the small room high in the house in New York—when she had tried to understand what was happening to her, and it began to feel like looking too long at the sun. In these moments, it felt that she was living too close to the center of experience, that the reality of the moment was too much to bear and an accommodation had to be made, and that accommodation was this splitting of herself, this drift away. "Honora," she said, out loud this time, and the sound of her own voice saying her name steadied her, and she said in her head, It will be all right. You will be all right.

She stopped walking and put a hand up to her eyes to shield them from the sun. She took the rifle in her other hand and held it out so that it stood next to her, away from her body, easy for the rider to see. If you must shoot, she had told herself all through the dark warm night, shoot the horse first, and then shoot the rider when he's down, and this time don't make the mistake you made with Ignatius. This time make sure he can't come back for you. Finish the job, Honora.

But shoot the horse first. Shoot the horse first.

The rider was coming toward her, very slowly, and it was as if he were descending out of the sun itself and he and the horse were black outlines against it, impossible to make out. Should she hold the rifle in front of her, point it at him? Her hand tightened around the stock, squeezing and releasing it in time with the beat her heart was keeping, too fast, too fast. Why did he move so slowly? She could not see where he carried his gun. She could not see his face. Should she shoot now?

The rider was almost directly in front of her, nearly on top of her, before he seemed to separate from the sun and she was able to make him out. Prosper had been right: he was an Indian.

She had seen Indians on the trail, and some in the town where she and Prosper had been married and made their claim, but she had never spoken to one. Best policy with Indians is to keep away from them, Prosper said. The farther the better. They're a passel of trouble, and whether that be their own fault or someone else's, I don't know, and I don't intend to find out. The farther away we are from them and them from us, the better it is for all parties concerned, he said, and that's all we need to know about the Indians.

The horse stopped.

"What do you want?" she said.

The evening wind was beginning to rise now as the sun set, and the horse turned its head to it and the promises folded into it. She felt the wind as if it were inside her, expanding her and pulling her at the same time toward the sky, toward the pale sinking sun.

The Indian was watching her.

"Where did you get that pony?" he said.

His voice broke curiously on the words; it was too high and too low in all the wrong places. He's speaking a language that isn't his own, and his own language, the memory of it, resists this new one, tries to strangle it in his throat: I recognize the signs, she thought.

"What pony?" she said.

"Painted pony you got down in the corral," he said.

She turned to look at the corral, as if it contained a multitude of painted ponies and she needed to determine which one he was talking about.

"It's my husband's," she said, because that sounded serious and correct, and then she told herself, Don't turn your back on him, Honora, and she turned back. She felt like hitting herself across the head with her gun for her stupidity.

"I've seen you ride it," he said.

He had been watching her, and she didn't know when or for how long. She looked up at him. The horse was moving backward and forward now, made restless by the wind, and the man's face was lost to her in the movement. She was looking directly at him, and yet she couldn't see him at all.

"Yes," she said stupidly.

She was the only one who could—who did—ride the pony. He would not let Prosper saddle him, would barely take a bridle from him.

"You sell it?" said the rider.

"No," she said, without thinking.

The pony was hers. She had nothing: hardly any clothes, only one plate to eat from. For two years she had lived in a pine cabin that let the wind in during the winter and overheated in the summer and was full of dust and dirt all year round no matter how often you cleaned it. The pony was hers. Prosper had given him to her, and she wouldn't give him up.

"It's my pony," she said. She wished she hadn't said before that it was her husband's, defeating her own argument even as she was making it. "I don't want to sell him."

"It's a Cayuse pony," said the rider. "What if I take it."

"You can't," she said. "It is my property."

He looked down at her. It seemed like he was a great distance above her, as far away as the sky or the sun in it, on his black dancing horse. She couldn't tell if he was looking at her with pity, or disdain, or some other emotion that she couldn't name.

Then he said, "I take it."

He picked up the reins of his horse, put his heels to its sides, and went away from her down the hill at a lope. She stood for a moment, watching him go, dumbfounded into inaction. Then she began to run.

She ran down the hill, so fast that it felt like she was falling. The Indian was at the corral already, and so was Prosper, standing in front of the gate. The three horses in the corral were running against the rail, kicking out at each other and calling out to the Indian's horse.

"You get on out of here," Prosper was shouting, but the Indian was riding toward him and then was next to him, and then he was at the gate and opening it against Prosper.

She had the rifle. Prosper didn't even have a pistol in his hand.

"Close the gate, Prosper," she shouted.

The horses would flee, and they could not buy more, and without them, what would they do? Everything they did—plowing, hunting, clearing the land, everything—depended on the horses. She had looked after these horses for a year; she knew them like people, and they meant more to her than many people she had known, and they would not be taken from her like this.

The piebald was already out of the gate. The Indian backed his horse up in one smooth movement, turned it in an easy arc, and rode after the piebald. Prosper, shouting, his hands in the air, ran at the two horses who were fighting to get out of the corral; they jumped back, away from him, and he swung the gate closed on them.

He is only taking the pony, she thought as she ran. He is leaving the other two, though he could easily have had them too.

The Indian was trotting toward her now, and the piebald was by his side, following him as if tied to him by an invisible line.

Shoot him, she told herself. Horse thieves were to be shot; that was the law. Shoot him, and take back your horse, and take his horse too.

She raised the rifle. The Indian was coming toward her, straight at her at a steady trot, very fast, too fast for her to think clearly. Then the piebald was going past her, and she put her hand out to grab at its mane; if she could get hold of him, she could mount him and ride him to safety. She reached for the piebald's flank—the pony gave a whinny of acknowledgment at her touch. Then the Indian gave a click of his teeth, and he and the piebald broke into a lope. Before she had time to act, they were already behind her, and then they were gone away from her, up the hill and over the top of it, into the dying sun.

She had missed her moment. She had hesitated and made the wrong choice, and the piebald was gone now because of her mistake.

He didn't want you after all, Honora, she told herself. He only wanted the piebald, and he got him.

Everything had happened so quickly that it was hard to understand that it was already over. The appearance of the Indian, the flight of the pony seemed at once as unreal as a dream and a distillation of everything that had ever happened to her, all at once.

The trotting horses had raised a cloud of dust that was settling; the horses in the corral were standing next to each other, their heads down; the wind was quieting; it was as if the land itself were conspiring to pretend that what had just occurred was right, regular. The Indian, his horse, the very air around them—a stone had been thrown into the deep calm water of the day, and now the water was closing over the space the stone had made; order was being restored, returned. The world thinks that what has happened here is the natural order of things, she thought, and it hurries to restore that order.

Prosper was standing with his back to the corral, watching her.

She had put her hands on her hips, and she was looking down at her feet, trying to catch her breath. She was still wearing the boots she'd been given by the maid in New York, though they were nearly worn through, and the laces had fallen apart even before the first winter on the homestead. I hate these boots, she thought, suddenly furious. I've always hated these boots. She remembered doing up the laces in the tiny room in New York the night she and Mary had fled, and the cold in that room, the fear in her chest. She still remembered too much, too often.

She had not yet learned how to forget. I wish I could forget everything, she thought. I wish I could cast off the past like I want to cast off these old boots and be free of it all, of the memories, of the shame, of the fear.

She started to walk toward Prosper, and in response, he pushed his hat back on his head and turned away from her, opened the gate, and went into the corral, to the horses. He put his hand on the neck of the horse closest to him and kept his back to her.

"You let him take the pony," she said to his back.

"I couldn't have stopped him without trouble," he said.

"He took the pony; he stole from us, and you let him," she said.

"You had the rifle," said Prosper, turning. "I didn't see you doing any shooting."

He sighed.

"It was a good-for-nothing Indian pony anyway."

He looked down and then across at her out of the side of his eye, trying to read her reaction. One of the things she had liked about Prosper at the beginning was the openness of his face; whatever he was feeling moved across it like a pale shadow, come and gone like light. It was impossible for him to conceal his emotions. He felt something; you saw it on his face; he acted on what he was feeling. She'd known people who could make their faces empty as the sky—Mary could—and those were the people who were hiding something, or hiding from something, someone. Those were the ones you needed to watch.

Prosper, she could see now, was worried, and watchful, and then as she came toward him, she watched his face change again, fill with hope.

"We've still got two, and they're the two that count," he was saying, but she went past him and to the big bay. She put the rifle under her arm and with both hands took hold of the horse by its mane and jumped so that she landed on its back, on her stomach, and then she pulled herself up by kicking back, threw one leg up behind and over the horse, and sat up straight with the rifle lying in front of her, resting across the base of the horse's neck.

The hope had gone from Prosper's face, like water run away.

"No, Honora," he said.

"You shouldn't have let him take my pony," she said. She put her heels to the horse's sides. "Come on," she said.

The corral gate was open, but if Prosper decided to try to close it, she would jump the rail. She had the bay at a trot now, and she was heading for the gate. Prosper didn't move. The rail was high, triple-barred and solid, and it would have been hard to jump with so little a run-up, but she would have tried it, and Prosper knew that; he knew it was useless to close the gate on her. She headed for the open gate at a fast trot all the same, in case he decided, at the last moment, to try, and with her legs tucked up on the bay's neck and a hand on the rifle, in case he tried to grab her and pull her off the horse as she went past him, but as she neared the gate, she heard him run back to the last horse left in the corral and shout at it to stay. She went through the gate, and Prosper, just behind her, closed it against the lone horse just in time, though it kicked at him, and he cried out in protest.

She kicked at the bay, and it broke into a canter, and they went across the open land beyond the corral. At the bottom of the hill, she put the horse into a lope. It was a big broad-backed horse, not difficult to ride without a saddle, and it could cover ground better than any horse she'd known. He should have taken this horse, she said to herself. It's faster, better tempered. He should have left the piebald.

It would be dark soon, and she had never been out on the prairie at night. Don't think about that now, Honora, she told herself. Keep going, and then to distract herself from the fear that was rising up in her chest, she began to think. The next time I get on a horse in these boots, I will remember to tie some rope around them, because I have to keep my heels well down to keep them on my feet, and it's only a matter of time before I lose one, and what will I do then during the long hot summer and me as barefoot as I was in Doolough. There was a quiet voice in her head that was whispering, You go out on this prairie in the night, and being bootless will be the least of your worries. Ride away from that voice, Honora, she told herself. Keep going on.

She went up over the top of the hill and down toward the setting sun. Ahead of her lay the flat plain of the prairie, stretching long against the horizon, painted gold by the dying light. In the distance, but not so far away that she could not make them out, were the black forms of the Indian and the piebald. They were proceeding at the same steady pace as before. The calmness of that trot suddenly enraged her almost more than anything else that had happened to her that day. He is in no hurry, she thought, because he does not even consider it a possibility that someone will come after him. He is keeping the horses to a trot because he has some distance to go and doesn't want to burn through them. He is considered, relaxed. He has taken my pony, and he does not even think to look over his shoulder.

She went down the rest of the hill at a steady lope, and when she got to the bottom, she pushed the bay into a dead run. He was a sure-footed horse, brave and steady, and he did not stumble on the rough ground or refuse what she asked of him, though he hadn't been ridden so hard since they'd come to the homestead, and many a horse would have refused to head in a direction other than home at this time of the evening. "Go on," she shouted, more to herself in wonder at what the horse could do than to him, and her voice was thin, insubstantial against the glowering evening, and in her head, she heard her voice echo, *Go on, Honora.* The prairie was endless, open, treeless, flat, a sea of space, and she watched the earth fly past her under the horse's hooves. I will never find my way back, she realized. It all looks the same, and I thought the Indian was close, but he is not; this place eats up distance and distorts, and I should not have come out here. Then she heard the piebald call to her.

The Indian had stopped and was watching her ride toward him. She slowed the bay to a trot; the horse was going so fast that the switch of paces made her slide to the side, and for a terrible moment, she felt that she would fall off. Then, because she had no bridle, no saddle, she had to whistle him to a stop. She felt ridiculous, whistling like a child—the Indian would be able to stop a horse without whistling at it, she knew. The bay pulled up, too hard, in front of the Indian and the piebald, and she pitched forward onto his neck and almost dropped the rifle.

She sat up. Her hair was all over her face; there was dust in her mouth, in her eyes. Her body was shaking. She had to hold onto the horse's mane to steady herself, to hide her shaking hands.

The Indian observed all of this without moving.

It was quiet on the prairie, though the wind had started to rise again, gently this time. Annie and Elizabeth had said that the prairie was at the end of the world, but they had been wrong about that. It was the gateway to another world, a world between worlds, and a middle point, a center.

The evening had turned blue now. The sun was gone, though there was still light enough to see by, and the darkness of night was so close by that she could smell it on the wind.

Look at him, she told herself. Look him in the face, and he looked back at her calmly.

He knew why she was here; she knew what his response to her would be. There was no need to say anything, to explain things.

"He didn't come after you," he said eventually.

"Who?" she said.

"The man at the corral," he said. "He let you come out here alone."

She had not thought of that. Prosper could have ridden after her. He could not have prevented her coming, but he could have come with her.

"I'm taking my pony back," she said.

She had to make this clear. Saying it out loud made it seem more likely to happen, somehow. And she wanted to turn the conversation away from Prosper and his absence.

When he did not respond, she said, "I don't want trouble."

Her hands were still shaking, and her eyes were streaming with tears. She wished she could say, *It's the dust that makes them water so; I am not crying.* She sat up straighter and moved her rifle so he could see her do it.

"Where have you come from?" he said.

"What?" she said, to give herself time. "Ireland," she said then. She moved her hand across the prairie, as if she were drawing a line across it with her palm. "Very far away." She paused. "I came on a ship." She looked down at the bay's neck. "We had no food, so we had to leave. I had to leave. Whoever was left alive, left."

He was still looking at her in the same calm way. Why didn't he say something? Why was she telling him this? He was probably getting ready to pick up his gun and shoot her in the face. She was surprised he hadn't already. Maybe he meant to try to do something else with her first, before shooting her. If he came closer to her, she would shoot him. She would kill before she let another man have her.

"What is your name?" he said.

"Honora O'Neill," she said.

It had been a long time since she had said the word *Ireland* and even longer since she had said the name of her father, the name she had been born with. *Honora O'Neill.* The words moved across the evening air, were picked up by the wind and taken away.

The bay shifted underneath her and then trembled under its skin, as if it wanted to shake off something that had landed on it. Say again that you are taking your pony back, Honora, she told herself, and then just ride up to him and take the pony and have done with it one way or another.

"What is your name?" she said.

"Joseph," he said.

"Why are you here?" she said, and she meant, *Where have you come from? Where are you going?*

210

"I came from far away," he said. "Where I came from, there was trouble, and we had to leave. Whoever was left alive had to leave."

Was he mocking her? It was impossible to tell. He had long hair nearly down to his waist, and the wind whipped it about his face, and he kept looking at her, kept his eyes on her; she kicked at the bay and went toward him and put her hand on the pony's mane. She had no rope. You are a fool, Honora, she told herself, to have come out here without even a rope. How will you get the piebald to go back with you? She looked down at her dress. It was a thin, poor cotton; she could easily tear a strip from along the bottom and tie it about the piebald's neck, but it would break if the horse even pulled back from her, and was she to start ripping at her dress in front of the Indian? He would think her touched in the head, at the least. She could jump onto the piebald and try to ride him, but what if he refused to go with her? What if he wanted to stay with the Indian? She would look ridiculous then, more ridiculous than she did now, even, a bareheaded girl wearing someone else's boots without even a rope in her hand.

She grabbed a fistful of the piebald's mane.

"I'm taking my pony back," she said.

Why didn't he speak? If he would say something, she could answer him, convince him and herself that she could do it.

"It's my pony," she said, but she sounded like a plaintive child now, shouting into the wind.

She could think of nothing else to say. Everything she had ever had, or wanted, had been taken from her, but not this time, not now. There was nothing else to say, but she would not give up the pony.

"It's an Indian pony," he said. "Doesn't belong to you."

They looked at each other.

"I'll give you this horse," she said, and she put her hand behind her and on the bay's flank. "You give me the painted pony."

"That horse is a better horse," he said. "Why don't you keep it?"

"Why don't you?" she said.

The bay was growing restless. It backed away from the pony, put its ears back, and threw its head up. Don't start to give me trouble now, she thought. She put her heels to the bay's sides, kicked hard, and together they moved forward again. I am running out of time here, she realized. It is dark already, and the smell of the night and all the wild things in it will make these horses unmanageable soon. She lifted her face to the wind. It was a strange thing, this wind, violet colored and with a ghostly, searching voice to it, and it was telling her something she couldn't understand.

"Honora," said the Indian.

His voice broke on her name, broke it into two, and he rolled the *r* against the back of his throat and put the emphasis on the final part of the word, down on the *a* at the end. It sounded like a different name, on his tongue.

Sometimes I hear my name being called, she wanted to say, *and when I turn, there's no one there, and still the voice calls me.*

"You won't find your way back in the dark," he said. "No moon tonight, and a bad wind coming up. I will take you. I will take that horse; you keep the pony."

"Why?" she said, astonished.

Why had he changed his mind?

He laughed then, a short bark.

"I don't know," he said.

His horse jumped under his heels.

"Come on," he said, "Honora."

XIV

They stopped at the top of the hill; below them was the cabin. Prosper had put the lamp in the window, and its small light was a lonely thing against the great darkness of the prairie. Joseph was looking at the cabin as if he were waiting for something to happen, and she thought of him telling her how he had seen her ride the pony: Had he watched her from up here? How long had he watched her? He looked across at her then and nodded. Go on, the nod meant, you are home.

"Are you hungry?" she said, and at the same time she was saying to herself, Stop, Honora. Do not do this.

He had turned back to look at the cabin; he didn't answer her.

"We have food," she said. She put her hand to her mouth to signal food and immediately regretted it. He understands you perfectly, she told herself. If he doesn't answer you, it isn't because he doesn't understand you. "If you want to eat, come," she said, and she wanted to say, *You can rest your horse, too; feed it; you can leave in the morning with the sun, and you said yourself there was a bad wind tonight out on the prairie. Where are you going, where are you going in this darkness, out on this land, alone?*

She swung her leg out behind her and slid down from the bay. Look like you mean business now, Honora, she said to herself, and so she slung the rifle into the crook of her arm and walked to the pony, purposefully, and took hold of his mane and gave a practice hop and then jumped up on him, but he moved as she jumped, and so she had to scramble, inelegantly, to save herself, with her legs kicking out behind her and her skirt way too far above her knees, pulling and pushing herself up, and all the time she was conscious of Joseph watching her. The pony broke into a slow trot as she mounted him, and for a moment, she was sure that she was going to fall. She had a sudden, dark vision of landing on the ground and losing the rifle and the pony running away from her and then her having to chase him up and down the hill and him trotting away from her, very slowly and always just beyond her reach, teasing her. It wouldn't be the first time he'd done such a thing. Prosper was right, she thought. You are a bad horse. You don't have a loyal bone in your swaybacked body, and yet I stick with you. She gave herself one more push up, and then she was on the pony. "Bad horse," she said, under her breath. The pony coughed, shifted. She leaned back and held the rifle out straight at her side for balance and put her legs forward, kicked at him, harder than she meant to, and the pony, surprised, affronted, bucked, and then broke into a skittish lope down the hill, toward the corral. He will drop a shoulder now to throw me, she thought, and in readiness, she wrapped her legs around his sides and caught onto great fistfuls of his mane.

She could hear horses behind her. The bay, maybe—maybe it was following her. It is only the bay, she thought, deliberately fooling herself, for she knew the sound of more than one horse as well as she knew anything, but she wanted to keep herself in that place of not knowing for as long as she could manage it. It was too much yet to try to understand what it would mean if the Indian came, or if he didn't, and why it mattered to her. When you are inside the corral, off the pony, then you can turn around, she told herself, and then she was, and she did.

Joseph was coming down the hill, riding at a slow, steady walk, with the bay at his side.

The cabin went dark and the door opened and Prosper came out, holding the lamp above his head. He came into the corral and put the lamp down carefully, took his time closing the gate slowly behind him. He went past her then, straight to the pony. He's not going to look at me or speak to me, she realized. I am being punished for riding away.

Here I am, Prosper, she had to stop herself from saying. I haven't been shot or stolen. And I have the pony. Can you see? I have come back. Are you not glad that I have come back?

"I said we would feed him," she said. He will respond now, at least, she told herself. "The Indian. He brought me back. He could have left me out there, on the prairie."

Prosper was walking around the pony now, running his hand up and down its legs, picking up its hooves, checking it over. You've never shown this much interest in him before, she felt like saying, and, maybe you think it wouldn't have been such a bad thing, after all, if I'd been left out on the prairie.

You didn't come after me. You let me go, so easily.

"I've swapped the bay for the pony," she said.

Prosper straightened up slowly, but he put his hands deep into his pockets and kept his eyes down on the ground.

"Honora," he began. Then he stopped. She watched him decide to begin again. "That Indian stole from us," he said. "And now you are giving him our best horse. He stole from us, and you are helping him to steal again. And on top of that, you want to feed him."

"I couldn't let him take the pony," she said, but her words sounded weak, ridiculous.

She held the rifle out to Prosper.

"Here," she said.

Prosper took the rifle. He began to check it, turning it over and over in his hands.

"Well, I guess I have a right to a feeling," he said. "To an opinion. Lord knows you got plenty of them yourself. And it's my opinion that we shouldn't be feeding a thieving Indian in our house when we barely have enough for ourselves."

"I will do it," she said. "You don't have to do anything."

Prosper made a sound. "Huh."

She had no skill in the kitchen. When they were still only settling the claim, Lina Olson, their neighbor from the nearest homestead, had come to show her how to churn butter, how to make buttermilk and bread—on the trail out here, the women had prepared the bread on the back of the wagons!—how to salt the meat, prepare and cook a bird. Lina was big boned and fair haired, and she made a show of smiling, but Honora saw her smile stop when she didn't know that she was being watched, and she was a great friend to Honora when the men were present, and short with her when they were alone. You need to learn how to cook for your babies, Lina said to her the first time they met, and for the men they will grow into, and for your husband too. You need to be a homemaker. She'd put her hands on her hips when she'd said that and had looked at Honora unsmilingly, and so, even though Honora wished she could answer, *This is not my home, Lina,* she had nodded, yes, and she had tried to learn, to do as Lina did. But she spoiled the butter by skimming it in the wrong way; her bread never rose and always tasted of ash; the meat she cooked was black on the outside and raw through. There was no ease between her and Lina, and being in her company made Honora feel tired and dull, and she suspected that Lina felt the same around her, and soon enough she began to make excuses not to come, and then she stopped coming altogether.

She could guess how Lina had recounted her efforts with Honora to her husband, John, how she had framed the story so that it ended with John telling her how lucky he was to have her, and her cooking too. At least you kiss better than you cook, Prosper had said with a laugh when she'd told him the lessons with Lina were over. I am a hopeless case, she'd said, but he'd smoothed her hair back from her face and kissed her. I'd better keep on kissing, she'd thought then, and all the rest of it, as well, and hope I grow to like it too.

"He speaks English, this Indian?" said Prosper.

216

"Yes," she said.

"That's a bad sign," said Prosper, and he turned away from her, back to the pony, to indicate that the conversation was finished, and he was the one finishing it.

She went to the gate, opened it wide, and went out of the corral. She thought for a moment of leaving the gate open behind her, to make Prosper have to scramble to close it, and then she told herself, Don't do that, Honora. Then she closed the gate and walked away. The pony whinnied behind her, but she didn't look back. I've had enough of you, she thought, and your unreliable ways. She went into the cabin, leaving that door to swing wide behind her. There was light enough from the low fire, but she lit a candle anyway and put it in the window, as was her habit every evening. She set out the two tin plates on the table, two knives, two spoons. They had no more than two of anything; she would have to share Prosper's. They could have the potatoes she'd cooked yesterday, and biscuits, and corn. They didn't have bread because she hadn't made any, again. There was no butter because she'd ruined it only that morning, trying to heat and skim it too quickly. She had no patience with cooking, Lina Olson had told her more than once, as if that would make patience come. She wouldn't take out the dried meat, or the sugar, or the coffee; that would be too much to ask Prosper to bear, she knew.

She sat down at the table and looked at the things on it. They seemed as unreal to her as objects in a painting, removed, eternal. It was hot in the cabin, but the cool wind from the prairie was coming in the open door and pulling at her hair, her dress. She touched the plate of biscuits, moved it, adjusted the position of a spoon. She picked up a tin plate, and there was her face, coming up at her out of the plate's dark surface as if it were rising up out of the waters of a black lake, black as the lake in Doolough. She put her hand to her cheek, to her mouth. There was dirt on her face, she thought, or it was a shadow on the surface of the plate; it was hard to tell. Her hair had come out of its plaits, and it was in her face and hanging down her back in the way that Prosper didn't like—he said she looked wild with her hair loose. It was too late now to do anything about her face, her hair. She looked in the plate, and her reflection looked back at her, grave, serious, and with that same slight frown she'd always had that Mary used to make fun of. *Mary.* She watched her face as she said the name in her head; she didn't even blink; her face didn't change at all. It was as if she'd never even said the word aloud.

She saw a light move beyond the window, and then Prosper came in and set the lamp down on the table so that its bright white light was between them. He looked at the set table.

"Should I wash up for our guest?" he said. "Put on a clean shirt?"

He sat down then as heavily, unexpectedly, as if he had been pushed. He put his elbows on the table and his hands in his hair.

"I don't know, Honora," he said, "what it is that you want."

I want someone to say to me, "Here we go," she thought, and then I want to go, just for the sake of motion itself, because there is freedom and beauty in it, and that's what the wind is saying to me. It's saying, "Let's go," and the suddenness and clarity of the realization made her feel like she'd had the breath knocked out of her.

She turned away from Prosper and toward the door. There was a noise outside, and then Joseph was standing on the threshold.

Prosper stood up. He had the rifle in his hands.

Joseph will turn and go away when he sees the rifle, she thought. He will not come in.

She went around the table and stood so that she was facing Joseph. He was taller than she had expected—she had to look up at him—and younger too: he was not so much older than she was, surely. She could smell the cold night from him, and it was a good smell, sharp and dry. It was hard to look at his face and take all the parts of it in at once; it was too much for her. She looked at his mouth, and then she opened her mouth to speak, and no words came out. Not now, she thought. Do not let this happen to me now. Her hand went up to her throat, fluttered at her mouth. She stood there, opening and closing her mouth and trying to talk, and the only sound in the room was from the low fire behind her, and from the horses, outside in the dark.

"If you want to eat, come in," said Prosper.

She turned to Prosper. *Thank you,* she wanted to say, and she hoped her face said it for her. He had been on her side since the day she had met him; he was steady and patient and rarely deliberately unkind. And yet with him I am not free, she thought, and it burns at me like a fire in my mouth, that I am not free.

Joseph came into the cabin.

"Sit down," said Prosper, not looking at him and sitting himself. He picked up a knife in his left hand, stabbed a potato, and began to eat it, skin and all. He had the rifle in his free hand, and he kept it standing up against him as he ate.

She went and sat next to Prosper. She put her hand on Prosper's spoon, to show that she and Prosper were sharing the things on this side of the table and that the things on the other side were meant for Joseph. Then Joseph sat, too, with the open door and the open prairie behind him.

"There's nothing to drink," said Prosper.

She had forgotten the tin cups.

She stood and got the pitcher of water, the cups, and put them on the table. Joseph picked up a biscuit.

"You took our horse," said Prosper.

"It's an Indian pony," said Joseph. "I told her this already. It has no mark on it. It's not trained to the saddle. How much did you pay for it?"

She knew that a blacksmith had given the pony to Prosper for nothing, to be rid of him. It was a shame, he'd told Prosper, to have to think of shooting a young, strong horse, but it had been a source of vexation since the day a cowboy had abandoned it at his forge, and if Prosper would take it off his hands, he wouldn't charge him for shoeing the bay, and he'd give him a good saddle, too, used, but well looked after. It had seemed like a good deal at the time, Prosper had told her, a deal I've come to question since, but at least I got the saddle out of it, and a story, too, a story for you, Honora, for your collection.

She couldn't look at Prosper now.

"I don't see how that is your concern," Prosper said. "Unless you intend on making me an offer for him."

"That pony was stolen," said Joseph.

Prosper put down his knife.

"Are you calling me a horse thief?" he said.

"I'm not saying you stole it," said Joseph.

He stood up from the table and slowly put the biscuit back down on the plate.

"Keep the dark horse," he said to Honora. "Keep the pony too."

He went out of the cabin so quickly that it took her a moment to understand what was happening. He had tethered his black horse to a tree, and even though she was running, he was at the horse already. If she didn't move faster, he would be gone into the night and only the memory of him would be left, and then she saw that he had stopped moving, that he was watching her come toward him, waiting for her, and then they stood before each other.

"You think you will ever go back?" he said. "To the place you came from?"

"I can't," she said, stunned into speech. "I can never go back. The ships we came on—they call them coffin ships because so many die on them, on the way, and because leaving Ireland is like dying. You can't go back on those ships."

The wind was high again, and it cried to her, longingly, like the lonely wind in Ireland.

"My people are gone," she said.

She didn't know why she had said that about the ships. That wasn't the reason she couldn't go back. She couldn't go back because there was nothing there and no one left to go back to. There was no one there who would know her now. When I speak to Joseph, she thought, I say things that I do not mean to say: the words come out of me, unbidden, and it is only in the saying of them that I realize the truth; and the truth, she knew, was that she wanted to make Joseph understand that she was alone in the world. It was essential to her that he understood this. That she was the only one left from Doolough. That they had walked as they had been told to walk, that they had always done everything they had been told to do, and it had all been for nothing, and she was the only one left, and she didn't know why, why she was left and not the others, and what was she to do now, all alone, and where was she to go in this world, and what was to become of her?

"We believe that when it is your time, you have a dream, and in the dream, you see clothes cast off in the middle of a path in the forest, and you hear laughing and talking up ahead. Then the ones who have gone ahead of you come and take you by the hand, lead you down the road. We all see each other farther down the road," said Joseph.

"Who are your people?" she said.

"Cayuse," he said.

"Will you go back to them?" she said.

"I don't know where they are," he said. "We had to leave our land and move on. I left, went off on my own."

"Where are you going now?" she said.

It was impossible that he was not following someone or searching for someone—she didn't understand. He was looking for something; she knew that as well as she knew her own name. Wasn't he looking for something that he had lost?

"Just going on," he said.

All the people I have known, she thought, they came into my life like they were just walking into a room, and they walked out as easily as they had come in; and she thought then of the robin that had flown into the house when she was being born and how everything that had happened to her afterward had been colored by it, as if the robin's flight were a thread that had been pulled through the fabric of her life.

"They say I was born under a curse," she said. "A piseog." The curse was tied up in the sound of the word: *pish-oh-ig*.

He does not know that it is not an English word, she thought. He does not know that it is Irish. He does not, probably, have the English he needs to describe many things. He cannot say what he wants to say, fully. Like me, she thought. Like me. We scrabble in the stones of English, looking for what we need and never finding it.

He bent down and picked up a handful of earth, stood up, and threw the earth over his shoulder.

"Gone now," he said. "Never there."

There was a voice in her, and it was rising up, and it was saying, Do not leave me here. Take me with you.

"Will I see you again?" she said.

"Farther down the road," he said, "Honora."

He turned from her.

"We need help here," she said.

He had his hand on his horse's mane. One more movement and he would be on the horse, and then he would be gone.

"If you are looking for work, you could stay," she said. "We need help with the horses, with the harvest." She stopped. She was afraid to think, nearly afraid to breathe. "We couldn't pay much," she said.

He turned and looked at her. "I'm not a farmer," he said.

Do not ask him again, she told herself, and so she said nothing, and stood straight, facing him as he stood looking at her. Then before she understood what was happening, he had moved back from her and mounted the horse.

"What about the pony?" she said.

"Doesn't belong to me," he said. "Doesn't belong to anyone. But you look after it. Ride it without a saddle. Don't let them put a mark on it."

She put her hand out toward his horse, and as she did, he was already going away from her. He went past the corral at a lope and into the folding darkness beyond it. He was out of sight then, but she could hear him still going, the sound of his horse's hooves getting lighter and lighter until she was only imagining hearing them, and after that, there was nothing left at all but the sound of the wind.

XV

After Joseph left, Prosper changed, but if he'd been asked, she knew, he would have said that it was she who'd done the changing.

When they had first set out together, many of the words he'd used were strange to her. She learned what they meant by listening to how and where he put the words in a sentence, and by paying attention to the action described that matched the word. To understand what a word meant, she had to translate it first into Irish, and from there back into English. But all her life she had been living between languages, and learning what the word meant was the easy bit. The hard part came after, when she thought to use the word, but felt too shy to, not least because when she said a word she'd learned from Prosper, she said it with his accent, and she sounded ridiculous to herself then, like she was pretending at being a different person. Her Irish accent had been a burden to her since she'd come to America: in New York and at Mrs. Egan's, people had laughed at her English, made a joke of her soft *t*'s, her hard *th*'s. It would only complicate matters to add in words said in another accent entirely.

Stay silent, she told herself during those early days with Prosper on the homestead, or as silent as you can manage without seeming strange, at least. Silence hasn't served you too badly until now, and you've time yet to learn what to say, and how to say it.

So before Joseph came, Prosper had talked, and she had stayed quiet, and as the months passed by, she had grown quieter, and he had talked more, and the words he used became more difficult to interpret. *Those horses sure like to nicker to each other in the evening*, he said one day. *Nicker*: she couldn't imagine how that was spelled, or what its equivalent was in Irish. Was it like *nickel*? Or *to nick*? *A knife nicked me*: she knew what that meant. That word, *nick*, was the same as the thing it described, she thought, and she would remember then the feeling of Ignatius's knife against her neck. But *nicker* confused her. *I once had a big sorrel, long teeth on him like a beaver; he'd jump a creek as soon as look at it with nothing but a rawhide bridle on him. Sorrel. Creek. Beaver. Rawhide.* There were no words for these things in Irish, and she couldn't understand what they meant in English. She gathered the sounds of the words to her as she had picked up small stones in the river and put them in her pockets when she still lived out in the woods in Ireland; now she was collecting a new language for this new world full of strange new things. One day, she hoped, the sounds of the words would make sense to her, and she could empty her pockets—until then, she stayed quiet, and listened, and learned.

I like to lie with you, but sometimes I think I like to talk with you just as much, Prosper had said to her one winter's night. *Feels like with you there's space for talking. It's been a long time since I had anyone to talk to, maybe forever, and it sure does feel good.* She hadn't said anything when he'd said that. *He doesn't even realize that I'm not talking back*, she'd thought. *He just wants to talk, and me to listen.*

But after Joseph left, it was Prosper who stopped talking.

"What did you say to him?" he had said to her when she came back into the cabin after Joseph had ridden away. "Why did you go running out there after him?"

She hadn't answered him. She had gone past him, wordlessly, to the fire; it had needed wood—it was burning too low. She'd put the kindling on, and then she'd gone down onto her haunches and watched

225

as the fire took light, slowly. Oh, how she hated this badly burning fire, the greasy cooking pot on it, and the hours she spent at both of them, trying to make something to eat.

"You're not going to talk, I guess," Prosper had said. "Same as always. But that's the easy thing to do, Honora, to stay quiet, and let everyone else do the talking."

He had gone out, then, to check the horses, she supposed, and when he came back, she was already in bed, lying facing the wall. She hadn't washed her face or taken off her dress; the dust of the prairie was still on her, in her mouth. She'd heard the match flare, then the chair being pulled across the floor, then the dull thud of the saddle and bridle being set on the table. The candle, the chair, the horses' tack, the cabin, the land it stood on—and all of these things connected to each other, like they were in some kind of a chain—to have them, to own them, meant freedom. This was what she had always understood to be true. But I am not free, she had thought, I am not. I have never been less free in my life, and this cabin and the things in it and the life I have here and what it asks of me—this is all the opposite of freedom. Ownership, possession: these are not what it is to be free. Joseph had said that he did not own the painted pony; neither did she. Neither did Prosper. They didn't own the pony, and they didn't own the land he ran on. It had seemed absurd, in that moment, to think of owning the land, as if one could think of owning air, and she had wanted to sit up and tell Prosper what she had realized, but he was angry with her, and she didn't want him to think she was talking to him as some kind of apology, and anyway, he would have dismissed what she said as ridiculous. Prosper believed that if something could be sold, it could be bought, and if you bought it, you owned it, be it a pony, land, or a person. He had paid for her at Mrs. Egan's. She had been part of a transaction. And now they were married, and in the eyes of the world, she was no longer a person; she was just a part of Prosper. She was his; his name was his mark on her. He owned her, like the landlord in Ireland had owned the land, and the people on it.

She had fallen asleep eventually that night, and Prosper had stayed at the table, and when she had woken in the darkness from a terrible dream, he was still there; he had watched her get up and walk outside, and he'd said nothing; and all the day after, he said nothing, still; and then the weeks began to pass, and still he said nothing. He was not the kind of person who recovered from an argument quickly, she was learning. William had been. So had Mary. But Prosper held on to feeling wronged for longer than she had expected, longer than she was prepared to bear.

~

It had been three weeks since Joseph had left, and every day of those weeks was like a ditch she had to climb over, and still Prosper wouldn't speak to her.

It was after sunset, an airless, hot night. Every evening she went out to look for a rider on the hill, but she looked, knowing Joseph would not be there; she knew he would not come again. He was gone, and she was still here with Prosper, in this cabin, on this land that seemed to want their blood before it would produce anything. Still, she watched the hill every evening, and waited, and then when the light began to fade, she rode the painted pony a way across the prairie, and sometimes, if there was enough light, she took him down to the creek that ran behind the hill and waded him along it, all the way down to where the trees met over the water like a bridge. She would get off the pony there and sit by the water and make a study of the grass, of how it was burned yellow at the bottom, then turned green and leafy and then pale yellow at the top, and sometimes she would walk through the knee-high grass and let her hand trail along its top and watch the grasshoppers jump from stalk to stalk in front of her as she moved, and sometimes she would lie by the creek and listen to the wind in the grass, in the trees. The world of the prairie made sense to her. Its trees were books she could read. The beauty of its lines—the line of the land against the sky, the lines of the blue mountains in the far distance—settled her. Out on the prairie, she was alive, free.

Prosper never commented on her absences or asked her where she had been, told her to take care. This was all part of her punishment, she knew. The days went by easily enough, because they each had their separate work to attend to, and the early part of the evenings she spent outside and was at peace, but the nights they spent confined to the cabin were growing more difficult all the time.

She stood in the open doorway, facing the hill. It was a particularly beautiful blue evening, full of rich light and sound, and she didn't want to go inside; it was too hot and still too light to sit in the dark, smoke-filled room, and the silence this evening would be as oppressive as on all the other evenings since Joseph had left.

She turned to look at Prosper. He was sitting at the table, working on a piece of wood with his knife. He'd already made chairs for the cabin—the table, the shutters for the windows, the head of their bed. Such a busy bee, she thought. Buzz, buzz. He was proud of his industry, she knew, and considered her wanderings out on the prairie and her lack of productivity in the house a kind of moral failing. She understood this, though she suspected that Prosper himself did not realize what he thought or believed. He only knew what he felt.

I will not sleep in this cabin again unless I am made to, she thought suddenly. From now on, I'll sleep outside, under the trees, near the creek.

Prosper shifted, sat up straight, and looked at her. He sees some expression on my face, perhaps, she thought, that makes him wary.

"What is wrong with you?" she said.

"What's wrong with me?" he said. "Ha. Nothing, Honora. Nothing at all."

He held up the piece of wood to her, as if it were proof of all that was right with him.

"You don't talk to me," she said.

"That's funny," he said, "coming from you. The queen of talk."

"You haven't talked to me properly since Joseph left."

"The Indian?" he said. "I didn't know you knew his name. I didn't know you two were so well acquainted."

"If you don't stop this, I will sleep outside," she said.

"Sleep where you want," he said. "It's not like you sleeping in here makes any difference anyway."

He stood up very suddenly and put his hand on the back of the chair, and she thought for a moment that he meant to throw it at her; she remembered him kicking over the chair at Mrs. Egan's and breaking it. Now she understood the petulance of that action, the lack of control it indicated.

He came around the table and toward her. She had to stop herself from moving away from him. Don't make him chase you. Wait, Honora, she told herself. Wait.

"Why do you go out every evening onto that prairie?" he said.

He was standing directly in front of her now.

"I like to ride when the heat of the day is gone," she said, and as she spoke, she realized that she'd had this answer prepared in her head, ready for this question.

"That's not it," said Prosper, "and you know it."

He took hold of her by the arm.

"You are not the same since that Indian came," he said. "You're unsettled. You're outdoors more often than indoors, and even when you're inside, you're watching the door. It's like you're waiting for someone. Who are you waiting for, Honora?"

She said nothing. Let him keep talking, she told herself. He'll talk himself out of it, surely.

"I don't expect you to say anything," said Prosper. "You never do, and you're not likely to start now, I suppose. But that Indian is not coming back. You are safe here. He is not in the employ of anyone. You have no need to worry anymore. No one is coming for you, Honora. No one knows where you are."

She closed her eyes so that he could not see any expression in them. What is it like to be you, Prosper, she wondered, and to be so sure of your world that you are sure, too, of how the people around you are thinking, feeling?

She opened her eyes, and Prosper put his hand out to her, and she took his hand, and he pulled her over the threshold and into the cabin, toward him, and then he spun her around so that she was facing away from him and he was behind her, holding her, his arms locked tight around her. He put his face next to hers and his mouth in her hair.

"I'm sorry if I've been sore," he said. His voice was muffled, rough. "I guess I was mad after you went out after that Indian, brought him into the house, because it was just so senseless, and then it all got me to thinking, ruminating on the whole ball of wax."

He pulled back from her a little.

"I started thinking that we've been here eighteen months now, and nothing is happening." He sighed. "John and Lina Olson, they've been on their claim as long as us; they haven't even been acquainted as long as we have, and their baby is six months now near as much, and she is having another one after the summer John told me, the last time I saw him."

So this is it, she thought. I should not be so surprised we have come to this, already. And then she thought, The thing that he is making—it is a cradle. How can I not have seen?

"Don't you find it burdensome, Honora?" he said. "This waiting for a child? I guess it must be worse for you than for me, even, with you being the woman. That's what John says."

She had to fight the desire to pull away from Prosper's hold. She had never liked being held, even as a child, and she liked it less as time went on. It was difficult to breathe, to move, and she hated to be restricted so.

"I know you struggle with the want," he said. "I know how you think; I know you better than anyone who's ever known you. I think the want makes you unsettled in yourself, affects your nerves. I understand, Honora."

He put his hand on her breast. He began to kiss the side of her face, her ear, her hair.

"I understand you; do you see?" he said, quietly. "Do you?" She recognized the urgency in the strained whisper. She knew what it heralded. "I understand you because we're the self-same people, you and me."

His hands were at her dress now, tearing it down and pulling it up, and he was pushing himself against her, and then he turned her around and began to kiss her hard, forcing his tongue between her teeth, and now he was moving her back against the wall of the cabin with such violence that she stumbled and almost fell.

No, she thought, no, no. And we're not the same, at all. You think because I have told you the things I wanted you to know that you know me, but you know nothing of me, of what I have seen. You have never known hunger. You haven't lost your baby and with her the only chance of having others. You left your home because you wanted to. You have had choices where I have had none. Everything you feel, you choose to feel.

She put her hand against Prosper's chest and pushed him hard and then harder, and then she realized that she was making a sound as she pushed, a kind of roar that was coming from somewhere deep inside her, and it was a terrible sound, shameful, exposing. Prosper fell back from her. He put the back of his hand to his mouth and wiped it. He was breathing very heavily, and his face was red, mottled.

"Get out of this house," he said. "Get away from here."

This is your chance, Honora, she thought. Walk out that open door and get on the pony and ride away and don't look back. Go on.

She took a step backward. Behind her was the emptiness of the prairie and in that emptiness her memory of all the things she had lost. Go on, Honora, she told herself.

It was night now. Prosper wouldn't let her take the rifle with her if she left. She didn't know how far she would get on the pony, with no saddle. She would have no money. She couldn't go to the Olsons for help: she had spurned Lina Olson's offer of friendship too often; besides, she wouldn't even be able to find her way to their homestead—she had been there only once, with Prosper, in the daytime. She didn't know the way. She didn't know the way anywhere. And it had been months, in any case, since they had seen the Olsons. And she had no food. She would be hungry by morning.

She could not be hungry again.

She had to think fast. There was something in Prosper's voice that she hadn't heard before. You never know a person's limits until you cross them, Prosper liked to say. Have I reached your limit, Prosper? she wondered. Can I come back from this?

"I'm sorry, Prosper," she said. "You're right. It is hard for me." She took a step toward him. "Every month, I wait and I am disappointed. I begin to grow melancholy in myself, I believe."

"I have done my best by you," he said. "I built you this cabin, made you everything in it, gave you the pony."

"You got me out of Mrs. Egan's," she said. "You've stood by me all this time." This is true, she thought. No one had done as much for her as Prosper. "And I am a disappointment to you. I do not give you want you want. I am a failure."

"There's no need to overdo it," he said gruffly, but she knew now that she could turn him.

"Any woman would be glad to have you as a husband." Say it, Honora, she told herself. Tell him what he wants to hear. She took another step toward him. "Who am I but a penniless girl from Ireland, by way of Mrs. Egan's." She stopped moving, put her head down, and covered her face with her hand.

She heard Prosper take a step toward her, hesitate, and then he came at her all in a great rush. He put his arms about her, very tightly, as if trying to hold her together.

"It's all right, Honora," he said. "Don't fret. We will just have to practice patience, I guess."

She sniffed. If she had to, she would cry.

He pulled back from her, took her chin in his hand, and lifted her face up to his.

"Oh, Honora," he said. "I've never seen you cry before."

He kissed her forehead, her eyes.

"You need more rest," he said. "You ride too much out on that prairie. No more riding from now on. You need to stay home more, stay quietly in the kitchen, and not excite yourself on that pony."

"Yes," she said quietly. "Maybe."

"Bedrest is what you need," he said, and he smiled at her then, and she knew she was safe. "What we both need."

Smile at him, she told herself, and she did.

"And I believe we should start by going to bed right now," he said.

He leaned down and kissed her again, and this time, she made herself kiss him back.

~

It was not difficult to go on pretending at being sad because they had not yet had a child, at pretending that she feared Joseph coming back, at pretending at being someone else entirely. She had had practice enough at being someone else. She was good at it. The hard part began to be holding on to who she was, at all.

Prosper hobbled the painted pony by tying his front and rear legs together with strips of bark rope, and then he tied him to the corral rail. It was for his own protection, he said.

And he watched what Honora ate, how much she rested, that she did not try to ride even the bay. He threw her boots away; he said he would get her some new ones the next time he had to go to the town for supplies, before the winter, maybe. It didn't matter that he had taken the pony, her boots; she hadn't gone when she had had the chance, and that was what counted. Prosper hadn't stopped her from going. He wasn't making her stay now. You are a coward, Honora, she told herself, a coward as William never was, and you've spent your life blaming everyone else for your troubles. When the moment came, you couldn't leave; you couldn't free yourself. You chose to stay. That's what matters.

Why can't you be a good girl, Honora, her father used to cry at her, and the question had held in it the acknowledgment that being a good girl was impossible for her; it had been a lament more than a question. She had always done as she was told, done her best, but it had never been enough, somehow. Maybe if you change what you do, you'll change who you are, she thought now. Maybe if you stop running, and searching, and fighting, you'll be a different Honora. Maybe you'll turn out to be a good girl, after all.

It was a relief to have Prosper smiling and talking to her again—she had missed his sweet, slow way of speaking—and he did smell good, and he kept his fingernails short and clean and his chin smooth, which was more than could be said for most of the men she'd known, and learning to accept lying with him as often as he wanted was just a matter of considering things from a different angle. If they lay together every morning and evening, as he preferred, then each time took only minutes; sometimes she didn't even have to turn to face him as he did his business. There were advantages to every situation if you just looked at things the right way; Mrs. Egan had told her that. Prosper liked her to go out only to attend to the poultry, or the vegetable garden, and she found that the less she went outside, the less she wanted to, anyway. She put the wooden bird that Prosper had carved her on the window ledge, and soon enough he made her other animals, too—a horse, a pig—and she lined them up together, her little wooden world, so that they looked out at the sun. She worked hard at learning in the kitchen and discovered that she could make a passable loaf of bread, and butter that didn't taste rancid, and from her efforts at making cheese, and buttermilk, they had enough to eat, finally. And in the long summer evenings, it was not unpleasant to sit inside the open front door and watch the chickens scratch around the yard for scraps. The light in the evenings was pale now; the sky was often high and violet, and there was no wind. The world seemed still, hushed, drawn up into itself. She slept late in the mornings and retired early to bed and often found that she needed to sleep in the afternoon too. "I am tired," she said to Prosper, in wonder, for she had never rested so much, and he replied always, "Sleep, Honora; give the body what it needs."

He is right, she thought, and maybe he is right, too, to think that if we keep trying, a baby will come. She had told herself there was no need to tell him of the baby she had lost. He does not need to know, she reasoned, that the doctor said I will not have another child. Those were facts that pertained to a different person, almost, who had lived in a different world, and this was a new world now, and she a stranger to even herself in it. A baby may come, she thought. It cannot be impossible, surely.

She slept more and woke less, and more and more she began to feel like she was living in a kind of dream, and it was a dream that was increasingly hard to wake from. The longer I stay here, in this house, she thought, the more I speak like Prosper, the more I sound like him. With each day that passes, I will become less like myself. In time, I will perhaps fade away completely, become someone else altogether. And who will know?

No one. No one is coming. No one even knows I am here.

XVI

"There's a robin that's been following me at my work these last days," said Prosper.

He had come in from a day in the field. The skin on his lower arms, face, and neck was burned brown, and when he took his shirt off at night, his body glowed white against the brown.

She was at the table. She had spent the day before picking berries from the garden, and now she was hulling them, getting ready to boil them down in the pot for the preserves that would see them through the winter. Lina Olson had shown her how to do it, and had loaned her sugar, too, for the boiling.

"That's curious," she said, which was the response Prosper wanted, expected.

She did not stop working as she spoke. She had found, over these last weeks, that if she kept going at a chore without talking, without thinking, the work came more easily to her. The important thing seemed to be to give yourself over to the task at hand, to go at it mechanically, in an ordered fashion, to forget who you were in relation to it.

"When I go out to the field in the morning, it flies up onto the top of the fence as if it's been waiting for me to come," said Prosper. "It sits there and watches me, and when I move, it follows on behind. It's like my shadow, all the day long. Yesterday evening, it tried to fly into the house after me, and I had to close the door on it to keep it out."

She looked down at her hands. They were stained bloodred from the berries, red like the robin's breast.

"Back home, we say that you must not let a robin in the house," she said, very quietly. "It's bad luck."

"Huh," said Prosper. "Here we say a wild bird in the house means a death is coming. Same kind of thing, I guess."

He leaned toward her and took a berry from her basket, put it in his mouth.

"Sure is strange the way that robin follows me, though. Feels like it's following me for a reason, almost." He winked at her. "Almost makes me nervous."

He did not seem to notice that she had stopped moving now. He did not see how she barely breathed. He was so cheerful in himself these days that he only saw good spirits in all those around him; he was blind to anything that was not a direct reflection of his own mood.

"You could make a good pie with those berries if you have some left over," he said.

"Yes," she said, looking down at the berries and seeing nothing.

"It's hot in here," said Prosper. "I don't know how you can bear to sit in this heat. And it's dark too. It's not good for you. Why don't you open the door, let some air in?"

He went to the door and opened it. The evening was hot, still, silent, and when the whinny came from the corral, it cut through the dusk like a knife through butter.

"It's that Indian pony," said Prosper, annoyed.

She felt something in her mind go click, and she thought then of the sound the gun had made as she'd readied it to fire at Ignatius in the alley in Bolt. It had been a clean, light sound, clarifying, simplifying. Click.

She stood up from the table.

"I'll go check on him," she said.

She picked up the knife from the table. Prosper would not let her take the gun; the knife was better than nothing.

"Leave him," said Prosper. "It's suppertime. Sun's near dipping beyond the prairie."

"It may be there's a coyote," she said. "I'm stiff from sitting at this table all day anyway. I'll be back in a moment to fix supper."

He nodded at her, but he was frowning a little. He had grown quickly accustomed to having Honora do what he expected when he expected it, and he did not relish even a tiny change to their routine.

She walked out of the cabin and toward the corral without thinking. Go on, Honora, something was saying to her. Go on. She remembered the voice that told her to turn to Alice, the voice that talked her onto the boat, the voice that told her to leave New York. Go on, Honora.

The pony lifted his head and watched her approach. She opened the corral gate and left it open behind her. She went to the pony and leaned down to the ground and cut the strips of bark rope binding his legs together, and then she unwound the rope that had been wrapped too tightly around each leg. The bark rope was cruelly thin and sharp, and she felt like crying out with anger and pity when she saw how badly marked the pony's legs were. She ran her hands up and down his legs and over the cuts—they were thick with dried blood—and under her breath she was saying over and again, "You are all right; you'll be all right."

Don't let them put a mark on him, Joseph had said.

You should not have done this, Prosper, she thought.

She stood up and untied the pony from the rail. He put his nose against her hand.

"Hello, my friend," she said.

It had been weeks since he had been ridden, and his mane was matted; his coat looked dull; he was too thin. She put her face against his and breathed in the sweet warm smell of him. The pony waited.

"*Mo chara*," she said. My friend. "*Ar chaill tu me?*" Did you miss me?

"Why are you speaking in that language?"

Prosper had followed her out of the house, and she hadn't even noticed. He had his rifle in his hand, and it shone darkly at her. She knew that if she asked him, he would say that the rifle was for the coyote, but he wouldn't waste a bullet on a coyote. *Give me the rifle,* she wanted to say suddenly. *I should be the one holding it.* She turned back toward the pony.

"An imeoimid?" she said. Will we go?

"Stop it," said Prosper. "Stop speaking in that language. Come back in the house. It will be dark soon. It's suppertime."

He came into the corral, closed the gate behind him, and began to come toward her.

She put the handle of the knife between her teeth and her hands on the pony's mane.

"Honora," he said, and he made the word a warning.

She was on the pony with one leap. She felt a shudder run through him as she leaned back on him, and it was a gathering that she recognized, a readying. She put her heels down and rolled her knees in and gripped tight with her thighs, and the pony drew himself in, put his head down, and when she put her legs to his sides, he responded so willingly that she knew he had been waiting for the signal to go. He broke into an easy canter, and then they were in a lope going around the corral, and then they were heading for the rail and clearing it. My God, she thought as they went through the air, he will break his heart jumping this rail, but they landed without even losing pace, and she turned him easily by shifting her weight so they were facing the hill. He has given everything to jumping the rail, she thought; he will not be able for more, but he broke into a lope that knocked the breath out of her. Don't look back now, Honora, she told herself. Go on.

They went up the hill. At its crest, the pony slowed for a moment, listening to something in the wind. What is it? she said to him in her mind. She could hear nothing but the sound of the land breathing in and out. Before them, the empty prairie rolled, unfolded like an endless sea. The moon was rising above the horizon, and it was a full orange-colored moon. Whatever happens, she thought, I am glad I have done this, and I won't go back. Everyone does what they want to do, in the end, or what they are meant to do. Mary had said that, and she hadn't agreed with her when she'd said it. But you were right, Mary, she thought, about that, at least.

In her mind she said, *Fagfaimid.* Let's go.

The pony turned his head and whinnied again. There is another horse close by, she thought. That is the noise he hears, and then she thought, It will be Prosper, on the bay, following me. She did not think, We cannot outrun the bay, and she did not think about what would happen when Prosper caught up with her.

She took the knife from between her teeth and put it flat against her palm so that she could close her fingers around it and hold on to the pony's mane at the same time.

"All right," she said to the pony. "Come on, so."

They went down the hill so fast that it would have frightened her if she had let it. She couldn't hold the pony. If he falls at this speed on the slope, he will break his leg, she thought, but he didn't fall, and as he went on, she began to understand that he was not running from something, but toward something. He knows where he is going, she realized. Something is pulling him forward.

They were going across the prairie now, and all there was in the world was the sound of the pony's hooves lightly drumming on the hard earth and the feeling of his mane and the wind in her face; she was beyond thought, and when the pony went down, it was more than a moment before she understood what was happening. He stumbled—it was not even a fall—but because they were going at such speed she lost her seat and then her hold on the mane, and she fell forward, unbalancing the pony so that his head went down and she went up onto his neck and then under it. She had hold of the mane yet, and she was hanging upside down under the pony's neck, and he kept galloping, galloping, but he was falling now as he was galloping, and if she could, she would have cried out, *Stop*, but then she was letting go and going down, under the pony's hooves. She had fallen from the horses on the homestead, many times, but not like this, and not in the dark: the pony couldn't see her to avoid her, and she couldn't roll away from his hooves quickly enough, and then she felt his hooves against her face.

The pain was a cold bang, and there was pain in her hand, too, and a terrible pain in her leg that made her want to be sick. She was lying on her side, but she dragged herself up so that she was half sitting, and she tried to feel her leg in the dark. Even to touch it made her cry out with pain. She lay back down, on her side. The pain in her hand was from the knife, of course—it had cut into her palm as she'd fallen. She'd dropped the knife, in the dirt, in the dark, and she was bleeding from the side of her head—I know that warm, soft feeling against my skin, she thought—and the pony was gone, into the night. He'd fallen onto his knees, she was sure, and he would have cut them and now he would bleed. And every coyote for a hundred miles around will smell that blood, and they will smell yours, too, Honora, she told herself, and you are finished now, you and the pony both.

She got up onto her knees and tried to stand. If I had Old Alice's stick, she thought, I could walk, perhaps, but Ignatius had taken her stick, as he had taken all the rest. Her leg gave way underneath her, as she'd feared it would, and she fell back down onto her side, but slowly, as if she were on the listing deck of a ship in a storm and she couldn't keep her balance. She could crawl, but not far, and certainly not all the way back to the homestead, in the dark. Find some shelter, Honora, she told herself, and rest, and in the morning, Prosper will come for you, but even as she was thinking this, she knew that Prosper would not come. He had no skill as a tracker, and in any case, he would not leave the homestead unattended. He would think that she had gone to the river for the night; she had done this before. It could be a whole day before he thought to look for her, or to ask for help in looking for her, and then there would be little chance she would be found: she had ridden fast and far, she thought, on the pony, and her tracks would be erased by tomorrow.

A wave of panic began to rise up in her.

She fell forward onto her hands and crawled toward some scrub. She could crawl no more than a few paces, even less than she had thought possible, because of the cut in her hand. She could hardly put her hand flat on the ground, and there was blood in her eyes from the cut in her head and in her mouth. She stopped by the scrub and turned to lie on her back so that the blood flowed away from her face and into her hair. She lifted her hand to the September moon and made it into a bird and flew her hand across the moon's pale face. I'm glad I can see the moon, she thought. When I was a small girl sleeping out in the woods, the moon was no stranger to me, and I never had a bad night out under such a full moon. Her hand felt heavy, and her arm weak; she let her hand fall back down to her side. She was very tired suddenly, tired of crawling and riding and fighting and walking and starving and working; all she wanted now was to sleep. *The fight has gone out of you, Honora,* Mary would have said to her. *You're the quiet girl now,* Ignatius would have said, *now that the world has taught you a lesson. I told you to be a good girl,* her father would have said, and *did you listen, did you try? You didn't, not even once.* She closed her eyes against the idea of Mary and Ignatius and her father; she had the feeling now of being in warm water, and she felt peaceful, almost comfortable. I'm rising, she thought, drifting, and then she slept.

When she woke, the sun was already at the highest point in the sky, and she turned her face from it. She opened her eyes. Coming toward her, from a great distance, as if he were emerging from the horizon itself, was the painted pony. I am dreaming, she thought, or I am losing my reason, and now I see two ponies, and she almost felt like laughing then, at herself. She tried to raise her head, but the pain was too much. She squinted against the white sun. She had been right: there were two ponies, and there was a rider too. And then she saw: it was Joseph.

The horses and Joseph stopped some way from her. In the hard light, they seemed like figures from the world of Old Alice, from a place that was suspended somewhere between heaven and earth, and a place it was, too, of unsettled spirits and restless souls.

She didn't understand why they had stopped, what Joseph was doing, whether he was coming toward her or going away, and she almost didn't care; she was so tired still that she wished she could keep sleeping; if Joseph came, he would try to stop her from sleeping, and she resented him for that. She closed her eyes against the light.

Then Joseph was holding her mouth open, too roughly, and pouring water down her throat, and she was coughing and gasping for air. *You are hurting me,* she wanted to say, but she found that her tongue was so swollen in her mouth that she couldn't move it, and in any case, he'd stopped pouring the water now and was turning her hand over and pulling at her leg, and now he was kneeling and sitting her up and throwing her over his shoulder, and now putting her across the back of the black horse and climbing up behind her himself. Then they rode. She lay against Joseph, and he rode with one hand against her back to keep her on the horse, and as they went, she drifted in and out of a kind of sleep. They rode for many hours; how many, she could not have said. Sometimes as they rode, she opened her eyes and saw the bare golden land going past, as in a dream, and sometimes she saw the high hot white sky ahead in a line against the land, and sometimes she saw only Joseph, above her, and only ever looking straight ahead.

∼

It was dark when she woke. She was under a blanket, next to a fire.

"How long have I slept?" she said. Her tongue still felt enormous in her mouth, and her lips were cracked and so dry that it was hard to move them.

"Two days," said Joseph.

The horse and the pony were tethered to a line that ran between two trees. The fire she was lying next to was well established. There was a saddle blanket on the other side of the fire, a rolled-out pack, water bags hanging from a low bush. This was Joseph's camp. She tried to sit up, but she couldn't move well. There was a wide stick strapped to the side of her leg with rawhide, as a splint.

"Bone is broken," said Joseph.

I fell from the pony, she wanted to say, but he knew that. He had found the pony, tracked its trail back to her, brought her here.

"What is going to happen to me?" she said. There was no point in talking to Joseph like she talked to other people, pretending that she didn't know what she did, asking questions she didn't want to know the answer to.

"Leg will heal," he said. "Not straight, though. Maybe you'll walk crooked after."

He gave her a look, almost a grin.

"The hand?" she said. Her hand looked bad. It was gashed open, and the wound had been packed with a paste that had dried hard.

"Hand is fine," he said. "Knife went clean through. Your head, where the pony kicked you, fine too. You were lucky."

I'll have a limp for life, she thought, but for me, this counts as luck.

Joseph stood and came behind her, put his arms around her chest, and pulled her up into a sitting position. He handled her roughly, like she was a rag doll. Then he turned and took the skillet from the fire and moved to set it on the ground next to her.

"Eat," he said.

There was a kind of stewed meat in the skillet, and she ate it with her hands, pushing it into her mouth. The meat was good, soft, though she hardly tasted it. I did not think I would know such hunger again, she thought, but here I am. Here I am.

"You been hungry like this before," Joseph said.

She stopped eating.

"Me too," he said. "Eat."

"When?" she said.

"Always," he said. "Eat."

He went back toward the fire, took some corn bread from the griddle, and gave it to her. When she started to eat again, he nodded and sat down across from her so that the fire was between them.

"Where were you going?" he said. "On the pony."

"Away," she said.

I didn't get too far, she thought, and she looked at him and saw that he was thinking the same thing.

"How is the pony?" she said.

"No good for riding anymore," said Joseph. "His legs have gone. Only good as a packhorse now."

That pony broke his heart for me, after all, she thought, and I never even gave him a name, not even in my head, and it's too late now to start naming him as an apology.

"Why are you here?" she said.

"I went into the town," he said. "Then I came back here, set up camp."

She waited. There is more, she thought.

"Trouble coming," he said.

Trouble coming, Old Alice had said, too, and there was something in the echoing of her words that made Honora feel as cold and still as she did before the hunt.

Her mouth was still full of corn bread, and her face was caked with blood and dirt. Her dress was wet; she had passed water while she had slept, and her thighs burned from the urine. I wish I had some water, she thought suddenly, so that I could wash, and ready myself. Afterward she would almost laugh when she recalled thinking that: that if only she could fix her hair and tidy herself, she would be ready for what was to come.

"Some time back, I met a tracker," Joseph said. "Navajo. Could track a fish through water. He told me he was looking for a girl—shot a man in Bolt and near killed him. Girl was in the company of a ranch hand from Tennessee, and they were riding with an Indian pony, Cayuse, marked with a black circle around the eye, four white legs. The Navajo was working for the man the girl shot. Good tracker." Behind them, the pony shifted restlessly. "Not as good as me."

Her mind was a penny falling down a black well with no bottom to it.

"I found you," said Joseph. "Then I met you. Then I didn't want the money for you anymore."

"Why are you telling me this?" she said. It was hard to open her mouth, and the words had to find their way out between her teeth.

"Tracker's found you," he said. "Told the man looking for you where you are. That man is coming for you now."

Joseph had been looking for her, after all. You were right, Honora, she thought, about him looking for something, and the something was you, and that doesn't even matter now. All that matters is that Ignatius has found you, that he is on his way to you.

"When is he coming?" she said.

"Four more days. Maybe five," he said, lifting his hand up, as if he were holding in it the idea of time itself. "He's a bad rider, they say, a bad traveler, but it's a day since he left the town, so four, five days."

"What would you have done if I hadn't ridden out?" she said.

"You ask the wrong questions," said Joseph. "You need to rest your leg for as long as you can. But before the man comes to this part of the country, you need to leave. You must ride through the night so you're not seen and go to territory where no one will find you. I will take you. We can go into the hills," said Joseph. "No white man will go there."

"Prosper is in the cabin still," she said.

"This man is looking for you," said Joseph. "Not him."

"He will kill Prosper," she said.

Joseph made a sound in his throat like a bark, and the sound meant, So be it.

"I have to go back," she said.

"You go back, he'll kill you," he said. "Maybe he'll have help with him, a hired gun. You don't know what you will be up against if you go back."

I don't know what I'm up against if I stay out here with you, she thought, but she said nothing. She looked out at the land in front of her, at the night on the eternal prairie. She put her hand out to the night air. It had texture, weight; it had a pulse to it like a person.

"He's really your husband?" said Joseph. "The man in the cabin?"

"Not in my heart," she said. "But he has been a friend to me."

"He is not one of your people," he said.

"You know nothing," she said, "of my people."

He lifted his chin, and for what felt like a long time, he just looked across the fire at her. Keep on looking, she thought, and then she realized, I'm not afraid of him looking at me, and what's more, and what is more surprising, I like it, that he considers me like this.

"Why do you have no food in your country?" he said.

"People came from another country," she said, "took our good land, and the land we were left with was poor, and our crops failed, and there was nothing to eat, and then we were hungry."

Things sound so simple, she thought, when you put a shape on them with words.

Joseph looked away from her and out to the dark night.

"These people," she said, "they say we are savages, and wild, that we are less than people."

Joseph turned back to her, and his face was different. This is who he is, she thought. Now I see him.

"I used to think it was our fault for being poor, and hungry, and dirty, and wild, because we are; we are those things. But since I have come here, I begin to think it is not our fault. I begin to think we were made like that. I begin to think that who we were before, the things we believed in, the way we thought and spoke and lived were so different from the ways of these other people who took our land that they couldn't understand us, and the easy thing was to think us less than them, less than people, and then to believe it their right to take what we had."

She had never said so much before—she had never in her life said such things, or even thought them.

Her hand, she realized, was burning with pain. She'd leaned on it and opened the wound, and fresh blood was running down her wrist now.

Joseph came around the fire and kneeled next to her and took her hand. He unwound the rag that he wore around his wrist and wrapped it around the wound. She watched the top of his head bent over her hand.

"Why are you here, Joseph?" she said.

It was the first time she had called him by his name.

He let go of her hand. She was sure that he would stand and walk away from her. When he finally looked up at her and she saw the expression on his face, it stopped her heart in her chest.

"Because I want you," he said.

"When my mother was birthing me, a bird flew into the house," she said, "and then my mother died. I had a baby who died, and my people are gone too. Everyone who has been dear to me has gone. I have no people now. That is the curse I told you of. I am bad luck."

"We say," he said, "that a bird in the house is good luck. The bird flies in, flies out, and its passing through is like life passing on. The house is the body; the bird flying through is this." He put his hand to his chest, to his heart. "The other people in your life were unlucky. You are the lucky one. You are the one with the blessing on you."

Look for the one who sees the blessing.

"Honora," he said, "my people are your people. If you want it. People of the horse."

"I cannot have a child," she said.

"Better," he said.

He had put his hands in her hair and was looking at her mouth, and then he leaned toward her and put his mouth on hers, very gently. She tried to open her mouth to say something, and their tongues touched and her whole body jumped, and then they were kissing as she had never kissed or been kissed before, and then he was kneeling on top of her and they were pulling at each other's clothes, and then they were lying on the ground, fighting each other, and it was a fight they were both winning and losing at the same time.

~

She had never known anyone who spoke as little as Joseph. Hours passed without them speaking to each other. They didn't need to speak. They would be sitting by the fire, or he would be with the horses by the trees, and they would give each other a look, and that look was louder than any shout she'd ever heard. He would come to her then, and every time was better than the last as they grew freer with each other. She was embarrassed by the strength of her desire for Joseph, and at the same time she marveled at it, the desire, and allowed herself to be submerged in it like she was going underwater. If someone had asked her, afterward, what she thought of when she thought of those days with Joseph on the prairie, she would have said, *desire*. The force of the desire was so strong that she almost didn't think about Ignatius coming across the prairie for her, about Prosper waiting in the cabin, about what would become of her once she had to leave the camp. The desire for Joseph was almost stronger than thought.

He was as easy and silent in his movements as the wind, and was as much a part of the world as the wind, or the sky. There was no separation between Joseph and the land, or the air: the fire lit for him without smoking; the horses responded to his every gesture. Every tree, every animal, every rock, even, held a kind of significance for him. He knew what the weather was doing, when to go out to hunt. To her, this part of the prairie was a difficult, sage-filled country, but to Joseph, it was a book of wonders. He knew which plants to pick to make into a paste to pack into her hand, what to use to take the swelling down from her leg, how to make a cooling mixture for her cracked lips and sunburned skin. He moved through the world as if he and it and everything in it were one. Because of this, she understood, Joseph didn't need to speak. Words had fallen, noisily, from the mouths of everyone else she had ever known: they had needed, she saw now, to understand the world through talking about it. Joseph had no need to put the shape of words on things that, for him, made sense already, and in any case, existed outside language.

One evening, she let herself imagine telling Mary about Joseph, and she heard Mary's voice saying, Well, Honora, there's no going back now, and in her head, she answered her, That's what I want. She and Joseph barely had a language in common. She knew of no society—hers, his—that would welcome them.

Oh, Mary, she thought, when I am with him, I am set free, and as for the rest of it—it doesn't matter.

~

On the fourth day, her leg began to feel stronger, and that evening, when they sat by the fire, she told him so.

"Tomorrow morning, we go," he said.

He had been out at the hunt for longer than usual today, and he had seemed distracted since he had come back. Something has happened, she thought. Or he has learned something.

"The man looking for you," he said. "He will be at your house tomorrow night, or the morning after."

He picked up a long thin stick and poked at the fire, sending sparks up in front of them.

"I will be able to ride if you tie my good leg to the stirrup," she said.

Joseph looked at her leg in its splint. It was lying away from her body at an odd angle. That does not look right at all, she thought, and then she thought, Do not think about that now, Honora. She put her hand on the leg and pulled it back toward her and tried to line it up with her other leg. She didn't want Joseph thinking that she couldn't get on a horse.

"I have to go back," she said.

He hit the fire with his stick.

"Why do you say nothing?" she said. To this, she thought, He must say something.

He looked at her, and it was a cold look that made her turn away, toward the fire. He was right, maybe, that she asked the wrong questions. But that didn't mean she didn't want answers. *I will not be easily silenced,* Joseph, she wanted to say, *and the sooner you know this about me the better.*

"Where is your family?" she said, to the fire.

If he won't answer any questions, she thought, I might as well ask him what I really want to know. To put the question to him is nearly enough.

"Honora," he said.

"What kind of people did you come from?" she said. Keep going, she told herself, even though she almost wanted to stop now. "Where are they?"

Still, he said nothing.

"What is the right question, Joseph?" she said.

He gave no sign that he had heard her, and he was silent for a long time. Then he said, "My mother, my sisters, got sick, died. Many of our people got the white man's sickness and died, from the sickness, and then from the hunger. After they died, my father was weakened, died too. My people had fought a long war and we lost it, so we had to leave our land and move to where the white man told us. The night before we were set to leave, I took the black horse and I left. I wanted to be on my own, out on the prairie, free to go where I wanted. Since then, I am alone."

Ask him, she told herself. Do it.

"What is your real name?" she said. "Is it Joseph?"

He said nothing.

"I don't think it's Joseph," she said. "Is it?"

William had named the baby Aine, she thought suddenly, and that was all wrong, and I never righted it.

"I left my old name behind with my mother, my father, who gave it to me," Joseph said. He moved his hand through the air as slowly as if he were moving it through fast water. "It was a Cayuse name, and I didn't want to take that name with me. It belonged to that world, that land. I let the wind take it."

"Anyone looking for you wouldn't be able to find you with the name Joseph," she said, And that is maybe why you left your name behind, she wanted to say, so that you can't be found, so that you can stay lost.

"No one's looking for me," said Joseph, and he stood up.

Nothing there and no one left to go back to, she had thought about Ireland, but she saw suddenly that what was important was not so much the place left behind as the act of leaving it, which never ended. What would always be true and continuous in her life and in Joseph's was that they had left the place they were from, and that they would always be leaving it; they would always be in motion. They could never go back, having left, because the people they had been before they left were gone. And she had been wrong to think that there was nothing left in Ireland and no one left to go back to. There were people there, yet. Others had stayed. Others were there still. The Cayuse still existed; the Irish did.

"Sleep now, Honora," said Joseph. "Tomorrow, we ride."

She watched him walk away from her. His legs were bowed at the knees and he had a curious rolling way of walking that filled her with a hunger for him. Whatever this thing is between us, she thought, it is stronger than reason. And Joseph had been right, she realized, not to have wanted to answer her questions. What had happened to them both before today—it didn't matter anymore. It was the past, and it was finished, gone, as the people they had once been, the names they had once had, were gone. She lifted her face to the night. The people you have been, they are ghosts, now, Honora, she told herself. Let them go. Set them free, and concern yourself only with going on, from now on.

In the morning, she woke while Joseph still slept. Every other morning, she had awoken after him; usually he had watered the horses and fed the fire before she stirred. She stood and put her hands to her mouth, to her hair. Her hands smelled of Joseph; her tongue tasted of him. He lay next to her, with his gun under his arm and his hair across his face. She had never seen him sleep like this before, and she took her time looking at him. His body was scarred, marked, but his beautiful face, in sleep, was clear and open.

She stood and began to make her way to the pony. She had to drag her leg after her, and she had been wrong; it did not feel stronger at all, and it hurt her terribly, and so did her hand. She put her hand on the pony's flank and then rested her head against it. How am I to do this? How can I face down Ignatius, when I can barely walk, when I will struggle to hold a gun? For a moment, she felt like she would cry out in anger, in fear. The pony, under her hand, was still, listening; his blood beat, thrummed, at her touch.

"The pony is finished," said Joseph from behind her. "I told you. You cannot ride him."

He walked to the black horse and was on him in one movement. He kicked at the horse and took two steps toward her and then leaned down and held his hand out to her. He nodded impatiently at her, come on.

"I'm going back to Prosper," she said.

"The only way you can go back is with me," said Joseph. He lowered his hand down more to her.

She took a step back. Joseph straightened up and took hold of the reins with both hands. The black horse danced away from her. He will leave now, she thought, and you will have sent him away with your fear, your hesitation.

"My name," said Joseph, "was Blue Horse. For a horse so black it looked dark blue, that my mother rode when I was in her belly."

Life turns on a point, she thought, turns over, and again.

She walked toward the horse and held her hand up to Joseph, and he took hold of her by putting his hand in the crook of her elbow, and he swung her up in front of him. He fixed her bad leg against his and put her hands deep in the horse's mane, then put his arms around her waist and leaned into her so that she could feel his bare chest against her back, through her thin dress.

He smelled of the sky and the wind.

He smelled like her.

XVII

"I don't believe you," said Prosper.

In the time that she had known him, he had often not responded as she had expected him to: it was because his way of thinking was so different from hers that she could not always guess at what his reaction to something would be. It was one of the things she found interesting about Prosper, this unpredictability. She didn't mind, usually, being surprised by him. It kept her alert to him, made him visible to her. But to not believe her now was born out of more than seeing the world from a different viewpoint. To not believe her now was born out of mistrust.

"What do you mean?" she said.

"It is simple, what I mean," said Prosper. "Are you simple? Perhaps. It would explain a lot, certainly."

He had been sitting at the table, with his hands folded on it, facing the door, when she had walked into the cabin. It was dark in the cabin, because the only light came from the dying fire—the fire was too low! He had not kept it going, and how was tomorrow's bread going to be prepared now, and then she remembered—You'll make no more bread here, Honora—and it was very hot. Why was Prosper still in his work clothes? Why was he sitting at the table in this strange, stiff fashion, with nothing at hand to occupy him, with this curious expression on his face? *Stand up, Prosper*, she wanted to say to him. *Stop sitting there like that.*

"I knew you would come back," he said with a satisfied, narrow smile. "By the way."

He has been sitting here, waiting for me, since I left, she realized. How long would he have stayed waiting like this?

"I have come back because Ignatius is coming," she said.

"And I have told you that I don't believe you."

"Why would I lie?" she said, astonished.

"Because you went out onto the prairie and had a fall, and after a few days of sitting in the sun with a sore leg, you realized that you had made a mistake; you wanted to come back, and you needed a good excuse to do so. This is not a good excuse, Honora." He gave her the same thin smile. "Something less fanciful would have served you better."

"I am with Joseph," she said.

Prosper stopped smiling.

"You mean the Indian?" he said.

"He's had word," she said, "that Ignatius is on the way."

"Oh," said Prosper. "Oh, that clears things up. If Joseph says it, then it must be so. Let us tarry no more; let us ready ourselves for action." His face hardened. "You're funny, Honora," he said. "I never realized how funny you were, until now."

"Ignatius will be here by morning," she said. "He was by the Olsons' only yesterday."

Prosper stood up.

"Yes," she said. Now he stands, she thought, at the idea of his reputation with John Olson being tarnished.

"How does he know this?" he said.

"What does that matter?" she wanted to shout, and then she realized she was shouting already. To stop the shouting, she let herself put her hand to her throat, to her mouth. "He will be here by morning," she said.

Prosper was looking at her, and his eyes were dark, empty. He came toward her until he was standing right in front of her, put his hand out to touch her, and then stopped, as if there were a wall of glass between them. He let his hand drop back down to his side.

"All right, Honora," he said quietly.

His rifle was leaning against the wall, next to the door. He picked it up and went outside. Joseph was standing by the trees next to the corral with his black horse and the painted pony, and Prosper was striding purposefully toward him now. *He means to shoot him,* she realized. *He means to kill Joseph.* She began to try to run on her broken leg, though the pain made her bite her tongue until blood came. *Do not try to kill him, Prosper,* she wanted to cry out, *because he will kill you first. Do not try to kill him, because I fear that I will kill you myself if you raise your gun to him,* and oh, Honora, she thought then, there is no way back for you now.

Prosper stopped walking and turned to watch her coming toward him.

Don't look at him, she told herself. Don't look at his face. Just keep going. She went past Prosper, dragging her leg behind her, and went to stand next to Joseph so that their arms were touching, and it seemed to her that even Prosper must feel the way the air changed around them when they were together, had become charged like the air before a storm.

Prosper looked at Joseph, then at her. She saw him seeing her hair, her torn dress, her hand wrapped in Joseph's rag and her bruised mouth, and she saw the understanding begin to spread across his face.

"My God," he said. He began to rock backward and forward on his heels, and then he leaned very far back with his fingers in his belt loops so that he was looking up at the sky. "With an Indian, Honora? You know what that makes you?"

You met me in a brothel, Prosper, she felt like saying. *What did you expect?* He had put his hand through his hair now so that it stood up on his head, and she was hit then by the memory of him leaning back against the iron bedstead in the bedroom at Mrs. Egan's, running his hands through his damp hair. As things start, so they end, Mary had said to her once, and things between her and Prosper had started in the wrong place and had stayed there.

"You are never coming in the house again," he said. "You can live now without a roof over your head like the whore you are."

Next to her, she felt Joseph begin to move.

"Ignatius may not be alone," she said quickly to stop Prosper saying more. "It is better we wait for him in the house, that we give him no sign we are expecting him."

"He is not coming in," Prosper cried to her, not looking at Joseph. His face was twisted and ugly now in a way she had never seen; he looked like he was in pain.

"He has a gun," she said. "We will need all the help we can get. Take the help, Prosper. It is not your fault that this has happened. Take the help, and survive."

"I wish I'd never met you," he said.

"I wish a lot of things hadn't happened that did, but here we are," she said.

He will pick up the rifle and try to shoot both of us, she thought, or he will shoot the painted pony, to punish me, or he will go back in the house—all are now equally possible. Life turns on a point.

He picked up the rifle. It was impossible to read from his face what he meant to do, because he was still deciding, she thought. Next to her she felt Joseph move, very quietly. She knew he was reaching for his gun. *Don't try to shoot him, Prosper,* she wanted to cry out. *You're a bad shot, and you can't win, and you'll be doing Ignatius's work for him if you start shooting now.*

Prosper looked down at the ground, studying it, and then without looking up, he turned on his heel and went toward the cabin.

She and Joseph watched him walk away.

"I come in that cabin with you, and if we are alive tomorrow, you leave with me," said Joseph.

"Yes," she said.

"What is happening here is not my concern," he said. "You know why I am here."

"I understand," she said. Blood on the moon, she thought, and me born under such a moon, and still not free, not yet free.

"You want to come with me?" said Joseph, and she could only guess at how much it cost him to ask her.

She turned and looked up at him.

"Yes," she said. "Yes, I do."

~

The wagon came at dawn. Its white canvas cover shone as bright as the sail of a ship in the raw early light. Honora watched it come over the top of the hill, watched its team of mules make its ungainly way down toward them.

At last, she thought, and she felt something like relief, for they had spent the day and the night in the cabin not sleeping, not speaking, not knowing how long they would have to wait, and at times through the darkness, she had thought that the wait was more than she could bear; more than once she had to stop herself from rising and running out the door and running away. Whatever lies out there, she had thought, it cannot be much worse than what is in here, for this house is full of anger and fear and violent feelings. Now, at last, at least, the wait is over, and I have been waiting a long time for this, she realized, for such a reckoning.

"He has traveled all night," said Joseph. "That was a bad plan."

"Will I open the door?" she said.

"No," said Prosper.

"Yes," said Joseph.

She picked up Prosper's hat from the table and put it on, tied it under her chin. She had always liked this hat, the color of it, the shape of it, the way it sat low on her head and covered her eyes. Now it covered her bruised face, threw a shadow over her broken lips. I am going to keep this hat, she decided. I'm going to need it more than Prosper will.

She fixed her hair under the hat and brushed down her skirts. She wished she had some boots: her bare feet looked childlike under her skirts. Don't think about that now, Honora, she told herself. If you do things right, Ignatius will be looking at things other than your feet.

"Will you give me the rifle or the gun?" she said to Prosper.

He was standing by the window, watching the progress of the wagon and holding the rifle. His handgun was in his belt.

He didn't turn when he answered her.

"No," he said.

"Prosper," she said. "I have a better chance than you."

She didn't want to say more. She didn't want to have to lay out how much better a shot she was than him.

She made herself wait for him to speak. Often, with Prosper, you had to wait for a response; if you tried to push him to reply, it just slowed everything down. Better to wait, and as she thought that she suddenly felt that she would cry, for she knew him as few people knew each other, surely, and one way or another, their time together was coming to an end.

"Give me the rifle," she said more harshly than she had intended because she was working to stop herself from crying, and when he turned, she saw the surprise on his face, and he held out the gun to her, wordlessly.

She took it. Joseph was standing with his back to the wall by the door. He looked at her, and she knew what he was saying to her as clearly as if he had spoken the words out loud: Hold the gun high and half cock it as soon as you stop walking. Be quick and easy in your movements, and don't be afraid, because the world is with you. He nodded at her, and that was her signal to look ahead. He opened the door, and she stepped outside. She lifted the gun with her good hand

and set it against her shoulder, and then she started to walk forward. She had to swing her leg around in a half circle to move forward: the leg from the knee down seemed to be facing in an entirely different direction from the leg above the knee, and she could tell that even after the bone had healed, the limp would stay. The important thing now was to try to hide the limp from Ignatius as best she could. She did not want him to see her weakness.

The air was sweet, damp; she could hear the horses stirring in the corral, and the wagon was coming, more quickly now, and then it stopped. The wagon was at the foot of the hill now, and she stood facing it. The driver pulled up the team, and she stopped walking, fixed the gun. The strange morning light was throwing shadows, and the sun was in her eyes, and because it was sitting behind the wagon, it blocked out the wagon, outlining it in black and making it impossible to see who the driver was. Was it Ignatius? It was a slight-enough figure, and the hat was Ignatius's; she was almost certain of that: it was Ignatius, surely.

Then she heard his voice. "Honora," he shouted. "I have come for you, Honora."

The driver lifted the reins and lashed at the mules, and the team broke into a stumbling gallop toward her.

Ignatius, she thought, I did not take you for such a fool, and then she thought, there is something else here.

She raised the gun, settled it against her shoulder, and put her wounded hand under it, keeping her good hand free for the trigger. She breathed into her stomach.

Shoot the mules, she told herself. Don't shoot the driver.

The mules were coming at her in a great, clumsy gallop. She had six bullets, and there were four mules, but she only needed to hit one to bring the team down. You can do that, Honora, she told herself. This is not difficult for you. There was dust everywhere, in her eyes, in her mouth, and Ignatius was screaming at the mules to go on, and the wagon sounded like a ship that was coming apart in a storm. Now,

Honora, she told herself, and she raised the gun and let her eye travel down its barrel as she cocked the hammer and then released it, slowly, gently, and fired. The mule at the front of the team, on the left, went down with a cry, and the other mules fell on top of and over it until they were all on the ground in a terrible crying confusion. They will have broken their legs, their necks, coming down at that pace, she thought, and how wrong it is, this world.

The wagon was on its side now, and one and then two mules were trying to stand and pull away from the harness, and the wagon was being half dragged along the ground still.

She kept the gun raised high, moving backward until she was inside the cabin. Joseph closed the door; she put her back to it, and the gun against her shoulder. Her mind was empty, like a cleaned-out room.

"He expected me to shoot the driver," she said.

"Now we see what happens," said Joseph.

"There's someone in the wagon," she said.

"Yes," said Joseph.

"Look," said Prosper.

He was at the small window. He put his hand out to her, and she took it, and he pulled her to him. Something so surprising has happened it has made him forget he hates me, she thought. She stood next to him so that their arms were pressed together, and they looked out the window.

"Look who is here to see you, Honora," shouted Ignatius. "Come and say hello to your friend."

It was Mary. She was dressed in a man's suit, and she was wearing Ignatius's hat, and Ignatius was holding her by the shoulder and pushing her forward. Then he pulled the hat from her head so that her red hair came free. It was Mary, and she was holding a child by the hand, a child who was dressed in white and had the same red hair as her mother. Ignatius had a rifle set against his shoulder, facing the cabin, and she could see a gun belt at his waist too. Oh, how he has prepared for this day, she thought.

"Come out, Honora," said Ignatius impatiently. "Or I will shoot your friend, and the child too."

She looked across the room at Joseph. He shook his head no at her.

She was still holding the gun. She held it out to Prosper, and he took it from her. Don't start to think, Honora, she told herself, not now. Just keep on going on.

She went to the door and put her hand on it and looked at Joseph again. His face was closed, shut tight as a fist. She pushed the door open and stepped out into the cool morning air.

"Come closer so we can take a good look at you," shouted Ignatius. "And keep your hands out flat in front of you, palms up to the sky."

Mary was looking at the ground, but the child was watching Honora, and as she walked toward Ignatius, she put her hand out to Honora. She thinks I am reaching for her, because I hold my hands out, thought Honora. Oh, sweet child, she thought, and she made herself smile at her as she walked, and the child smiled back. Her hair was a wonderful color, darker red than Mary's, nearly the red of the robin's breast in winter.

"Here she is, Mary," called Ignatius, triumphantly. "Didn't I tell you we'd find her? It's a long road that has no bend in it. We've found her, at last. We are reunited, though she seems a shadow of herself with the limp on her and the broken hand, and wouldn't she have been better off staying safe and sound with us."

Honora kept her eyes on the child. Don't look at Ignatius, she told herself. Think of the wax man on Alice's star, and remember what you can do; remember who you are.

"What is your name?" she said to the child.

"Nellie," the child answered in a whisper.

"Stop that," said Ignatius, and he kicked out at the child. "Stop talking, or you know what will happen to you." The child moved as silently as a little ghost to stand behind Mary. Ignatius put his head on its side, watching her, and then he looked at Mary, and it seemed to Honora that he had forgotten where he was and what was happening, that he was lost in himself. Then he sighed heavily, as if he were tired from a difficult job. He is mad, thought Honora, and the madness has split his mind, and I have seen animals like this, made mad, and there is no law in this world or the next that they abide by. Ignatius turned back toward her, looked at her, and it took him a moment, she saw, to collect himself, to come back from the place he had been in his mind.

"You look like a witch from the woods," he said after a moment of considering her. "Burned brown, and with your hair like that. And the limp on you. Not like a respectable person, at all." He took hold of Mary by her hair and pulled her head back so that her chin snapped up. "Doesn't she, Mary? Doesn't your friend look like the witch she is now?"

Mary opened her eyes and looked ahead, not at Honora, but at the air in front of her, at nothing, and her eyes were empty of color, and her face was gray, hollowed out. There were ugly-colored bruises on her face, on her neck. He pulled her hair again, and she gasped in pain and opened her mouth, and Honora saw that her teeth were broken into stumps. *Oh, how proud you were of your small white teeth, and what has happened to you, Mary?* she wanted to cry out. *What has he done to you?*

"Mary's very quiet these days," said Ignatius. "She's gone as mute as yourself." He gave a small sigh. "Well," he said. "Down to business. I suppose your cowboy is inside?"

She said nothing.

"And I suppose he has his rifle trained on me," he said. "But that's all right, because we all know what kind of a shot he is, and he won't shoot now that I have you, unless relations have deteriorated so much that he's glad I'm here." He started to laugh hysterically. "It wouldn't surprise me. Thank God Ignatius is here, he's probably saying to himself. That's that problem solved, he's probably telling himself." He stopped laughing. "Because you're a problem, Honora, aren't you?"

He leaned toward her gently, and then he grabbed her by the arm and pulled her toward him, hand over hand, up her arm. "Now," he said very quietly. He put his fingers to her face, and there was something cold against her skin, and she felt it as the knife before she knew what it was. "Now I have all my girlies with me. Now I can finish what I started."

Mary, she wanted to say, *it is all right. We have come a long way, and oh, all the things we have seen, and done, and we did what we could—it is all right. And your betrayal—you did it for the child, and I would have done the same, and it is all right.*

Ignatius was smiling at her, and she felt something rise up in her that was as cold and concentrated as the feeling from the knife. She put her head back as far as she could and opened her eyes to the sky and opened her arms out wide, as she used to do when she was a child in the woods in Doolough and she had played at riding on the wind. The sun was a blazing white, and there was a bird above, flying across the sun, a hawk, maybe, and then she heard the painted pony in the corral. She moved her head against the knife and saw the child step away from Mary and put her hand out and point, and as one they all turned at the same time in the direction the child's hand was pointing, like they were a group being directed onstage, and she saw that Joseph was coming toward them. Ignatius dropped his knife, let go of her arm, and lifted his gun, but he was too late, too late by only a moment, and then Joseph was upon him. She saw the glint of the knife as it moved through the air—Joseph had it, and now he was raising it up, and now he was slicing down and forward, toward Ignatius's throat—and then she heard a noise like thick paper being pulled apart, and that was the sound of the knife cutting through flesh, she knew, and it was a sound that once you'd heard it, you never forgot it. Ignatius gave a gasp of surprise, and he closed his eyes and fell onto his knees, before Honora. The child was crying, and Mary was screaming, "Oh God, oh God," but everything in

Honora's mind was as quiet as land under falling snow. Joseph moved to stand behind Ignatius.

"Honora," Joseph said, and he made a clicking sound in the back of his throat and held the knife out to her.

"No," she said, and so Joseph, without waiting for her to say or do more, kicked Ignatius in the back so that he fell facedown into the dirt before her. She looked from Ignatius up to Joseph. *Leave him to bleed out in the dirt, in the sun,* she wanted to say. *It is right that his blood goes back into the earth,* and Joseph, understanding, nodded at her, yes.

All of this happened in a moment. If she looked up, she thought, the hawk would still be flying across the face of the sun. The knife blade was red still with Ignatius's blood; Joseph wiped it clean against his leg. The child was crying, but more quietly now, and Mary was silent, perfectly still. No one went to Ignatius, though he writhed in the dirt, and grabbed at the ground like he was looking for a rope to pull himself up out of a hole.

Joseph turned toward the mules, who were still thrashing against the traces.

"Help me free them," he said to Honora, and he went toward them, the knife held high in his hand.

~

"Did you ever think it strange," said Mary, "that we came all the way from Ireland and ended up in another cabin in a field?" and she jiggled the child on her lap, to show that she was making a joke.

Honora felt Mary look across at her, to check if what she had said was all right. She was still not the Mary of old, and she would never be again, Honora thought. Too much had happened to Mary, and she was permanently changed now. We might be in a cabin in a field as we were in Ireland, she thought, but we're not the people we were there.

You have gone away from the person you were, and I am going toward the person I am meant to be, whether I like it or not.

"I've thought about that, all right," said Honora.

She had laid out her blanket flat on the table, and on it she had put her winter dress, her winter coat. She folded the blanket around the clothes and around again, and then she tied the bundle around with a length of rope. She picked the bundle up; it felt amazingly light, insignificant. That was good, she told herself; the less she had to carry, the faster she could move. She would not let herself wish for boots. It was still summer; there was time to worry about boots before the winter came.

She looked around the cabin, seeing nothing; she put her hands to her skirts, to her hair, fixing herself. She took Prosper's hat from the back of the chair, put it on, and tied it under her chin. She felt better with the hat on, more prepared.

Prosper had his back to the door and his hands in his pockets, and he was leaning forward, looking down at the ground. She took a step toward the door, and he straightened up to look at her. He may try to stop me leaving, after all, she thought. That would be something to reckon with.

"Here," he said. He picked up the rifle that stood next to him, and he held it out to her. "Take it."

"You need the rifle," she said.

"Where you're going, you'll need it more than me," he said. "Take it."

She took the rifle from him; her hand shook as she reached for it. What would he think of when he thought of her, years from now? How would he remember her? All the things she wanted to say—*You love this rifle; how will you replace it?* and *I'm sorry, Prosper; I'm sorry,* and *Are you sorry for how things have gone?*—were better left unsaid now. They had never done that much talking, and it was too late to start now.

"The rifle will serve you better than my old hat and that broken-down pony you're so keen to have," he said.

She looked at him. *You tied the pony's legs,* she wanted to say, *and you kept him in that corral so that he wasn't used to loping, and if he's broken down, you're not innocent of it, and, oh, Prosper, I know that you are waiting for me to say thank you for the rifle, but I worked this land as hard as you; I helped build this house, and I deserve the rifle, and the hat, and the painted pony, and the bay too. And I'm leaving behind my name, on this land, the name that got you twice as much land as you would have had without it, and that's a fair swap for an old hat, a pony you don't want, a horse you can't ride as it should be ridden, and a rifle you can replace.*

"Are you ready?" said Mary.

"I am," she said.

I am, she thought.

Prosper stepped to the side, away from the door, to let her pass.

"I may be back one day," she said to him suddenly, and she almost believed it as she said it.

"You won't," he said, and he gave her his crooked smile, and the smile broke something loose in him so that he had to turn away from her. If he had looked at her again, she would have tried to say something, anything, but he didn't, and so she put her hand on the door, pushed it open, and walked outside into the light with Mary by her side and the child following them, and together they walked away from the cabin until it was far enough behind for them to be able to turn and look at it as a whole.

I spent a long time looking out from that house, she thought. It feels good to be able to look back at it from here.

In the early-morning light, the cabin looked small, safe, somewhere a person would be glad to come home to.

"This is a good place," said Honora. "Prosper is a good man."

"He did a good job building the cabin, all right," said Mary. "It's well made. And the land is well looked after."

"He will be good to you," Honora said.

268

She couldn't say to Mary, *Be good to him*; she didn't have that right. But Mary and Prosper would fit together: she was as sure of this as she had been of anything. Mary could make bread from water, nearly, could run a house with one hand tied behind her back, and one day she would be strong enough again to help in the fields. She had a child, and she could have more. It was right that Mary should stay here with Prosper, that she should take Prosper's last name, that Honora should throw off that name like a heavy coat as Joseph had thrown off his. All my life, Honora thought, I've been seeking something missing, missing something left behind, but I won't miss having Prosper's name. I'm happy to let that go.

"What will become of you, Honora?" cried Mary suddenly. "Out in the wilderness, with that man?"

Do you like ghost stories, Mary? she wanted to say. Because this is a ghost story, in its way. I was meant to wander between worlds, and so it is with Joseph too. We're both travelers in someone else's land.

The child cried out then, "Mama," and pulled at Mary's dress. Mary bent and picked her up.

It was strange to hear Mary being called Mama. It was a word Honora had never used, and would never be called. She thought of her own mother, in the cottage in Ireland; she'd been younger than Honora was now when she had died. She knew nothing, at all, about her mother, and then she told herself, Stop, Honora. Do not think about such things. It's as useful as wondering why the wind and the sea sound the same.

"Do you want to hold her?" said Mary. "To say goodbye?"

"She'll cry if I take her," said Honora, but she leaned toward the child and put her palm against her warm cheek. It would do no good to hold her and to start to think now on what had been lost, to remember everything she had tried to hold on to that had slipped away from her like a fish returning to the water.

She put her hand down to the neck of her dress, down to her heart, and took out Alice's feather. The feather had lain against her skin for so long that it was curled now into the shape of the curve of her breast.

If she looked at the skin where the feather had rested for so long, she'd find its imprint pressed there like the shadow of a fern against the earth, she fancied.

She held the feather out to the child.

"*Tugadh e seo mar adh orm,*" she said, "*in Eirinn, an la a d'fhag muid an sraidbhaile.*"

I was given this for luck in Ireland, on the day we left the village.

The child took the feather from her and closed her small hand around it.

"*Slan go foil,*" said Honora to Mary, to the child, and the child smiled up at her shyly.

Farewell, for now.

"You know I don't speak any Irish," said Mary, and she was laughing and crying at the same time now. "We're not all culchies like you." She rubbed at her nose, violently; her face was blotched red and ugly.

There was a sound behind them then, and Honora turned and saw Joseph coming down the hill at a lope. He was back from packing up his camp; he had a heavy roll tied to the back of his black horse, and he wore one blanket across his chest and the other strapped to his back. He was ready for a journey. Honora lifted her hand to him, and in reply, he raised his hand to her, as he had that first time she had seen him on the hill. From the corral, the painted pony and the bay whickered and broke into a restless canter along the rail. There was a wind coming up, and Joseph was coming at her at such speed now that thought was pushed away, and she turned to the corral, and then she was running to the horses, and as she ran, she began to smile to herself.

Behind her, she heard Mary calling, "Honora, Honora," but she didn't look back.

I always wanted someone who would say to me, Here we go, she thought. Well, Honora, she said to herself, Here we go, and then, she did.

AUTHOR'S NOTE

When I heard of the tragedy of Doolough for the first time, it felt like a story I'd always known. It seemed incredible to me that it was a story that wasn't more widely known. There's something mythical, almost ahistorical in its simplicity, about what happened on the west coast of Ireland in March 1849. A group of starving people sets out on a quest for help. They journey across mountains in the snow. Help comes too late, and the people die on the banks of a black lake. It's an intensely local story, rooted in a place, and a universal one too; it's something that took place in the past, but it could be happening today, here, anywhere. It's both outside of time and place, and of them.

Irish people are fascinated by the Famine; it's a blood memory for us. But when I started writing this book, I wanted to keep it fictional, for it to be only loosely inspired by the events of 1849. The book, however, had other plans for me. I'd write a section, do some reading, and then find that what I'd written had actually occurred. The people would have slept on banks of sand by the black lake, I decided, and then I discovered that that was exactly what happened. The more I wrote of the book, the more I felt as if I were tracing over an already written story, that I was bringing to life something that had been waiting, for a long time, to be told. You couldn't make it up, I would tell myself as I wrote—I almost didn't have to.

What would a survivor of Doolough have done? I asked myself (because all Irish people, in a way, are survivors of Doolough and what it represents), and I decided that she would have left Ireland and gone to America. She would have traveled west then, I thought, and she would have met an Indigenous man whose experiences mirrored her own. I started to look for historical connections between the Irish and the Indigenous Americans, and I found, again, a whole world of history waiting to be told. In 1847, the Choctaw Nation sent money to help the Irish during the Famine. In 1990, a group of Indigenous American people traveled to Doolough to complete the Famine Walk, in memory of the Doolough Tragedy (www.mayo.ie). In 1992, a group of Irish people walked the Trail of Tears, from Oklahoma to Mississippi, to mark the forced walk the Choctaws had undertaken in the 1830s. In 2020, the Irish donated 2.5 million euros to the Hopi and Navajo peoples who'd been badly hit by the COVID-19 pandemic. "We are kindred spirits," said the chief of the Choctaw Nation, in 2020, "with the Irish."

The story of *Sing, Wild Bird, Sing* was already there. I just had to tell it.

ACKNOWLEDGMENTS

Thank you to Anthony Two Moons of the Southern Arapaho, Zuni, and Dine peoples, whose support of this book and review of the Indigenous voice in it mean so much to me. Thank you to Marisa Miller Wolfson, for introducing me to Anthony. Thank you to my passionate and inspirational agents, Sallyanne Sweeney and Lisa Gallagher, for fighting for this book, and to my editor, Alicia Clancy, for believing in it. Thank you to Jonathan Myerson for your incisive readings of earlier drafts, and for encouraging me to keep on going on.

Thank you to my brother-in-law, Tom O'Mahony, who told me the story of Doolough, and whose passion for and knowledge of Irish history are a great gift to me, and thank you to my sister, Claire O'Mahony, for always being on my side.

Thank you to Genevieve Bates, Fiona MacDonald, Jennie Walters, Debra Hills, Melissa Russo Tzvetkov, Hannah Joseph, Svenja Weber, Annika Murjahn, and Caroline Conway Pendrill for your friendship and support and interest and ideas on books and writing and life.

Thank you to my children, Louis, Allegra, and Gigi, for showing me how fast time moves, and how to go at life with verve and joy.

Thank you to the plains and skies and hills of Montana, which are always in my mind's eye, drawing me on.

And most of all, thank you to Mike, for your love. There's no one I'd rather be traveling the road with than you.

~

This book was inspired by the story of the people who set out on a walk for help on March 30, 1849, in Doolough, Ireland. It was a hard story to hear, and a hard story to tell, not least because to separate the story from the history, the people from what had happened to them, was a difficult process. For a long time, I struggled with the idea of giving a voice to those who'd been silenced, of making them into characters in a story of my telling. Their history, their ending, is theirs alone. I can only hope that those who didn't survive Doolough, who didn't get to tell their own story, would have been glad to have had it recounted as it is here, and that they would forgive me any mistellings, omissions, or misunderstandings. This book is for them, and for the Cayuse people of the Pacific Northwest, who today form part of the Confederated Tribes of the Umatilla Indian Reservation in northeast Oregon. The Cayuse are, as they say, still here. The Irish and the Cayuse were banished to wander the world. May their souls, and the souls of their ancestors and their descendants, find peace in their ancestral homelands.

ABOUT THE AUTHOR

Photo © 2019 Nicola Schafer

Jacqueline O'Mahony was named Young Irish Writer of the Year by the *Irish Examiner* when she was fourteen. She took her BA in Ireland, her MA at the University of Bologna, and her PhD in history at Boston College and as a Fulbright Scholar at Duke University. She worked at Condé Nast as a stylist and editor for *Vogue* and at Associated Newspapers as an arts editor, and in 2015 she graduated from City University's MA in creative writing with a first-class degree. Her debut novel, *A River in the Trees*, was nominated for the Authors' Club Best First Novel Award and the Not the Booker Prize in 2020. Originally from Cork, Ireland, she lives in London with her husband and three young children.